"I'm going out," Cathryn announced

"What?"

"Out. I don't want to stay in tonight. I don't want to be—" she looked around her living room with the eyes of a hateful stranger "—here."

"Where are you going?" Tucker expected her to say Lauren's or Julia's, but instead she just shrugged.

"Out," she repeated, heading for the bathroom. She returned a short while later with her makeup repaired. "It's Saturday night, and I'm tired of playing by the rules. Why should I? No one else has." *Including my ex-husband,* she might have said—but didn't.

Uh-oh. Tucker's eyes swept over her for about the thirty-seventh time, and a premonition of disaster hit him. "Maybe that's not such a good idea."

"Don't try to stop me, Tuck."

Tucker knew she was angry and in a hell-raising mood. But then, why shouldn't she be? She had a right to rage for a night. And actually, a bit of rage might do her some good.

As long as she had someone to watch over her.

He lifted his hands in surrender. "No, I wouldn't do that. I just want to go with you."

Dear Reader,

During the writing of *Cathryn*, several people asked
me how I could possibly create a romance novel featuring
an overweight, happily married stay-at-home mom whose
hobbies include square dancing, sewing and choir. That was
the Cathryn McGrath they knew from her brief appearances
in *Julia* and *Lauren* (published in November 1998 and
December 1999 respectively). Each time I was asked, my
response was a rather smug "You'll see," accompanied by
a slightly dirty laugh.

I knew something, or rather *someone*, they didn't—
Tucker Lang, bad boy extraordinaire, who drops into
Cathryn's life needing to change his ways just when Cathryn
needs to change hers. From the very first line of the book,
I recognized the potential within such a situation. With that
line I also began my most enjoyable writing experience to
date. I absolutely loved being with these two buoyant people.

Cathryn concludes CIRCLE OF FRIENDS, my series about a
group of people who share the unusual experience of having
grown up together on a small fictional island off the coast of
Massachusetts. I hope you enjoy it.

My best to you always,

Shannon Waverly

CATHRYN
Shannon
Waverly

HARLEQUIN®

TORONTO • NEW YORK • LONDON
AMSTERDAM • PARIS • SYDNEY • HAMBURG
STOCKHOLM • ATHENS • TOKYO • MILAN • MADRID
PRAGUE • WARSAW • BUDAPEST • AUCKLAND

ISBN 0-373-70932-3

CATHRYN

Copyright © 2000 by Kathleen Shannon.

Visit us at www.eHarlequin.com

Printed in U.S.A.

To Paula,
who took a chance on me fifteen books ago.
For your always-judicious editing, lofty standards
and human understanding
(especially each time I was late with a manuscript),
thank you.

CHAPTER ONE

TUCKER LANG wasn't the sort of guy good girls cared to be seen with. Not if they valued their reputations. Good girls went out with clean-cut, law-abiding guys, the ones who stayed in school and went to church and had plans for the future.

Being with Tucker Lang was another matter, however—as long as no one found out—and by the time he left Harmony at the age of twenty-one, not many girls remained who *hadn't* joined him for a walk on the wild side. Tucker was trouble, all right, and nothing was more alluring than trouble.

Tucker even looked like trouble, from his long black hair to his scuffed biker's boots, which he wore both winter and summer and even to the beach. He also favored shark-tooth jewelry, black leather jackets, and sleeveless T-shirts, to display his sinewy musculature.

The vehicles he drove, both of which he'd rebuilt himself, looked like trouble, too. The first was a big, loud Harley-Davidson; the other, a Trans-Am with flames painted on the sides. Auto repair was, in fact, his trade while he lived on Harmony, one he'd stumbled into simply because it happened to be the family business. His great-uncle Walter, who'd brought him to the island from the Bronx when he was thirteen, operated the island's only garage, Lang's Auto Repair.

To the distress of Walter and his wife, Winnie, trouble

ran deeper than just appearances with Tuck, right from the get-go. He set off stink bombs in school, encouraged his classmates to smoke and swear, and pilfered candy and magazines anywhere he found them for sale.

Another reason the Langs turned gray so fast, beyond the fact that they were both sixty when they took Tucker in, was that he seemed perpetually involved in dangerous activities, usually on a dare. One day, for instance, he dived off Little Harbor Bridge—nothing unusual for island kids, except that in Tucker's case his hands were tied behind his back. He once camped out all night in Morgan's Hollow, where if the ghosts didn't get you, the deer ticks would. But the incident that made Tuck an irrevocable Harmony legend was his getting struck by lightning, a gigantic bolt that passed right through him, yet left him totally unharmed.

Tucker was combative, too, a trait that became more prominent as he grew older and began hanging out in bars. He wasn't the largest or strongest guy on the island, but he was arguably the toughest, and he never backed down from a fight.

In addition to all this, Tucker drank hard, swam nude, danced dirty and spent more than his fair share of nights in jail paying for his sins, the sum of which, alas, only added to his appeal and, in turn, the sullying of even more female reputations.

Not mine, though, thought Cathryn McGrath a bit smugly as she drove across Harmony on a slushy, colorless Valentine's Day. She was on her way to attend the afternoon visitation at D'Autell's Funeral Home where Walter Lang was laid out. Cathryn's virtue had remained intact—although, to be honest, Tucker had never tested it.

For one thing, she'd been off-limits. She'd gone steady with Dylan from the age of fifteen until they were married four years later, and Tucker had respected that. Also, her parents and the Langs were neighbors. They did what good neighbors do—traded news and recipes and tools, and lent each other help whenever it was needed. For some odd reason, that bond seemed to affect Tuck's attitude toward Cathryn. That, and his being four years older. When he wasn't ignoring her, which he often did, he unfailingly treated her like a kid sister, someone meant to be endured and occasionally protected, but not seduced.

But even if he *had* hit on her, she was positive nothing would've come of it, because, quite frankly, the appeal of Tucker Lang, bad boy extraordinaire, was lost on her. Although other girls had swooned over his dark eyes and rugged unshaven jaw, Cathryn had much preferred Dylan's blond and blue-eyed all-American looks. In fact, Tucker's aggressive demeanor had sometimes scared her, and his behavior had positively turned her off.

She didn't find Tucker Lang exciting or irresistible, the way other girls did. Cathryn's idea of irresistible took the form of respect, loyalty, industriousness and being family-oriented, all of which Dylan possessed in spades. Rather, she considered Tucker confused, immature and pitiable, and the girls who allowed him to use them were fools.

Slowing her van for the stop sign at Four Corners, a central marker on the fifteen-square-mile island, Cathryn's rambling remembrances also came to a stop, and she realized with some annoyance that she'd spent an unwarranted amount of time thinking about Tucker Lang today. She hadn't seen the man in nearly fifteen years, and before that they hadn't exactly been bosom buddies. He probably didn't even remember her. Yet, from the moment she'd heard about his uncle's death and realized he'd probably be home for the funeral, he'd been drifting through her thoughts like a low-grade obsession. *Probably because, despite all his shortcomings, I liked the guy,* she thought with a slow smile. *We were oil and water, but we always got along.*

Cathryn set her van in motion again and soon arrived at D'Autell's, located near the cemetery rather than within the touristy harbor district, which the Chamber of Commerce seemed to appreciate.

There weren't many cars in the parking lot, Cathryn noticed as she shut off the engine. Most people probably intended to pay their respects during the evening visiting hours. She sighed in dismay as she gathered up her purse. It would be easier to leave quickly and unnoticed if there was a crowd, and she definitely wanted to leave quickly. She was eager to get home and continue decorating the dining room.

Because it was Valentine's Day, she'd planned a special dinner—beef stroganoff, Dylan's and the kids' favorite, with a heart-shaped raspberry-chocolate cake for dessert. Actually, she wasn't aiming to make this Valentine celebration special; she was aiming to make it perfect. She already knew what Dylan intended to give her, and only perfection on her part would do.

She'd found the gift by accident last week. Normally she didn't go into Dylan's business files, but a supplier had phoned with a question about an order, Dylan had been out and she'd figured the information must be somewhere in the drawer.

It was. So were the diamond earrings. Not rhinestone, not cubic zirconia. Diamond, the real McCoy. The sales slip was in the bag, as well, and when Cathryn saw the bottom line, she'd suffered serious heart palpitations. Dylan's landscaping business was doing well—but eight hundred dollars for earrings? Was he out of his mind?

But then she'd found the card, also hidden under the files, its verse so romantic and intimate it had brought tears to her eyes. And at that moment she'd decided that being impractical once in a while was perfectly forgivable in a man. In fact, it was perfectly...perfect.

She'd kept the discovery a secret, even from her best friends, Julia and Lauren, but it had been difficult. Heavens, diamond earrings! Usually Dylan's Valentine gifts ran to flowers or chocolates. Was he finally going to say, yes, he'd like to have another child? Was this his way of making up for the disagreements they'd had whenever she'd broached the subject? God, she hoped so.

When Bethany, their youngest, had entered first grade in September, Cathryn had thought she might get herself an outside job. Dylan had thought the time was right, too. But after considering several positions and becoming mysteriously anxious and depressed, she'd come to the conclusion that she was just a natural-born, stay-at-home mom, a one-hundred-percent throwback to another era. Trying to be otherwise was fighting against type.

Her family and home were the core of her life, and unlike a lot of women she knew, she loved taking care of them. She loved everything domestic and was never happier than when she was cooking or sewing, gardening or helping with homework. And having a toddler underfoot just seemed like an integral part of the picture.

Smiling, Cathryn recalled that there was one more reason having another child would be fun. Last summer she'd jokingly proposed to Lauren and Julia that they all have babies at about the same time. That way, she'd said, they could share prenatal joys and woes, and later help each other with child-rearing. She'd seen the arrangement as great fun and a wonderful way to broaden their already deep, lifelong friendship. Her friends, however, had predictably considered the idea absurd. At the time, Julia had been content simply

being a newlywed, and Lauren hadn't even been dating anyone.

Well, Lauren's baby was due in August, and, to no one's
surprise, Julia had recently announced that she was two
months along. Now it was Cathryn's turn, and she had a
strong hunch that was the message behind Dylan's extrav-
agant gift. He'd just needed a little time to get used to the
idea.

Cathryn suddenly felt the urge to skip the wake and hurry
home. Unfortunately, though, some things couldn't be
sloughed off. Paying final respects to an old neighbor was
one of them.

She angled the rearview mirror toward her, fluffed her
long sandy bangs—and squeaked in horror. She was still
wearing her Valentine earrings, the dangling hearts that
looked exactly like candy. One said, Kiss Me, the other, Be
Mine. Not quite right for a wake. After removing them and
tossing them on the dash, she fingered off a tiny smudge of
pink lipstick from the corner of her mouth and tried not to
think about how much heavier Tucker was going to find
her. Each of her three pregnancies had left her with ten extra
pounds, then a couple more. Sly devils, had slipped in all
on their own. Ah, well. There was nothing she could do
about it right now. With a resigned sigh, she opened the
door and stepped out into the slush.

Inside the foyer, Cathryn signed the guest book and took
a bolstering breath before walking into the viewing room.
It was overly warm and smelled of carnations and dusty
velvet. Serene harp music, meant to create a celestial am-
bience, drifted from speakers poorly hidden behind the cof-
fin. To Cathryn's chagrin, her attention zoomed straight to
Tucker. Not to poor Walter, the reason she was here.
Tucker. He was sitting in the first chair in a short receiving
line of relatives, talking quietly to the elderly woman on his

right, Walter's sister-in-law Sarah from Barney's Cove Road.

Oh, Lord. He looks like a Mafia hit man, Cathryn thought. It was the maroon shirt that did it. With a white or otherwise pale shirt, Tucker's charcoal sports jacket and fitted black pants might almost pass for normal. But that shirt, all that head-to-toe darkness, distinctly marked him as an under-world figure. Maybe not *the* underworld, but an underworld nonetheless.

Cathryn's first glance also registered that he'd grown a beard, a feature that in her opinion added absolutely nothing to his appeal. Moreover, in disregard of current fashion, he still wore his hair long.

Cathryn changed her mind. Tuck didn't look like a hit man; he looked like an aging rock star.

He was neither, of course.

She remembered her father once remarking that Tucker, being unusually charismatic and street-smart, had the poten-tial to become somebody really special someday, a top-flight salesman, for instance, or a politician—if he got the right breaks. But with bad breaks, getting involved with the wrong people, for instance, he could turn into a bum, a hood or even a criminal. He was walking a precarious fence rail, her father had theorized. Tuck's life could fall either way.

Like most people grafted to Harmony's grapevine, Cath-ryn knew that Tucker had drifted through several trades be-fore settling into the one that currently occupied him— stock-car racing. According to Walter, it was an occupation that provided Tuck with a good living and the opportunity to travel, so Cathryn surmised he'd "fallen" well. Not that she condoned his racing. She knew how much the old wid-ower had worried about his great-nephew's safety, but at least Tucker wasn't living out of a shopping cart or doing time in San Quentin.

As for his personal life, Winnie and Walter had long ago given up on his ever getting married or settling down. They'd gone to their graves believing he'd be a skirt-chaser forever. And they were probably right.

Cathryn's curious perusal, which couldn't have taken more than a few seconds, was cut short when Tucker turned to see who'd just entered. Quickly, she shifted her attention to the casket.

After saying a short, silent prayer and wishing Walter well in the hereafter, Cathryn made her way over to the family. Tucker got to his feet, one knee cracking.

"I'm so sorry for your loss," she began with automatic formality, gripping Tucker's hand while staring at the small garnet stud in his left ear.

"Thank you. It's kind of you to..." His polite response trailed off, and suddenly his dark eyes took on a rich gleam, their outer edges creasing as he broke into an unabashed smile that erased her earlier cynicism about his looks. "Shortcake?" he exclaimed, loudly enough to elicit chuckles from several people.

Heat climbed up Cathryn's neck. Not that she disliked the nickname Tuck had pinned on her when she was young. The character Fonzie on the old TV sitcom *Happy Days* used to call Joannie Cunningham "Shortcake," and that was clearly an expression of brotherly fondness.

"Hi, Tucker," she said, dropping the formality. "I wasn't sure you'd remember me."

"Not remember you? How long did we live next door to each other?"

"Eight years," Cathryn answered and then winced, realizing the question had been rhetorical. "You're looking well," she said. And he was. Trim, fit, tanned.

"So are you," he replied, and before she could refute

him, added, "Married life agrees with you, I guess." It seemed more a question than a statement.

Tucker had disapproved of her becoming engaged while still in high school. In fact, he'd called her crazy for agreeing to marry the only guy she'd ever dated.

"Yes. I'm very happy," Cathryn replied.

He lifted his broad shoulders in a concessionary shrug. "You were right."

"Uh-huh," she hummed slowly and with just enough needling for him to hear her unspoken "And you were wrong."

He asked, "Where are you living these days?"

"West Shore Road." When his brow furrowed, she explained, "It's new since you left." Although she was brimming with questions, she was beginning to feel self-conscious. Standing in the condolence line at a wake was not the proper place for such a conversation. "Maybe we should catch up later, Tuck?"

"Oh. Sure."

"Again, I'm really sorry about your uncle. He'll be missed."

Tucker nodded and let her move on to his great-aunt Sarah. Cathryn extended her sympathy, then told Sarah in an undertone, "I brought my coffee urn and warming trays."

The elderly woman's plump face crinkled with a smile. "Oh, wonderful. Thank you for remembering." With a rustle of black crepe, Sarah turned to Tucker. "Cathryn's lending us some buffet things for tomorrow's brunch. Do you think you could move them from her car to yours?"

Tucker flicked a brief smile at Cathryn. "Sure," he said. "Whenever you're ready to leave."

She nodded, made her way down the line quickly, then hurried to the back row of chairs. About a dozen people, all friends and neighbors, sat ahead of her conversing quietly, and some not so quietly. Walter had lived a long, full life and would've been the first to say there was no need to overmourn his passing.

The minutes ticked by slowly. When Cathryn checked her watch and found that a respectable amount of time had elapsed, she began to button her coat. Simultaneously, Tucker left his seat and headed in her direction. They said nothing until they were outside, under the portico at the front entrance.

"I thought you'd never leave," he grumbled, reaching inside his jacket. "I've been dying for a smoke."

"You haven't quit yet?" Cathryn exclaimed incredulously as he struck a match and lit up. He didn't bother replying, just took in a lungful of smoke. Watching him, Cathryn felt the urge to cough on his behalf.

He tossed the extinguished match toward the receptacle by the door. "You still ready to chew my head off?" He squinted at her, looking fierce, and for a moment Cathryn found herself holding her breath. But then his mouth tipped up at one corner, deepening a groove that on a less masculine face might be considered a dimple.

"You bet. You shouldn't smoke, Tucker. It's a terrible habit. It'll take years off your life. And anyway, it's so passé. Nobody finds it attractive anymore."

He angled a glance at her that was full of devilishness, even as he drawled in exasperation, "You always were a pain in the ass."

"Oh, please, no praise."

He laughed and made a sweeping gesture toward the parking lot with the hand that held the cigarette. "Which one's yours?"

"The blue van."

"Figures." He touched her shoulder and urged her forward. Although she wore several layers of winter clothing, she still felt the tingling warmth of his fingers. "So...how've you been?" he asked, as they tramped through the translucent slush, which only yesterday had been pristine snow.

"Great. How about you?"

"Oh, can't complain."

Cathryn noticed he was wearing black leather boots. Not quite the atrocities he wore as a teenager, but in the same general family of footwear.

"And Dylan?" he asked.

Cathryn beamed. "He's just great."

They arrived at her van and she slid open the door. "He runs his own landscaping business."

"Oh, that's right. He went off to some sort of agricultural college, didn't he?"

"Yes." Four years of letter-writing and carrying on a long-distance romance, but somehow she and Dylan had endured. "When he graduated, he worked for another landscaper, but after a few years he ventured out on his own. It was shaky at first. We had a mortgage and a toddler and another baby on the way."

"You have two kids?"

Cathryn reached into the van, batted away a basketball, pulled forward the box containing her thirty-five-cup coffee urn and deposited it in Tucker's arms. "No. Three."

"Three!" The box slipped a little.

"Yes." Cathryn lifted two warming trays. "Where to?"

Pointing with the cigarette clenched between his teeth, Tucker indicated a black sedan, a rental, across the lot. They mushed on.

"Anyway," she resumed, "before long, business picked up and Dylan hasn't looked back since."

"Doing well, I take it?" Tucker's shapely winged brows

lowered just enough to remind Cathryn that his disapproval had included more than just her early engagement. For reasons beyond her comprehension, he'd never seemed to care for Dylan, either. In fact, one afternoon just before leaving the island, having spotted her and Dylan on her porch, Tucker had crossed the lawn between their houses and stomped up the wooden steps in his trademark boots. "You be good to her," he'd warned Dylan in a deceptively soft voice. "Or I'll come back and break your kneecaps." A joke, but oddly no one had laughed, least of all Dylan.

"Yes. He's very busy," Cathryn replied. "Very much in demand. Even today, only February, he's consulting with a client about a spring project. Gone are the days when we had the winter months to ourselves."

Tucker unlocked the trunk of his car and laid the box inside. Cathryn fit in the warming trays. When he began to lower the lid, she cried, "Wait. There's more." And they slopped across the parking lot once again.

As she handed him a large chafing dish, he growled, "Jeez, what do you do, Shortcake, run a restaurant?"

"No, I just—" she shrugged "—have things like this. Families often do, you know."

Tucker grunted, and they headed back toward his car. "So, tell me about your kids."

As usual, a request to talk about her children set off an internal geyser of love and pride. "Well, my oldest is named Justin. He's eleven and into sports, big time. Cory is eight. He's my scholar, quiet, always reading. And Bethany, who's six, is my little shadow. She loves to bake and sew and do all the things I enjoy. Incidentally, she's the reason I couldn't attend Winnie's funeral. I was in the hospital giving birth to her."

"That right?" They'd reached his car. He tossed his cigarette, deposited the chafing dish, and after closing the trunk, turned his full attention on Cathryn. "Who do they take after?" he asked, bracing his foot on the bumper and leaning on his thigh.

"Justin clearly looks like Dylan, but the two younger kids are a blend. Each has features from both of us. Beth, for instance, has my hazel eyes and Dylan's blond hair. Cory has Dylan's smile, but my build." She added "unfortunately" to herself.

"I bet they're great kids."

"They are, if I do say so myself." Cathryn began to grow uneasy under Tucker's close regard. While she spoke, he gazed straight at her, his eyes unwavering. She couldn't remember the last time anyone, especially a man, had listened to her so interestedly or watched her so intently, and for a moment she thought she understood something of Tucker Lang's fabled appeal. "So, what about you, Tuck?" she asked, hoping to deflect his attention.

"Me?"

"Yes. What've you been up to?"

He dropped his foot, straightened to his full six-foot height and shifted his attention to the fog swirling over the meadow across the road. "Oh, just the same old same old."

She had no idea what that meant. "I heard you've taken up car racing...?"

"Uh-huh." He nodded rhythmically for several seconds as if that might take the place of further conversation.

"So, where are you living?"

He shuffled his feet and added a few more inches to the distance between them. "Alabama."

"Really? I've never been to Alabama. I haven't been anywhere, really. Except Florida. We went to Disney World with the kids two years ago. Best vacation we ever took." *Only vacation we ever took.* "Ever been to Disney?"

Tucker pulled out his cigarettes again, stared at them a moment and then repocketed them. "Uh...no."

She swallowed. "Anyone special in your life these days?"

He didn't actually answer, just made a face as if to say, "Are you kidding?"

Cathryn knew a stone wall when she was hitting one, especially when that stone wall was so familiar. Tucker hadn't liked personal questions when he was a boy either, particularly when they involved his life in New York. A couple of times she'd heard him lie about it, but mostly he'd just clammed up, holding the truth, and all the pain that went with it, tight inside him. Until one day when she was ten and couldn't take it anymore and admitted to him that she knew his background, knew his mother was a hooker and a drug addict. She'd overheard her parents talking. And if he wanted to discuss it or cry or go for a fast walk like she did when she was angry, that was okay with her. She only wanted to help, and she wouldn't tell anyone about it, honest. Tucker, being Tucker, hadn't cried. But he had talked. A little. And he had walked. A lot. Damn fast, too.

What did he have bottled up inside him now? she wondered. Anything? Nothing? And whose business was it, anyway?

Even as Cathryn was still musing, Tucker glanced over his shoulder toward the funeral home and said, "Well, I'd better get back inside before someone sends out a search party."

"Oh. Of course." She clutched her purse in two hands and caught her lower lip in her teeth. "It was good seeing you again, Tuck."

His grin returned, all confidence and male sass. "I know."

Cathryn laughed. Some things never changed, and she was just as glad they didn't.

TUCKER STOOD under the portico of the funeral home, puffing on a cigarette and feeling a sense of loss after Cathryn drove away. Not that he wanted to continue their conversation, especially considering the direction it had taken. Rather, his sense of loss rose solely from himself. Cathryn's role had simply been to remind him of it, of the life he'd made a religion of avoiding until now. Married life. The life of a husband and parent, home-owner and mower of lawns, coach to Little Leaguers and reader of bedtime stories—the life of a responsible adult. "And look where that's landed you," he muttered in self-disgust.

Clamping his cigarette between his teeth, he brushed aside his jacket, unsnapped the leather pouch at his waist and lifted his cellular phone. He'd pressed in half of Jenny's number before remembering she was out of range. Way out of range. Cursing around his cigarette, he returned the phone to its case and paced the portico like a caged bear.

He wished there was someone he could call. Normally, he disliked sharing his problems. After fending for himself most of his life, he was accustomed to handling crises on his own. But right about now, it might be nice to bounce ideas off another person.

He considered the guys he hung around with and dismissed them as quickly as they came to mind. How could he admit to the yahoos he called friends that at the ripe old age of thirty-five he'd gotten a woman pregnant? They'd never let him live it down and they'd certainly be no help. Jenny didn't want to marry him. What was the problem, man? To them, the problem would be if she *did* want to get married.

A car swashed into the parking lot and a moment later

an elderly couple got out. Strangers to Tuck, they nodded, lips pressed in sorrowful regret, as they walked by him, taking careful little steps, and entered the building. He sighed. Ah, yes—Walter. Automatically his lips pressed in matching regret. This wasn't the time to be thinking of Jenny or impending fatherhood. It was time to mourn the generous man who, together with his patient wife, had rescued his sorry-ass life and changed him from a punk into...less of a punk. And for that, Tucker was truly sad. He wished he could've turned out better *more quickly* for them. He wished he hadn't caused them so much trouble—all those calls from the principal and Charlie Slocum, Harmony's now-retired chief of police. He wished he had finished high school here, not in some far-off GED program, so they could've watched him receive his diploma. He wished Walter had seen him race at least once, even if he was just on the stock-car circuit. He wished he'd bought Winnie a clothes dryer before she caught pneumonia from hanging out laundry. He wished...he wished Jenny would change her mind and marry him.

And with that his thoughts went over to the other side again. A barrel-deep moan rose from his chest. He'd been embroiled in this emotional tug-of-war for days, caught between his sadness over his uncle's death and his angst over his love life. Pulled in two directions, he was doing neither justice.

Well, he was tired of it. It was clearly time to focus. Or at least do something about one or the other.

Tucker dropped his third cigarette into the trash receptacle and headed inside. Old man D'Autell was sitting in his office at the end of the center hall, changing a tape for the P.A. system. More harp diddling. Leaning in the doorway, Tucker asked, "Is there a phone somewhere in this building where I can make a private call?"

The long-faced mortician gazed at him with a wariness that slightly offended Tucker. As far as he could remember, D'Autell had never been the target of any of his boyhood pranks.

"Will it be long distance?"

"Yeah, but I'll use my calling card."

D'Autell cranked himself out of his chair, giving the phone a slight push in Tucker's direction.

"Thanks," he said as the old man walked by.

In place of "You're welcome," D'Autell grumbled, "Don't touch anything."

Tucker closed the door, went to the phone and punched in a Missouri number. Jenny answered on the third ring.

Hearing her voice, Tucker tried to summon up an image of the woman who was carrying his child and was disturbed when he couldn't. He could see short auburn curls and grass-green eyes and a pointy chin. And freckles. Yes, there were definitely some freckles. But he wasn't able to put all the parts together and see a cohesive whole.

"Hey, Jen," he began, sitting down in the chair D'Autell had vacated. "It's me, Tuck."

"Oh." Her voice sank, leaving no question how she felt about hearing from him.

"How's it going, darlin'?"

"How's it going? I just spent the morning puking my brains out. That's how it's going."

"Oh, I'm sorry."

"Yeah, well, you should be."

"Sorry," he mumbled again, wincing.

"So what do you want, Tuck?" Somehow she managed to sound both bored and impatient.

"Just to talk."

She sighed heavily. He tried not to take offense.

"Are you coming over?" she asked. "Are you back in town?"

"No. No to both questions. I'm in Massachusetts. I had to fly home because of a death in the family."

"Home?" Her surprise underscored how little they knew about each other. "You're from Massachusetts?"

"Sort of. I was born in New York, but…" He felt himself closing the gates of communication. But if he and Jenny were meant to live the rest of their lives together, it was time to start sharing. "When I was thirteen, I came here to live with my grandfather's brother Walter and his wife Winnie. Walter just passed away."

"Oh." Jenny's uncertain exclamation betrayed an encouraging softening. "That's too bad, Tuck."

"Yeah, it is. He was a great old guy. Played a mean hand of whist."

"What happened to your parents?"

He swallowed, faced with the question he'd had to answer all his life. "My father died in Vietnam when I was three, and when I was twelve my mother…was the victim of a drunk driving accident."

"She died, too?"

Jenny was astounded and incredulous. As well she should be, he thought. It was an astounding, incredible story. A lie, actually. Not the part about his father dying in Nam; Tuck had worn the Silver Star posthumously bestowed on his father right until the day the clasp broke off. The part about his mother was a lie. He'd chickened out again. He couldn't admit his mother had been sent to prison when he was twelve and had overdosed five years later.

"Anyway, I'm at the wake now, taking a break, and I had to call. You've been on my mind since last weekend."

"Where in Massachusetts?" she asked, steering so

sharply away from the subject, he could practically hear her tires screech.

He sighed. "Harmony. It's a small island ten, twelve miles off the southeast coast. Not far from Martha's Vineyard."

"Harmony? Never heard of it."

"Understandable. It's small. Not many people here during the winter. Last I heard, the count was around seven hundred."

"*You* lived on an island with only seven hundred people?" She infused every word with sarcasm.

"Yep. Peel away the outer layers and I'm really just a small-town boy at heart."

"Yeah, right." Not the sharpest comeback, but she made her point.

Tucker massaged a place on his forehead where a headache was gathering force. "About the discussion we had last week…" he tried again. "It's been bothering the hell out of me, Jen."

"Which part? You asking me to marry you, or me turning you down?"

"The last part. I don't regret asking you to marry me. I'll never regret that. I meant it when I said I want to do right by you and the baby."

She laughed a tinkling, cascading laugh, hitting every note and nuance of condescension along the way. "Tucker Lang, you wouldn't know right if it smacked you square in the face."

Tucker drummed his fingers on the desk in mounting frustration. "I know enough to feel responsible for my kid and to want it to have a good home life."

"And what's that, Tuck? You being gone three-quarters of the time? You saying good-night over the phone from some motel room half a world away?"

"No!" Inadvertently he thought of the kind of home Cathryn must have, how loved and secure her children must feel. *That* was what he meant.

"No? You're planning on quitting racing then?"

Tuck swallowed with difficulty. "That isn't fair. You know racing is how I make my living."

"Tell that to our kid when he's ten and doesn't know you."

Tucker regretted calling without having prepared. He wasn't doing very well. When it came to playing for keeps, he didn't know the lines. "I can cut back. I can do other things...."

"It wouldn't matter." Jenny sighed dismally. "You're just not father material, Tuck. And you certainly aren't cut out to be anyone's husband."

"What do you mean?" As if he didn't know. Hadn't they met at a party swarming with racing groupies and hadn't he flirted with her and arranged to call her, even while his date for the evening stood less than ten feet away?

"Don't get me wrong, Tuck. You're a great guy and a lot of fun, but frankly, I don't trust you from here to the front door."

Her accusations stung. "I'd be different if we were married."

She burst out laughing.

"I would," he insisted, realizing how serious he was, how deep was his desire to claim his unborn child and raise it well, protect it, be a good father. "Jenny, please, you've got to give us a chance. I swear on my father's grave I'll be..."

"No, Tuck. I'm sure your intentions are good, but you know what they say about the road to Hell."

Tucker pressed a tightly clenched fist against his forehead. After a long cleansing moment of silent swearing, he took a different tack. "But what'll you do? How will you get along? And don't tell me you intend to go on welfare because I won't allow it."

She huffed impatiently. "Listen, Tucker, I have to go. I have to be at the restaurant in half an hour." She paused. "A heck of a place to work when you're having morning sickness, huh?"

"You could quit if we—"

"No," she interrupted. "Really, Tuck. Thanks anyway, but you're simply not the type of guy I hoped to marry. That doesn't make you a bad person. It just makes you, you. And as for the baby, to be blunt, I'd prefer raising it without you. You'd only confuse our child, here today, gone tomorrow. And as it got older—" she swallowed as if this was difficult for her, too "—I can't imagine you being anything but a bad influence. In fact, I'd prefer you don't even visit."

"You can't mean that. I'm the baby's father."

"No. You're the guy I had unprotected sex with one night last November after one too many margaritas."

"Don't reduce it to that. We dated."

"And I'll remember those dates fondly, but now it's time for me to go my way and you to go yours. It's for the best."

Tucker started to protest but heard a click, followed by the insulting buzz of disconnection. Anger bubbled inside him. He wanted to hurl the phone across the room. Instead, he quietly dropped the receiver into its cradle and fought back the tightening in his throat.

Of all the ironies. After a lifetime of wanderlust and womanizing, he'd finally decided to settle down, and the mother of his child didn't want him. Far worse, she didn't want him anywhere near his child. He supposed there was a strange justice in the situation. He was reaping his due rewards.

But, hell, he didn't have to like it, he thought, surging out of the chair. He didn't have to settle for it, either. Fathers had rights. He'd take legal steps, and when his offspring came into the world next August, he was going to be right there to say, "Hey, son or daughter, this is your old man looking at you."

He sank to the chair again, dropping like a popped balloon. Bad choice, bringing in lawyers and demanding rights. That road led to bitterness, spite and fighting back. And maybe she'd win. He had to remember what he wanted— to be a vital, ongoing part of his child's upbringing—and the best way to do that was to convince Jenny to marry him. And who knew, maybe he could. He'd convinced a lot of women to do a lot of things they'd never dreamed of doing before.

Tucker didn't have a clue how he intended to accomplish this, but he would. He had to. For the first time in his life, he had something worth fighting for.

CHAPTER TWO

CHOCOLATES. A five-pound box of chocolates. This wasn't the gift Cathryn expected from her husband. Staring at the plastic roses that adorned the red-satin cover, she felt her smile crumble.

"Happy Valentine's Day," Dylan said, setting the heart-shaped box on her dinner plate and hurrying to his place at the head of the table. He was the last member of the family to sit. He had tumbled into the house forty minutes later than promised and had still wanted to shower. The stroganoff noodles had congealed into a big sticky pasta ball, and the green beans almandine had gone limp. Not quite the perfection Cathryn had been aiming for.

"Th-thank you," she replied with forced cheer. Maybe the earrings were coming later, during dessert, or after the kids went to bed. Sure. That was it. After the kids were asleep. Dylan had bought her a special gift and obviously meant to create a special moment when he gave it to her. The chocolates were just a front.

She opened the accompanying card and nodded with a knowing smile. It was a simple generic greeting, not the gorgeous card with the touching verse she'd found at the bottom of the file drawer. But, of course, that would come later, too.

"Thank you," she said again. "It's very pretty." She gazed at her husband across the candlelit table. He seemed bemused, his eyes fixed on the centerpiece. "Dylan?"

His head jerked up. "Huh?"

She chuckled. Sometimes he was worse than the kids. "Thank you."

"Oh." He waved his hand dismissively. "My pleasure."

"Can I have some?" Justin asked, eyeing the box lasciviously.

"Hey!" Bethany complained. "You've got your own chocolates."

"So do you, and I bet you want some of Mom's too."

"Whoa!" Dylan called. "Bring it down a notch."

Cathryn pulled her red linen napkin from a ring made from construction paper decorated with glittery stick-on hearts. Beth's contribution to the table. "Of course all of you can have some of my candy. Tomorrow. Any more sugar today—beyond dessert, of course—and you'll be swinging from the curtain rods."

Cory apparently found this funny and laughed. Milk came snorting out his nose.

"Eeiuw. Gross." Bethany scooted as far away from him as she could.

Cathryn gave her brood a glare of mock impatience. "All right, settle down. It's time to give thanks."

Bottoms wiggled on chairs, throats were cleared, and a semblance of order descended.

"Thanks" was a casual ritual at the McGrath house, an observance more conversational than prayerful. During thanks, they passed food, dug into meals, and sometimes strayed off subject. But Cathryn didn't mind. It worked. She could see a sense of gratitude taking root in her children, a mindfulness of the small blessings in their lives. With such an attitude, they'd be able to find happiness anytime, anywhere, no matter what calamity befell them.

"I'm thankful I got a seventy-five on my math quiz today," Justin said, the first to volunteer. With a sheepish grin he confessed, "I didn't study."

Dylan growled at him scoldingly.

Chewing a slice of cucumber, Bethany mumbled, "I'm grateful Jason Toomey stopped chasing me in the schoolyard."

"Yes, we're all grateful for that," Cathryn agreed, as she passed the basket of rolls.

Cory pushed his glasses up his nose. "I'm thankful for all the cards I got today in school."

Cathryn's heart went out to her middle child—her Charlie Brown. Had he thought he wouldn't get any?

"And I'm thankful for this table," Dylan said. "The food, the flowers and decorations, everything. It's wonderful, Cath. As usual."

"Yeah. Thanks, Mom," Justin said, and the other kids chimed in.

"Your turn, Mommy." Beth was the only one who still called her Mommy.

Cathryn had been so busy listening to others, she hadn't really thought about her own contribution. Off the top of her head she said, "I'm thankful that I have such a thankful family, even when I serve pasta that needs to be cut with a chain saw."

Everyone laughed and then settled into serious eating, and it was a while before Cathryn thought about the earrings again. Almost simultaneously she thought about having another child. The two ideas had become entwined. She and Dylan didn't need another child. Neither did the overpopulated planet, which was Dylan's strongest argument.

But maybe another child needed them.

Of course! They could adopt. She'd propose the idea tonight. How could Dylan object?

That night before going to bed, Cathryn showered,

donned her prettiest nightgown and spritzed on Dylan's favorite perfume. But when she waltzed into the bedroom, her husband was sprawled across three-quarters of the bed, already asleep. Swallowing her disappointment, she reasoned that falling asleep had been unintentional and surely he'd appreciate being roused.

She sat on the bed and gave Dylan's shoulder a gentle shake. Nothing. She bounced and jiggled the mattress, which earned her a dull moan. She turned on the radio and flicked the light, but the only response that elicited was a mumbled, "For Crissake, Cath, knock it off," before Dylan dropped deep into sleep once again.

With dismay pressing heavily on her, Cathryn slipped into bed and pulled the blankets to her chin. Where were her earrings? she implored the enshrouding darkness. Where was her mushy card? And what about the talk she'd hoped to have about another baby—to say nothing of the lovemaking she'd anticipated all week long?

Maybe tomorrow, she thought, sighing downheartedly. Putting off the surprise until the day after Valentine's would be odd, but obviously Dylan had his reasons.

But the next day dawned, and Cathryn got the kids off to school, and she and Dylan attended Walter Lang's funeral, and the likelihood of his presenting her with a belated Valentine gift grew more and more remote. During brunch at the Lang house afterward, she overheard him saying that as soon as he got home, he planned to change out of his suit and go scope out a new project.

Maybe tonight, Cathryn thought, struggling to keep her optimism buoyant. Maybe tonight...

Several guests had already left and Cathryn was helping Sarah round up used plates and coffee cups, when the front door opened and someone new arrived, a thirty-something blonde whom Cathryn recognized only vaguely. She certainly wasn't a permanent resident of Harmony. After exchanging a few words with Sarah, the newcomer approached Tucker, who happened to be talking with Dylan.

The woman was sleek, graceful and attractive in a wealthy sort of way. She'd given her coat to Sarah at the door, and now stood before the two men in a cowl-necked, black, angora knit dress that made an absolute drama of her rich blond hair, peaches-and-cream complexion and turquoise eyes. It didn't exactly detract from her figure, either. Cathryn felt like a frump in comparison, dressed in her high-collared Victorian blouse, gray cardigan and calf-length challis skirt.

For some irrational reason, she also felt she was needed at her husband's side.

The woman extended her hand to Tucker. "Mr. Lang," she said, her tone as soft and smooth as the angora that enveloped her, "I was unable to attend your uncle's funeral, but I couldn't let the day go by without coming over to offer my sympathy."

"Thank you," Tucker replied, one eyebrow arched and betraying the fact that he had no idea who she was.

"Zoe Anderson," she said, introducing herself. "I have a summer home out on Sandy Point, and for the past three years I've trusted no one but Walter with my Land Rover. He was a marvelous mechanic. Marvelous. I'll miss him terribly."

Tucker's eyebrow lifted higher. "You're a cottager?"

"Yes. From New York."

"What are you doing on Harmony at *this* time of year?"

She laughed musically. "The island has its charms, even in winter. In fact, lately I find myself spending as much time here during the off-seasons as I do during the summer." Unexpectedly she turned her smile on Dylan. "Of course, this man knows all about that. Don't you, Mr. McGrath?''

Cathryn glanced sharply at her husband. His face was flushed and he was widening his eyes at the woman. Cathryn was well acquainted with the expression, but didn't understand it in its present context.

"Dylan is my landscape architect," Zoe Anderson continued, her quick survey of Cathryn leaving her feeling invisible.

Cathryn glanced at her husband again. "Landscape *architect?*" she questioned him. Just when she'd adjusted to his upgrade from a simple landscaper to a landscape *designer*... he was changing what he called himself again?

Dylan shrugged self-consciously, avoiding her eyes.

"Last year," the Anderson woman continued animatedly, "we made extensive changes to the backyard. New perennial borders, trees, arbors, walkways. It's breathtaking. This spring we'll be overhauling the front."

"And that's—" Dylan paused to clear his voice which seemed unusually dry and squeaky. "And that's no mean feat, considering Ms. Anderson's front yard is more than an acre."

"But Dylan has been coming up with marvelous ideas. I hope you don't mind how much time he's spending on my project, Mrs. McGrath."

Cotton-mouthed, Cathryn replied, "No. Why should I mind?"

The woman laughed, shaking back her hair, and suddenly Cathryn discovered there was a very good reason why she should mind.

There on Zoe Anderson's earlobes sparkled Cathryn's Valentine earrings.

She lost her ability to speak, to move, even to breathe. All she could do was stare at the familiar eight-hundred-dollar earrings. And there was no doubt in her mind they were the same ones. The setting was just unusual enough to be distinctive.

All at once Cathryn remembered the card, the intimate verse, the romantic phrases, and nausea brought the taste of bile to her mouth.

Someone touched her arm and quietly asked, "Are you all right?"

Mechanically she turned and saw that the person addressing her was Tucker. Remembering where she was, she concentrated on composing herself and nodded with a reassuring smile. "Just a little queasy. I...I've been fighting symptoms of the flu all morning."

"Come sit down," Tucker said, urging her toward the sofa.

"No, I think..." She glanced at Dylan and caught him exchanging a look with the other woman that seemed too familiar, too fraught with communication. "I think I'll just go home."

Dylan escorted her to the van with a solicitous arm around her waist, but it wasn't concern she saw in his handsome, square-jawed face. It was fear. And guilt.

"Who is she?" Cathryn asked, her voice as shaky as her legs.

"Who?"

"That woman. Zoe Anderson."

"She's...a cottager. From New York. Weren't you listening?"

"Yes, but who is she to *you?*"

He pulled in his chin, in innocence and perplexity. "To me? She's a client, Cath. A client with a job big enough to pay for that sunroom you've always wanted." He helped her into the van, went around to the driver's side, and they started toward home under a cloud of tension, which he tried

to dispel by turning on the radio and humming along with
the song that was playing.

I should let it go, Cathryn thought. *I could've made a
mistake. Zoe Anderson might very well own earrings exactly
like the ones I found. Although they were unusual, surely
they weren't unique. Besides, this is Dylan I'm having
doubts about. Dylan.*

But the windshield wipers hadn't even had enough time
to clear a decent wedge of road grit off the window when
Cathryn decided she had to keep asking. She had to find out
for certain who Zoe Anderson was. She wouldn't rest easy
until she did.

By the time Dylan was steering into their driveway, Cathryn had her answer. She stumbled from the van, heading for
the house, but made it only as far as the walkway before
doubling over and throwing up.

LATE THAT AFTERNOON Tucker set off with the back seat of
his rental car rattling with cookware and serving dishes.
Sarah had suggested waiting. She said he was tired and
should get some rest. The neighbors who'd brought over
food were bound to drop by eventually to reclaim their
dishes. And even if they didn't, he could always return them
later in the week.

Trouble was, Tucker wasn't planning to be around later
in the week. There was a little woman in St. Louis who
needed to be sweet-talked into marrying him, and the sooner
he got to it the better. Right after Sarah had wrapped the
last leftover, declared the kitchen suitably neat, buttoned up
her overcoat and toddled on home, he'd put himself in gear
and packed the car. There was still too much to do.

Returning cookware was the least of it. Far more complicated was the chore of sorting through his uncle's belongings and deciding what to keep, what to throw out, what

to sell or give away. That could drag on for days. Then there was the house itself. Walter had left it to him, and while Tucker was deeply moved by his generosity, the gift didn't come without its problems—most notably, selling it. The garage presented problems, too, maybe more so than the house. Finding a buyer for a house wasn't unusual. But for an auto repair shop?

Sure, he could put off returning pans and dishes, but anything he could knock off the list now would be one less thing standing between him and his leaving Harmony.

Tucker decided to drop off the items that belonged to Cathryn McGrath first, since they took up most of the back seat. He was also a little curious to know how she was feeling.

With an up-to-date map of the island on the seat beside him and West Shore Road highlighted with yellow marker, he set off toward what should have been a setting sun. Unfortunately a gloomy gray blanket of mist continued to muffle the island, and the only evidence he saw of the sun existed in a paler shade of gray to the west.

Still, the landscape wasn't without its beauty, in a stark and empty way. Tucker turned off the radio and cracked open a window to better enjoy the mellow two-note bellowing of Harmony's competing foghorns and the screeching of its gulls. The cold brine-scented air blowing in invigorated his body. The long vistas, both seaward and skyward, invigorated his soul.

He used to loathe this time of year when he was a kid. There was a stillness to February, a nothing-happening hush as nature hung idle between winter and spring, that used to drive him crazy. Funny, how time could alter a person's perspective.

Tucker found Cathryn's address with minimal trouble. She lived in an area of new midpriced homes, each set on at least two acres, with SUVs in the driveways and swing sets in the yards. The McGraths lived in an extended Cape Cod house with white shutters, natural cedar shingles, and well-tended shrubs out front. Kid-made paper hearts, framed by ruffled curtains, decked the windows. Cupids lined the walk, and a red-and-pink Valentine flag hung by the front door. There were window boxes stuffed with pine and holly, flower beds waiting for spring, and tucked here and there, stone squirrels and bunnies and ducks. It was picture-perfect. And perfectly Cathryn.

Tucker was standing at the door before he realized he should've called before coming over. Although it was nearly dinnertime, the house was eerily still. He heard no children's voices within, no TV gabble, no clatter of pots or plates. He didn't even see any lights.

He stepped back, peering toward the attached garage. The double door was raised, revealing only one vehicle. Maybe the family had gone visiting. Or maybe to a restaurant…although Tuesday was an odd night to go out to eat, and Cathryn *had* been feeling sick.

For a brief moment, Tucker worried about Cathryn. Something wasn't right with her. She'd claimed to be fighting off flu symptoms all morning, but he'd seen her eating and nothing had been wrong with her appetite. He'd also noticed the abrupt change in her expression while the Anderson woman talked with her.

With a shake of his head, he tossed aside his suspicions. He was an inveterate cynic, seeing trouble where none existed, and that was all there was to it. Tucker set down the urn on the doormat where it couldn't be missed, then returned to the car for the rest of Cathryn's things.

With everything piled on the stoop, Tucker was ready to leave and head over to his next stop. But on a whim, he picked his way across the sodden mulch in front of the house, squeezed himself between two pungent evergreens and peered through one of the living room windows.

The room was dark, steeped in shadow, but he found an occupant anyway. She was curled into a fetal position on the sofa, as still as a shadow herself. Cathryn.

CHAPTER THREE

ALARM RIPPED THROUGH Tucker like a bullet, sending his heart racing. *Don't jump to conclusions,* he told himself. *Maybe she really is sick. You've played dead yourself a few times when you were under the weather and people knocked at your door.*

Despite what common sense was telling him, Tucker scrambled back to the stoop and tried the door. It was unlocked. "Cathryn?" he called, stepping inside and peering into the living room. She didn't move. With his heart caught in his throat and his imagination in overdrive, he crossed the room, dread in every step, and forced himself to touch her. "Cathryn?" he repeated, shaking her gently by the shoulder. It was warm, he realized with tremendous relief.

Slowly, very slowly, she turned her head and looked up at him. Her eyes were glazed and unfocused, like those of a person in shock. For a moment she simply stared without recognition. Then, "Oh, Tucker," she said in a soft, faraway voice. "I didn't hear...I must've fallen asleep." She made an effort to sit up, then sagged again.

Tucker wanted to accept that she'd been sleeping, but his cynical twin refused to let him. "What's the matter? Not feeling well?"

She swallowed. "No. Not very." Tucker *did* detect the faint odor of vomit drifting from her clothes. Not a pretty smell, especially when combined with the apple-cinnamon scent that pervaded the room.

The first strokes of embarrassment began to lash at him. He rubbed a hand across the back of his neck. "I'm sorry about walking in the way I did, uninvited. I hope I didn't scare you."

"No." She lay so still, as if moving might shatter her.

"I brought back your things, your coffee urn and stuff."

"Oh, yes?"

"Mmm. I was planning to leave it all on the front step, but then, just for the hell of it, I tried the door."

As if he'd strung together too many thoughts for her to process, she frowned and slowly massaged her skull, her fingers buried in her tangled hair.

With feigned nonchalance, Tucker cast his glance about the dusky living room. "Where's Dylan?"

"Out," she whispered hoarsely. "He's...out."

"And the kids?"

"With my parents."

"Can I...do anything for you? Get you anything?"

"No. Thank you. I'm sorry I can't be more..." She lifted the hand that had been massaging her head and held it limply poised, palm up, as if it contained the rest of her thought.

"I'll just bring in those things then." He backed up a step, turned toward the door when he heard her sniff. Damn! He retraced his steps. "Cath, where did Dylan go? Maybe I should call him or something."

"No, it's okay." Her face cramped into a mask of anguish underlaid with embarrassment. "Really. He'll...he'll be back soon." Her jaw began to tremble. She tried to steady it, but her lips took up the trembling instead.

"Hey, what's the matter?" Tucker squatted on his heels to be at eye-level with her.

"Nothing. Please... Nothing." But two plump tears slipped from her eyes and soaked into the couch pillow.

Every instinct Tucker possessed screamed at him to take flight. He'd walked into a domestic cataclysm. But he listened to the voice of responsibility instead, a voice that had been growing stronger ever since he'd learned he was going to be someone's dad.

"Cathryn?" he implored, brushing back her hair. It was softer than he'd expected. Her chest hitched and she made a tight hiccuping sound as she tried to suppress a sob. "Cath, at the risk of butting in, are you and Dylan having problems?"

The pain that scored her features answered him better than any words. Cursing under his breath, he gently pulled her to a sitting position and wedged himself into the space beside her.

"Do you want to talk about it?" he asked, wondering when he'd lost his mind.

"No." She began to tilt in the opposite direction, heading for another pillow. Tucker put his arm around her to keep her upright.

"There's nothing to say, really." She pressed her hands to her cheeks as her mortification deepened. "I'm sorry, Tucker. Please, just go. This has nothing to do with you."

So true. But, masochist that he was, he continued, "Does it have anything to do with that woman who showed up after the funeral?"

Cathryn had been trembling already, but now the potency of her tremors grew until they rattled Tucker, as well. He tightened his grip on her, felt the pressure building, until finally she seemed unable to contain it any longer and cried out, "Dylan's having an affair." With that she crumpled forward, covering her face with her hands, and wept with such misery that Tucker found his own throat thickening.

He rubbed her back, a feeble attempt to let her know he was still there. After a while he asked, "Are you sure?"

She nodded, still buried in her hands. "He-e to-o-ld me so-o himself." At least, those were the words Tucker thought he heard. They were too fractured for him to be really certain.

She steadied her voice long enough to say, "What's worse is, they've been seeing each other for...for over a year." And then she began to cry again, harder than before.

Tucker didn't know what else to do but pull her into his arms. "You didn't suspect anything?"

With her face buried in his leather jacket, she gulped down tears and shook her head. In her sob-broken way she added Dylan and Zoe had apparently been discreet, for which she was extremely thankful.

Overcome with self-consciousness again, she moved away, scraped the sleeve of her sweater across her eyes and inhaled shakily. "This must be so awkward for you."

"No, no..." he lied.

"Please, why don't you just go? This isn't your concern."

"You made it my concern twenty years ago when you invited me to one of your parties—a clambake on the beach, I believe."

"What?" She scrunched her nose in puzzlement.

"It didn't matter that I was an outsider and a punk and the last person anybody would want at a civilized party. You didn't want me to feel left out."

A weak smile briefly lifted her tear-wet cheeks. "Yes, but I was also relieved you didn't show up."

Tucker clasped his heart and gasped. "And all this time I believed you were a saint."

Using her sleeve again, she blotted her eyes and cheeks and surreptitiously wiped her nose. No great loss, in his estimation. The sweater, the same one she'd worn to the funeral, was an overly bulky, blah-gray thing better consigned to the ragbag.

He suggested, "How about I make us some coffee?"

She shook her head.

"Tea? Sure. You'd probably prefer tea." He was reaching to switch on the lamp near him when Cathryn emitted a strangled groan and shot off the couch. In the sudden illumination all he saw was her back disappearing down a darkened hallway. The next moment he heard the sounds of retching.

Whistling tunelessly, he bided his time until he heard the toilet flush. Then he got up, slipped off his jacket and went to help her. She was still hunched over the bowl, clutching her stomach and shivering. He found a washcloth in the undersink vanity, wet it with cool water and pressed it to her cheek. She nodded her gratitude and took it from him. Next he found mouthwash and poured a shot into a paper cup. After rinsing and spitting, she straightened and met her image—and his—in the lighted mirror.

She mewled. "Oh, God!"

He couldn't refute her. Her cheeks were blotched, her eyes were swollen and her nose was red as a June strawberry. Groaning, she made a futile stab at her hair, most of which had escaped its elastic and now hung in loose, wild tangles. "What a wreck!" she choked out, her gaze grazing Tucker's. "No wonder Dylan…" She let her sentence trail off, squinched her eyes shut and clutched the rim of the sink with desperate tightness.

Standing behind her, Tucker studied her reflection curiously. She was a woman he hardly knew, a woman he hadn't thought about in years and expected to forget again soon after he left. Yet, in those emotion-marred features he could still see the pretty little girl she'd once been, with bows in her hair, scabs on her knees, and a heart of pure gold. Although he'd often mocked her klutziness and fuss-budget ways, he really hadn't minded her all that much. And he'd always appreciated her generosity toward him, her compassion—from the nerdy pom-pom hat she'd knitted for him his first Christmas on the island to the party she'd helped Winnie organize the day he left.

Tucker smoothed her hair and smiled encouragingly. "If you're feeling better, maybe we can move to the kitchen?" She pulled in a deep breath and nodded.

Cathryn's kitchen was much like the rest of the house, what little he'd seen of it, anyway—cabinets in light country oak, stenciled walls, ruffled curtains, and handcrafted doo-dads everywhere. Towels, place mats and chair pads coordinated. Cookbooks spanned the entire top shelf of a hutch. The rest held bric-a-brac, Valentines and photographs. Kids' art and school papers patchworked the refrigerator, and a bulletin board that resembled command-central apparently kept everyone on track.

"Where do you keep your tea?" Tucker asked her.

"There. The cabinet by the fridge."

Tucker opened the door and a pantry unfolded. His eyes widened as he took in the well-stocked shelves. He was about to ask her what kind of tea she wanted—she had nine different flavors—when she said, "I really don't want tea. I'd much prefer brandy."

He turned, frowning. "Can your stomach handle it?"

"Yes. This nausea is all nerves. The brandy will actually help." She shuffled toward a cabinet near the hutch. "Sit. I'll get it. What can I get for you?"

Tucker marveled that, even with her world tumbling around her, she felt obliged to play hostess.

"No. *You* sit. Just point me in the right direction."

"No, I insist…"

After going back and forth a few more times, she deferred

to him and slipped shakily into one of the Windsor chairs at the kitchen table. Tucker poured her some ginger brandy and got himself a beer—*Dylan's* beer, he thought, wanting to kill the bastard.

"Do your parents know about this situation?" he asked, joining her at the table.

Cathryn lifted her brandy snifter with two hands to minimize the trembling, took a careful sip and swallowed. "No. I phoned my mother and asked her to pick up the kids at school and keep them overnight, but I lied about why. I said..." Her jaw quivered. She took another sip. "I said Dylan had surprised me with a belated Valentine gift—dinner and an overnight stay at the Old Harbor Inn. I know the excuse has holes, but it was the only one I could come up with. Dylan and I were in the thick of our...our discussion."

Tucker nodded understandingly. "Have you called anyone else? A friend maybe? Is anyone coming over?"

Cathryn bowed her head, tears gathering on her lower eyelids. "No."

Great. So he was *IT,* the ear for her to pour her troubles into, the shoulder for her to cry on. "Okay, Shortcake," he said as soothingly as he could. "Tell me all about it."

Hugging her waist, she slowly tipped forward until her forehead rested on the table's polished surface. Tucker sighed. The woman could not sit up straight to save her life. It was as if she'd lost all strength in her backbone.

"Cathryn?"

"Mmm."

"I understand your reluctance. I hate to talk about my personal life, too. But talking helps. At least that's what they say."

Cathryn raised her head and reached for her brandy. She was quiet so long, staring at the glass, that Tucker figured she'd decided to disregard his suggestion. But then, in a small, dull voice she began.

"IT ALL STARTED when I found a pair of earrings," Cathryn said, uncertain if talking to Tucker was a good idea. Who *was* he, after all? she thought. At best, a distant acquaintance she hadn't seen in years. At worst, a reprobate who probably *endorsed* extramarital affairs.

Still, he was here, and nobody else was, and maybe he had a point. Talking *would* make her feel better, regardless of who was listening.

Oh, but it was hard. She'd never talked about her marital problems before, and until now most of them had been minor. Her relationship with Dylan was sacred territory, not to be betrayed.

Then again, she'd been the only one playing by the rules, hadn't she? She went on with her story.

"...Finally I simply confronted him with the fact that I'd found the earrings, and since he hadn't given them to *me*..."

The brandy she'd sipped between sentences was having its desired effect. She was warming from the inside out, knots of tension releasing.

"I could see he was trying to invent an excuse but couldn't. He had nothing to say, nowhere to turn, so he admitted the truth, he's seeing her."

"And he's been seeing her for a year?" Tucker said unobtrusively.

"Fourteen months."

Tucker raised a skeptical eyebrow. "How'd they pull that off on such a small island?"

"Apparently they met off-island, too. Times when I believed he was at a trade show or buying equipment or some such thing." Despite the effects of the brandy, Cathryn felt a sharp echo of the shock and grief she'd felt upon first learning this. She pressed her fingertips over her lips and waited for the pain to subside, but it didn't. She was in the van again, sitting beside her husband on the edge of hysteria, while the world as she knew it shifted and slid. She kept hearing Dylan apologize. "I'm sorry, Cath. I'm so sorry." And then the crucial phrase, "I didn't mean for you to find out this way."

Unthinkingly she'd snapped, "Oh? How did you want me to find out?"

"Not…this way. I thought we might go away for a few days. Just the two of us."

She'd stared at him a long incredulous moment. What was Dylan saying? That he *did* want her to find out? Then, as understanding dawned, her already shifting, sliding world utterly shattered.

"Why?" she'd implored. "What went wrong? I thought we were happy."

"And did he give you an answer?" Tucker asked.

Cathryn was jolted out of her daze by his voice. Had she been talking all this time?

"He said it just…happened."

"It just *happened?*"

"Yes." Cathryn reached for the brandy bottle and poured another dose into her glass. "That's what he said, at first anyway. But I guess I kept after him, and eventually he got so angry he began to admit things he'd never intended to." She had to pause until the anguish gripping her released some of its hold. "Apparently Dylan's been unhappy with me for some time."

"With you?" Wide-eyed, Tucker looked ready to go ten rounds with her statement.

She nodded. "He said I ignore his needs. I spend all my time tending to the house and the kids."

Tucker laughed sarcastically. "Aw, poor baby."

Cathryn raised a hand. "No, he's right. I *have* become too absorbed with homemaking and the kids' activities. I *have* become complacent about us, Dylan and me." *Complacent* was Dylan's word, though. She'd always thought in terms of contentment, and it hurt more than she could express that he didn't feel similarly contented.

Cathryn blinked her burning eyes, battling tears, as she recalled the myriad complaints Dylan had registered with her that afternoon, each one an arrow straight to the heart.

"The son of a bitch," Tucker rasped. "He's caught having an affair and he turns on *you?* You should be outraged."

Cathryn swallowed, trying to loosen the knot in her throat. "I would be, except that much of what he said is true, and I'm not surprised he turned to another woman."

"Would you explain that to me, please?"

"Well, you know…" She cast about for something she could say that wouldn't lead to a discussion of sex. "The way I've let myself go, for instance."

"Did he accuse you of that, too?"

"Well, look at me, Tucker. I'm not exactly the girl Dylan married twelve years ago."

"That's right. You've improved."

"Ha! I'm a big, worthless hunk of fat."

Tucker sat forward, scowling with the fierceness of a lion. "Okay. So you've put on some weight, but you're hardly fat. To be honest, I kinda like you this way. Holding you, a guy knows he has a *woman* in his arms."

"Oh, please." She dragged her gaze away from Tucker. "On top of being fat, I'm stupid, too. Stupid for not realizing Dylan was so bored and unhappy."

"All right. That's enough of that," Tucker snapped. "You're not stupid, Shortcake—except for calling yourself stupid."

"Oh, yeah? What do *you* call a woman who doesn't know her husband's having an affair—for a whole year?"

"Maligned," Tucker shot back angrily.

Cathryn bit her lip to keep it from trembling. Yes, she did feel maligned. Maligned and betrayed. When she thought about all the things she and Dylan had done and shared over the past year—the hundreds of meals and chores, the socializing with friends, the lovemaking—oh, especially that...

Tucker got up and set his empty beer bottle in the sink, his scowl still in place. "Is he coming back tonight?" he asked, staring out the darkened window. Not a glimmer of daylight remained.

Cathryn needed a moment before she could answer. "No."

Tucker turned in hopeful surprise. "Did you toss him out?"

"No! Of course not. Dylan simply thought it would be better if he left. Otherwise, he said, the house would be too tense, the possibility of our arguing in front of the kids too great."

Tucker's narrowed eyes met hers. "Do you have any idea when he will be back?"

"To live?" She swallowed more brandy, welcoming its numbing bite. "No. I asked, but all he said was, he needs time to sort things out."

"Things?"

"How he feels, I guess. If he wants to stay in the marriage."

"Is he going to continue seeing the Anderson woman?"

"I don't know that, either." She'd been afraid to ask. Afraid, also, to inquire where he'd be sleeping tonight.

Tucker folded his arms and rested his hip against the counter. "What are you going to do about the kids?"

"Oh, God. My kids." Cathryn braced her forehead on one hand and closed her eyes. "They're going to fall apart when they hear about this." Out of the blue she burst into tears. She didn't want to cry. Crying was weak and dumb and humiliatingly messy. But thinking of her kids broke down every defense she had.

She felt something nudge her elbow—a box of tissues Tucker was pushing at her. She helped herself to several, and after a lengthy mop-up said, "Dylan's coming by tomorrow afternoon to help me tell them. He promised he'd be here when they got off the school bus. I'm not quite sure what we'll say or how we'll say it…" She'd never in her life felt so lost, so vulnerable. "Do you have any suggestions, Tuck?"

"Me?" He stood up straight. "Hell, I'm so out of my element here." He sighed heavily, shook his head and contemplated the problem. "I probably wouldn't say anything about the affair. You'll have to tell them eventually—assuming your separation continues; in such a tight community, they're bound to hear something. Better from you than some kid at school. But not tomorrow. They'll have enough to cope with as it is."

Cathryn plucked another tissue from the box and pressed it to her eyes, fighting back a renewed surge of tears. She nodded. "Yes. Better to take small steps, move the kids through this in stages."

"Also, whatever you do, make sure you and Dylan tell them you love them."

"Of course."

"And that you'll *always* love them, no matter what."

"Okay."

"And you'll always be there for them."

"Okay."

"And your problems are not their fault."

She kept nodding, filing away his advice.

"Other than that," he shrugged, "I don't know what to say. Sorry."

Cathryn gazed up at Tucker, standing at the table with his large, suntanned hands resting on the bowed back of a chair. She studied his hair, caught back in a low ponytail, his beard, his garnet earring, his belt buckle with its carving of an eagle in flight, gripping a rattlesnake in its talons. She saw a man who, in giving advice regarding her children, claimed to be out of his element.

He could've fooled her.

Just then Tucker's stomach growled. Loudly. "Oh, Tuck, I just realized how late it is. Have you had dinner?"

TUCKER BACKED UP a step. Hell, he thought, she was going to offer him something to eat. And although he was hungry, he'd much rather eat alone at his uncle's house where no one's problems but his own existed to give him indigestion. But he couldn't very well leave Cathryn in her current state.

"Not yet. Have you?"

"No. But I'm not hungry. Please let me get something for you, though. There's leftover stroganoff in the fridge, and homemade chicken soup, and tons of stuff in the freezer. Hamburgers, hot dogs, pizza..."

"Pizza sounds good. Which freezer?"

"The chest." She started to get up, swayed and gripped the table.

"I can get it. Frozen pizza is a bachelor's specialty." Tucker noticed she didn't argue this time. She smiled feebly and sat.

Tucker opened the freezer and his mouth gaped. It was full of food, the kind of food he'd forgotten existed—roasts, pork chops, whole chickens, huge economy-size bags of vegetables, ice cream bars, homemade pies, gallons of milk. He didn't even know milk *could* be frozen.

His aunt used to shop in bulk, too, stock up on the mainland a few times a year. He remembered the sense of security he'd felt looking into her storeroom, the sense of wealth, of provenance and self-sufficiency. Those feelings had been all new to him when he'd first arrived. Back in the Bronx, he'd often had nothing to eat at home and survived mostly by stealing.

He'd tried doing the same on Harmony, although he'd no longer had a need to. Stealing had just become a way of life. He'd gotten caught, of course. Here, proprietors recognized their customers and knew when stock had been tampered with.

He'd expected to be taken to the police station and then hauled off to juvie. But to his amazement, no one had prosecuted. Instead, they'd talked to him, helped him understand there was a different way to live. In exchange for his doing odd jobs, they'd given him spending money. Thus, he'd learned the value of working for a living; he'd learned decency and the true meaning of the phrase, "It takes a village…"

"Not the microwave!" Cathryn yowled. "That'll make the pizza inedible!"

Tucker shrugged diffidently and moved to the stove. On the wall above the burners hung a plaque that read, Martha Stewart Doesn't Live Here. But Cathryn McGrath Does!

With the pizza in the oven cooking properly, he turned and noticed Cathryn reaching for the bottle of brandy again. In three strides he arrived at the table and scooped the bottle away from her. "I think you should eat something. Drinking's only going to give you new problems." *Hypocrite.* If he'd been in Cathryn's shoes, he'd already be passed out on the floor.

"Tuck, I can't eat." She *did* look kind of queasy.

"I know, it's hard. You're hurting pretty bad. But think of your kids, Shortcake. In the days ahead, they're going to be hurting, too, and looking to you for comfort. To take care of them, you'll have to be strong, and whether you want to face it or not, emotional strength and physical strength go hand-in-hand." Tucker wasn't at all sure he knew what he was talking about, but she seemed to buy it.

"Okay. Um… Soup, I guess."

Tucker warmed a bowl of her homemade chicken soup—she conceded he could use the microwave for that—and set it on the table. "Eat slowly," he admonished, donning a cow-shaped oven mitt before fetching his pizza.

Cathryn ate about half of her soup dutifully before sitting back and raising her hands in surrender. Tucker didn't push the issue. He polished off his pizza with another of Dylan's weak-as-piss beers, cleared the table and thought longingly again about going home. He *needed* to go home, needed to sit on the porch, clear his head in the cold night air and figure out how people became married, not separated.

But that would have to wait a little longer. While putting their plates in the dishwasher, he'd noticed Cathryn's gaze drift toward the display of family photographs in the hutch, and there it remained.

"Cathryn?" he asked, wiping his hands on a paper towel. He wasn't sure if the coordinated cloth towels were meant to be used.

She swallowed, turned and forced a teary smile. "Yes?"

"Are you still friendly with that redheaded girl? What was her name? Laura?"

The question surprised her and dried her tears. "Lauren?"

"Lauren. That's it. Is she still around?"

"As a matter of fact, yes. She returned to Harmony just

last year to buy her mother a house and ended up marrying her old boyfriend, Cameron Hathaway.''

Tucker, about to toss the wad of damp paper into the wastebasket, swung around in astonishment. "The kid who got her pregnant?''

"Yes.''

"Well, I'll be damned.''

"Why do you ask?''

Why? Because he needed help here. Because the situation was soon going to be more than he could handle. "Maybe we should call her, ask her to come over and stay with you.'' Primarily he was thinking about getting Cathryn showered and put to bed. He'd watched her trying to stand a couple of times and knew she'd had too much brandy.

"Calling wouldn't do any good,'' Cathryn said, yawning widely. "Lauren and Cam went to Boston. They're seeing *Rent* tonight. Not coming home till tomorrow.''

Tucker kept his curses silent. "How about your other friend, the one who used to do that show up at old man Finch's crazy little radio station? She still around?''

It pleased him to see Cathryn smile. "Julia came back, too.'' Her smile widened around another yawn. "Better watch out, Tuck. All she planned to do was attend a funeral, too, and she ended up marrying the editor of the island newspaper.''

"Thanks for the warning. I'll remember to keep up my guard. In the meantime, do you know Julia's phone number offhand?''

"Forget it. Jules now owns Preston Finch's crazy little radio station and is presently, even as we speak, doing her show. She won't be off the air until eleven.''

Tucker's heart sank. He knew enough not to ask about the other classmate who'd been Cathryn's friend. He'd heard about her death. "Looks like I'm *IT* again," he muttered in an undertone.

Cathryn blinked at him groggily, uncertain if he'd spoken. She looked so tired, he was sure that if he walked out now she'd fall asleep right there, head on the table, soiled clothes still on her back. Not that the clothes really mattered. But she might tumble off the chair and hurt herself. At the very least she'd wake up with a stiff neck.

"Okay, Shortcake," he said, clapping and rubbing his hands as if he were about to propose a great adventure. "How about we head to the bathroom and get cleaned up for bed."

She blinked again, her eyes widening with sudden alertness.

"I mean *you*," he said quickly. "*You* get ready for bed. I'll just be close by if you need help."

Her face flushed a deep pink. "Thank you, but you've done more than enough already. You should go home." Bracing on the arms of the chair, she pushed herself to her feet, and the color in her cheeks drained to ash.

Tucker flew around the table and supported her, one arm around her back, one under her elbow.

After a moment, she said, "I'm okay."

"Great. I'll hang on to you, then." That earned him a gratifying chuckle—and compliance.

He escorted her through the living room, up the stairs to the bedroom she'd shared until now with Dylan. An oil portrait of them, twelve years younger and resplendent in wedding gear, hung over one of the washed-oak dressers. Ever so slowly, she gathered up her nightgown, slippers and robe. Tucker remained at her elbow, urging her onward whenever her path crossed an item of Dylan's.

At last, he shuffled her into the adjoining bathroom, sat her on a brass vanity stool and removed her shoes.

"Tucker," she protested, obviously embarrassed.

"That's all. You can do the rest." He stepped to the tub and slid open the glass shower door, moved some towels closer and spread a mat on the floor.

"Tucker," she said on an exasperated chuckle. "I'm just tired and a bit tipsy. I haven't been lobotomized." She rose and pushed him out of the bathroom with surprising vigor. "Go home!" she ordered, shutting the door.

"Okay, see ya," he called back, dropping into a comfy-looking reading chair. The last thing he wanted was for her to slip and crack her head and be lying in there all night, alone and helpless.

His gaze roamed the room. It looked like something out of a J.C. Penney catalogue. Thick flowered comforter, matching curtains and table skirt and wall border. About thirty-two pillows on the bed...

Tucker's gaze drifted to the wedding portrait again. Dylan was a handsome guy, he couldn't deny that. But Tucker had gotten his number when they were still just kids. Although Dylan was a year younger than him, they'd shared a few mixed-grade classes, and Tucker had seen him cheating on tests. Later, he'd caught him cheating at cards. And there, standing beside the double-dealing bastard, was the straightest arrow Tuck had ever come across. Sincere, ingenuous Cathryn. Blind, gullible Cathryn.

Suddenly, the door to the bathroom opened revealing pink, naked Cathryn.

Cathryn screamed and ducked back into the steam. Wincing, Tucker eased to his feet with thoughts of tiptoeing out of the room. As if that would erase what had just happened.

"Tucker!" she wailed from behind the closed door. "You said you were leaving."

"I lied."

"No kidding."

The door opened again. She was bundled in flannel from chin to toe. Her wet hair, combed straight and sleek, framed a face that blazed.

"I'm sorry," Tucker sputtered, embarrassed too. "I didn't think."

"Oh…" She flapped an arm as if to finish her statement. "It's all right. With the beating my pride took today…" The sentence trailed off to another arm flap.

"Would you like some hot milk?"

She grimaced. "No. Please. Just my bed, although I doubt I'll sleep. My mind keeps racing."

"Well, at least give it a try. Remember, you have to be strong for the kids."

Tucker regretted taking that approach. Her expression filled with sadness. Still, she nodded and said, "You're right."

"I'm always right. Now, hit the sack, lady."

Cathryn climbed onto the bed on all fours, batting away pillows until only two remained. Real pillows. Then she flopped face forward into one of them. "Good night," she said, her words severely muffled.

Tucker tugged the comforter down, pulling it under her, until it cleared her slippered feet, then covered her with it and sat on the edge of the bed.

She turned her head and said, "Go home."

He smiled and placed his hand on her head. "I'll be downstairs if you need anything," he said, lightly stroking her wet hair. "I'll leave in the morning."

Cathryn swallowed, pressed a bunched hand to her mouth, and tears glistened along the lashes of her closed eyes. "Thank you."

"No problem." He could get up now, he realized. He could go downstairs and have another beer and watch TV. But he sat awhile longer, stroking her hair and wishing he could say everything was going to be all right. But he couldn't. All he could say was, "I'll be here," because his instincts were telling him that nothing was going to be right in Cathryn's world for a very long time.

CHAPTER FOUR

CATHRYN WOKE to the familiar sound of a cupboard door slamming. She sat up in alarm and glanced at the bedside clock. Oh, God, she'd overslept. Only fifteen minutes until the school bus came. Had the kids gotten up on their own? Made their own breakfast? Was Dylan up with them?

Her gaze shot to his pillow, his perfectly plumped pillow, and suddenly, painfully, reality came flooding back. No, her husband was not downstairs. He was gone. He'd left her for another woman. Cathryn toppled sideways onto his cool forsaken pillow, choking back a cry.

But there it was again, the thump of a cupboard door, and as suddenly as she'd remembered Dylan's betrayal, she remembered Tucker Lang. Tucker was here. He'd been here all night.

In a flash of agitation, Cathryn threw back the comforter and swung her feet to the floor. Ow! Her ribs ached from vomiting, and her head throbbed. Slowing her movements, she scanned the room for her bathrobe. Oh. Right. She was wearing it. Her slippers, too. She'd put them on last night after her shower.

No, not after her shower, she remembered, wincing. After she'd waltzed out of the bathroom wearing nothing but her certainty that Tucker had gone. Cathryn buried her face in her hands and moaned, suffering every bit of the embarrassment that had eluded her last night.

But then, another recollection hit her: today she and Dy-

Ian had to tell the children he'd moved out. And suddenly her embarrassment seemed trite and disappeared under an onslaught of dread and anxiety. How would the kids cope with the news? How would she cope with telling them? And why should they have to cope with any of this, anyway? That was the question. She still didn't understand why this was happening to them. Separations happened to other people, not to her and Dylan.

Forcing herself past her desire to crawl back under the covers and hide forever, she got to her feet and headed into the bathroom—and then wished she hadn't. Under the bright vanity lights, her eyes looked like puffballs, her cheeks held all the color of oatmeal, and her hair, wet when she'd gone to sleep, had dried crazily, flat here, bent there, a veritable 3-D Rorschach inkblot test.

Feeling defeated before she even began, she picked up her hairbrush, pulled it through the mess a few times and fastened it with an elastic. That done, she stared at the faucet awhile but lacked the energy to wash her face. She walked back to the bedroom, tugged on jeans and a sweatshirt and went downstairs.

"Good morning," she said, stepping into the kitchen. Despite her smile and determinedly straight posture, she felt fragile, like a glass mercury ball filled with sorrow just waiting to be spilled.

Tucker spun around from his perusal of the refrigerator's contents. "Oh, hey! I hope I didn't wake you?" His dark gaze swept over her warily, as if trying to assess yesterday's damage and today's mood.

"No, actually I overslept." This was just too weird, having big, bad Tucker Lang in her kitchen first thing in the morning. He'd apparently showered. His hair was damp and, like hers, caught back at his nape. Sadly, she noticed, the style looked better on him.

"Coffee! Oh, bless you." Cathryn hurried toward the cof-feemaker.

"Do you feel up to eating something?" he asked, car-rying a carton of eggs to the counter.

Grimacing and shivering, she shook her head. That earned her a growl of reprimand. "Maybe I'll have a piece of toast," she said. Somewhat mollified, Tucker continued pre-paring his own breakfast.

Their conversation was subdued as they ate, and focused mainly on chores Tucker needed to tackle that day. She hadn't realized there was so much to do. Had he mentioned any of it last night? Locked inside her own misery, she'd paid so little attention to him.

He probably thought he was doing her a favor by steering the conversation clear of her problems, but his thoughtful-ness only ended up burdening her with one more: guilt for having cut so deeply into his valuable time.

With the last bite of his three-egg omelet consumed, Cathryn insisted he be on his way. But he merely poured himself another cup of coffee and said, "Not until we get Julia or somebody else over here to stay with you."

"That isn't necessary. I'm fine. Besides, it won't be long before Dylan arrives."

Tucker shot her an impatient look over the rim of his coffee mug. "That could be five, six hours from now. Com-pany will make the time go faster."

"No. Please. I..." She decided to be honest. "I really can't face anyone yet. Not even close friends. *Especially* them."

Tucker tipped his head so that a shaft of winter sunlight fell across his face. "Pride, Shortcake? Is that what I'm hearing?"

She thought a moment. "Maybe. Everyone thinks of me and Dylan as an ideal couple, an institution practically. Solid as Gibraltar. Always here, year in, year out. They're going to be shocked and disillusioned and full of questions, and, quite frankly, I have enough to cope with today."

"Oh. It never occurred to me that friends might be more of a problem than a help."

"Today they would be, when everything is still so raw and in transition and hard to explain. Plus, this is a private matter between me and Dylan." After a heartbeat she added, "And the kids. We still have to tell the kids. I wouldn't feel right talking to outsiders before talking to them."

Rubbing his jaw, Tucker appeared thoughtful, a wry arch to his left eyebrow. "That puts me in kind of an awkward position, don't you think?"

Cathryn bit her lip. "I really am sorry you got caught up in this, Tucker."

Sighing, he shrugged. "Not your fault. You told me to shove off a number of times."

"Yes, I did." She attempted a smile, but it faded quickly. "You will keep this under your hat, won't you?"

"Goes without saying."

"Thanks. The gossip will start circulating soon enough. No need to prime the pump." Struck by a vision of her beleaguered life in the very near future, she slumped forward, moaning, and rested her forehead on her arms.

"Is that how you want your kids to find you?" Tucker chided sternly. "Is that how you intend to be strong for them?"

She popped up. "I'm okay."

His look sharpened, made all the more fierce by the sunlight slashing across his dark eyes.

"Honestly," she assured him. "Now, unless you're still hungry, can I finally convince you to leave?"

"What'll you do here all alone?"

"Oh, I have plenty to keep me occupied. Laundry. Vacuuming. A sewing project. Some calls to make for the PTO.'' Noticing Tucker's frown, she explained, ''Parent-Teacher Organization.''

''Well…'' Tucker glanced at his jacket hooked on the neighboring chair. Not a biker jacket, but black leather nonetheless. ''I really do have to get moving.''

''Then move.'' Cathryn got up, came around to his side of the table and lifted the jacket. ''Let's go, Lang. I'm throwing you out. Enough's enough.''

Smiling his dimpled smile, he hauled himself to his feet and took the jacket from her.

''How much longer will you be on Harmony?'' she asked, walking him to the front door.

''Four, maybe five days.'' He pulled a pair of leather gloves from his pocket.

''Well, don't leave without saying goodbye.''

''I won't.'' He opened the door and surveyed the hoary, frozen lawn through the glass storm door.

''I don't know how to thank you for everything you've done.''

He shrugged negligently. ''Buy me a beer someday, when this all blows over.''

''I will. Maybe even two.'' *If this ever does blow over.*

His gaze connected with hers. ''Hang in.''

Lips pressed hard, she nodded. ''I'll try.''

''And good luck with the kids. Remember to tell them you love them and the separation isn't their fault.''

She nodded again, unable to speak for the emotions clogging her throat, not least of which was gratitude toward this man who'd come to her door merely to return a coffee urn and ended up helping her through a night she would've been ashamed to share with a dog. She felt she owed him more than a thank-you, or a beer, but what? A hug? Too awkward. A promise to return the favor someday? Tucker never needed help. Before he left she really should find some way to express her appreciation.

Tucker opened the storm door, and a wall of thirty-degree air shocked her out of her musing. "Take care, Shortcake," he said with a wink and stepped outside. She watched him stride down the path, leather jacket creaking, black ponytail gleaming in the morning sun, an incongruous figure if ever she saw one.

"You too," she called back belatedly. And perhaps because she felt so indebted to him, she waited, shivering, until he drove away before closing the door.

It took Cathryn until midmorning to muster the courage to call her mother. Primarily she wanted to ask about the kids—if they'd done their homework, if they'd gotten off to school all right, and if they knew they were supposed to come home afterward, not return to their grandparents'. She didn't want to discuss her problem. If telling her friends was going to be difficult, telling her mother would be impossible.

Meg Hill thought so highly of Dylan, and she was so very proud of her daughter. Always had been, for as long as Cathryn could remember. Not that her father was any less proud; he simply kept his feelings to himself. "Cathryn has never given me a day's trouble," Meg would tell anyone who'd listen when Cathryn was a girl. "Not in school, not at home or with her friends." For the past twelve years her mother's praise had centered on Cathryn's home and domestic skills and, of course, her beautiful family. Dylan was the ideal husband, and the children...well, they were the absolute sun in Meg Hill's sky. Although Cathryn knew her mother's bragging sprang from love and genuine pride, it sometimes embarrassed her. But far worse, it also was a burden because Cathryn felt pressured to continually meet that praise. Disillusioning her mother was not something she was looking forward to.

After assuring Cathryn that everything had gone fine with the children, her mother asked if she and Dylan had enjoyed their stay at the inn. Here it was, Cathryn's chance to get the dirty deed over with.

"It was lovely," she replied.

After hanging up, she spent the next half hour crying. But when crying made her sick to her stomach, she decided she simply had to pull herself together. She had to make the effort or else suffer a rerun of yesterday. Dragging the vacuum cleaner out of the utility closet, Cathryn swore she heard Tucker's voice cheering, "Thatta girl, Shortcake."

It was after noon before she glanced at a clock again. After noon? Yikes. Dylan would be here soon, and just look at her! She dashed upstairs to change. Half an hour later she came down again, looking halfway human. Not that she thought her appearance would make any difference to Dylan, but maybe it would to the kids. If they saw their mother pulled together, they might be reassured the world wasn't really falling apart.

She knew she should have some lunch, but gave up on that idea on the way to the kitchen and just sat on the couch instead, munching on grapes and crackers—and watching the street.

Cathryn grew edgier as time ticked on and Dylan didn't show. Yesterday they hadn't discussed specifically what they'd say to the kids. They needed to devise a strategy. They had things to discuss, lines to rehearse, a story to corroborate…hearts to keep from breaking. So where was he? He'd distinctly told her he'd be here to share the task of telling the kids.

There was the school bus now. Was she going to have to face their questions alone?

The kids had barely started up the driveway when Cathryn noticed Dylan's truck skulking up the street. The timing was just too right. Obviously he'd been trying to avoid being alone with her.

The back door opened and the kids tumbled into the house as they always did, noisily. Backpacks thumped on the mudroom floor. Chatter and teasing filled the air as jackets and hats got hung on their pegs. "Mom!" Justin hollered his usual greeting as he tramped into the kitchen. "We're home!"

Out of sight in the living room, Cathryn's heart ached with love and terror. She pressed her palms to her cheeks, trying to sculpt a smile, then stepped into the kitchen. "Hi. How was school?"

Her question was met with various blithe answers of "good," "okay" and "highly forgettable." The children were too intent on rummaging for snacks.

"Hey, don't I rate a hug?" she said, hoping her flippancy disguised how desperately she wanted to hold them.

One by one, the kids obliged. Justin, with his flannel shirt unbuttoned and hanging outside his jeans—not how her mother had sent him to school, Cathryn was sure. Beth, her soft curls tickling Cathryn's neck, her pink Barbie sweater smelling of peanut butter. Cory, tripping forward on an undone shoelace.

"Are you okay, Mom?" Cory studied her through his round, wire-framed glasses, too observant for his own good.

Cathryn smiled and combed her fingers through his hat-swirled hair. "Of course."

"You look different."

"I put on a little makeup, that's all."

"Oh." Her eight-year-old dismissed his concern with the alacrity of a child raised in a home where serious trouble is simply unthinkable.

The door opened again and in walked Dylan, wearing the same clothes he'd had on yesterday. He'd forgotten to pack a change. Still, he looked as if he'd just stepped out of a casual men's wear catalogue. That was Cathryn's doing. She loved buying clothes for him.

Because his hours were so irregular, the kids weren't at all surprised to see him at midafternoon. They barely looked up from pouring milk and reaching into the cookie jar as they said hi.

His gaze met Cathryn's guiltily, then veered away. For the first time since he'd admitted to his affair, she felt a hot lick of anger. In avoiding her, he was only hurting the kids.

"Would you like some coffee?" she asked, challenge in her tone.

He slipped off his parka and hung it on its peg. "That'd be great. Thank you," he replied, polite as a guest.

Seated at the table, Justin stopped munching and looked from one parent to the other. "How was last night?" he asked with a touch of suspicion.

Cathryn glared at Dylan. Ready or not, the moment was upon them, and now what were they supposed to do?

With a heavy sigh, Dylan lifted his coffee mug, the one that said World's Greatest Dad, and sat beside his firstborn, the son who looked so much like him. Cathryn pulled out a chair next to Beth, who was cheerily emptying her backpack of the day's papers and arranging them in front of her. Cory, already immersed in a library book, sat at one end of the table.

"What's up?" Justin asked, aware that his first question still hadn't been answered. Cory lifted his gaze, sensing something peculiar in his brother's voice.

"We have something to discuss with all of you," Dylan began. He looked tired, distraught under his surface calm, and Cathryn's anger ebbed somewhat.

"Something important?" Cory asked.

"Yes, important and difficult, and I'd give anything if I didn't have to say it."

Then don't, Cathryn silently implored, desperate to shield her babies.

"What's wrong, Dad?" Cory and Justin asked simultaneously.

Dylan glanced briefly across the table at Cathryn, then down at his coffee mug. "Kids, your mother and I—"

Cathryn feared he was about to blurt everything and send the children into shell shock. "Before we go any further," she interrupted, "we want you to understand something. And this is the most important thing of all, so listen up." Her gaze circled the table. "Beth?" she said to get her daughter's attention. With everyone listening, she continued, "Your father and I love you. We love you more than anything in the world. And we will always love you, and be here for you."

Justin paled. "Oh, no," he murmured, two jumps ahead of his younger siblings.

"What?" Beth asked, head swiveling, curls flying out. "What's happening, guys?"

Cathryn had more to say, more words of assurance and comfort to impart, but Dylan, perhaps thinking she was done, picked up the ball with, "Your mother and I have hit a rough patch in our marriage." He swallowed, his Adam's apple working over the ribbing of his crewneck sweater. "And we've decided it might be best if I...if I moved out for a while."

There. It was said. Dylan didn't breathe, waiting for the children's reaction. Neither did Cathryn. She couldn't for the pain encasing her.

"What?" Justin shot to his feet. His lean face, which lately seemed so grown-up to her, became a child's again, soft and vulnerable.

Cathryn glanced around the table, from Justin to Cory to Beth, watching Dylan's words sink in. It was like watching her children being lined up and executed. This was abuse. This was consciously inflicting harm on them. And it shouldn't be happening.

"Sit down, Justin," Dylan said gently.

Justin sat with caution, as if the chair might not be there anymore. "What kind of rough patch?" he asked. "What do you mean? Did you and Mom have a fight?"

"Sort of. I can't really get into that right now. It's between me and her."

"You've had fights before," Justin argued.

"Yes, but this one was a little different." Dylan dipped his head to his coffee mug as if he were diving for cover. Cathryn noticed her two youngest had grown unnaturally alert and tense. They seemed to be absorbing the scene with the very cells of their skin.

"How?" Justin persisted. "How was it different?"

"More serious."

Cathryn could almost hear the gears of Justin's mind whirring, processing all the adult troubles he'd ever heard about. *No! Please let's not go there.*

Fortunately—or unfortunately—everyone was distracted by a hiccupping sound at the end of the table, and turned their attention on Cory, who was struggling not to cry. Embarrassed, he buried his face in the crook of his arm, but his sobs were audible anyway. Although Beth still didn't seem to fully comprehend what was happening, she sensed calamity and burst into tears, too.

Cathryn considered comforting them with words, but nothing she thought of was true. No, the situation was *not* all right. There *was* reason to cry. The only comfort she felt she could give with any honesty was physical—a hug, holding a hand or stroking a head.

"But where are you going, Daddy?" Bethany asked through her jerky whimpers.

Yes, where? Cathryn wondered.

"To Gram and Grandpa McGrath's farm. I'll stay in my old room."

With a fresh stab of pain, Cathryn thought of her in-laws, good, hardworking people both. She loved them, got along well with them, and considered them an inextricable part of her life. Now what? How would they relate to one another after this?

"When are you coming back?" Justin asked his father.

A heavy pause hung over the table. "I'm not sure, Jus," Dylan replied, staring at his tightly folded, white-knuckled hands. "There's no timetable to this."

"But why do you have to leave at all?"

"We...need some time apart."

Cory lifted his head off his arms, sniffing back tears. His face was mottled and stricken. "From us?"

"No! Not from you, Buddy." Dylan squeezed Cory's shoulder. "Not from you. I'll see you as often as I can," he said, only making matters worse by reminding the children he *wouldn't* be seeing them on a normal basis.

"But who'll take me to Scouts?" Cory asked.

"I will, same as always," Dylan replied.

Justin pouted. "And will you still take me to my basketball games?"

"Of course. In fact, I was thinking we could do something special this Saturday after the game. All...four of us. Maybe you could even sleep at the farm that night." If he expected to see smiles or eager faces, he was sadly mistaken.

"Why are you gonna stay at the farm?" Beth asked, still lagging in understanding.

"They had a fight, stupid," Justin snapped.

"Take it easy, Justin." Dylan patted his son's arm.

"But you *are* coming back, right?" Cory needed to know.

Dylan hesitated too long.

"You're not getting divorced, are you?"

Dylan's swallow was so dry his throat made a scratching noise. "No one's talking about divorce here."

Cory's expression crumbled as if Dylan had said just the opposite. "But who'll take care of us?"

Shivering with her own insecurities, Cathryn answered, "I'll be here. I'm not going anywhere, love."

"But—" Lack of confidence filled Cory's eyes.

"Hey!" Dylan interrupted sternly. "No one's abandoning you. I'm still going to take care of you. Don't you dare start thinking I won't."

His certitude seemed to assure the children somewhat, the youngest two at least. Cathryn could see that Justin's thoughts were leaping ahead.

"What'll we tell our friends?" he inquired, pulling repeatedly on the short blond hair over his right ear.

"You don't have to tell them anything," Dylan replied, growing irritated. "It's nobody's business."

"But they're gonna know." Tears glistened in Justin's dark blue eyes. "They're gonna ask about it."

"So?"

Cathryn shot her husband a quelling glance before saying, "You can tell them your parents are separated. Use the word *separated*. And if they want to know more, just tell them the truth, you don't know the details and, therefore, can't talk about them."

Justin sighed and fell into a sullen funk. "Easy for you to say."

"Does anyone want any more milk?" Cathryn asked, noticing half-full glasses all around the table. The children mumbled no and shook their lowered heads.

She gazed at Dylan, trying to delve his thoughts. Did he have anything to add? Any way to make this better? Apparently not. His eyes were downcast, too.

Justin got up and carried his glass to the sink. Cory and Beth followed his example, their bottom lips jutting and quivering. "Maybe I'll just go upstairs now and do my homework," he said. Seeing him hoist his backpack, the younger kids did the same.

"Do you have any other questions?" Cathryn asked. "Any concerns?"

"No," Justin answered and was followed by two echoes.

"Well, okay. I'll call you when supper's ready." With a knot in her chest that wouldn't loosen, Cathryn watched her children file out of the kitchen and up to their rooms where, she was sure, no homework would get done.

"Something tells me that didn't go very well," Dylan said, placing his coffee mug on the counter.

Cathryn fumed as she wiped cookie crumbs from the table. "You thought it would?"

"I don't know what I expected."

She pitched the dishcloth into the sink. "Then maybe you should've arrived earlier."

He nodded, brow pinched, and turned to face the hutch. "Sorry. I...have no excuse."

Cathryn leaned her hip against the counter, crossed her arms, listened to her speeding heartbeat. "Are you really going to stay at the farm?"

"Yes. I think that'd be best."

"Did you stay there last night?" When he hesitated, she explained, "I simply want to know if you told your parents, if they know about us, in case I run into them."

He shoved his hands into his Dockers pockets. "No. They

don't know yet. I plan to go over there now." With an evasive glance around the kitchen, he quickly asked, "Is everything all right here?"

"Oh, just great," Cathryn choked out, still smarting from his oblique admission that he'd left here yesterday and gone straight to his other woman.

Dylan stepped closer and stroked her arm, looking apologetic, but she was in no mood for apologies. "Don't touch me. Just…don't."

He dropped his hand and sighed. "Well, if you don't need me for anything else, I'd like to get some more of my belongings."

Although her heart felt like the Titanic, she reciprocated with, "Fine. But you'll excuse me if I don't help you pack." Then she turned her back on him and stared at the crumb-coated dishcloth in the sink.

"Cath." His voice reached for conciliation, but she could only shake her head. "I'm sorry," he murmured again, then slowly turned and went upstairs. The next thing she heard was the opening and closing of dresser drawers.

It wasn't until then that Cathryn realized how much anger her pain harbored. The previous night had been rough, of course, but seeing Dylan now, hearing him in the house again, reminded her too vividly of his affair. When she looked at his hands, she pictured him touching Zoe Anderson. When she looked at his mouth, she imagined them kissing. And when he came downstairs lugging two overstuffed gym bags, although she didn't want him to go, she couldn't bear to have him stay.

"I've already said goodbye to the kids," he said, standing at the door. Cathryn was gratified to at least see tears in his eyes. "I'll come by for them on Saturday around ten. Okay?"

"Fine."

"And I'll return them on Sunday, late afternoon?"

She agreed again with the tersest of nods.

"In the meantime if you need anything, you know where to reach me."

Yes. Both places, Cathryn thought, and closed the door after him.

THAT SUPPERTIME Cathryn omitted doing thanks. It would've been a mockery, and the kids certainly didn't bring it up. They picked listlessly at their food, and when asked about school, replied in sullen monosyllables. When the picking and mumbling had dragged on long enough, Cathryn took away their plates and suggested they go watch television or play a game. They pretended to do both, but whenever she glanced into the family room as she straightened the kitchen, they were unfailingly huddled in conspiratorial conversation.

She ached for them. They were confused, scared and swarming with uncertainties. But then, so was she. Without Dylan, the house felt different. *She* felt different. Disconnected. Almost disembodied.

Surrendering to her need to comfort and be comforted, she hung the dish towel and joined them on the braided rug, watching meaningless images flash across the TV screen. Before long, however, Beth had climbed into her lap and the boys were pressing close on either side. She waited, softly stroking their hair, and eventually, as was inevitable, they began to open up to her.

Their questions were the same ones they'd posed to Dylan earlier: Why was he moving out? What had he and Cathryn fought about? Who'd take care of them? When was he coming back? It was almost as if they expected a different answer from their mother, a more honest answer. Cathryn tried to accommodate, but it was difficult. So many issues had to be sidestepped.

The best she could do was follow Tucker's advice, reassure them they had done nothing to cause the problem, and their father still loved them as much as always. She also tried to convince them their lives would continue unchanged, but her own uncertainties must've come through, because just when she thought they were done, their questions resumed.

Finally, realizing they were capable of going over the same ground all night if she let them, Cathryn announced it was time for baths and bed.

"But, Mom…" they chorused.

"No *buts*. It's already quarter to eight." She roused them to their feet and up the stairs and into extra-bubbly bubble baths—and better moods.

But as she was tucking Cory into bed, Bethany tiptoed into the boys' room and complained she was afraid to sleep alone. "The house is scary without Daddy. Can I sleep in here?"

"Not with me, you don't," Justin balked. "You kick like a mule in your sleep."

Cory sat up. He was wearing his Patriots pajamas, the ones he wore only because Dylan was an avid football fan. "I have room," he said. He threw aside the covers, and before Cathryn could decide what was best in this situation, Beth climbed in.

"Okay, but this is an exception. Tomorrow night I expect you to sleep in your own bed." Cathryn bent to kiss her youngest and was startled to find the child's cheeks wet. "Hey, what's the matter, honey?" She sat on the bed. Within seconds, Beth was in her lap and the boys were at her sides, just as they'd been earlier. Would this awful day never end? she wondered. Would she never find reprieve?

"Mommy, please make it better," Beth said, wiping her eyes on her pajama sleeve.

Cathryn cradled her baby closer, feeling helpless, frustrated, alone and scared.

"Dad *is* going to come back, right?" Justin inquired for the umpteenth time.

"Oh, I hope so." Cathryn sighed wearily. "But this is all new to me, too, Jus. I really can't say what's going to happen from one hour to the next."

"But he has to," her oldest insisted, a quiver in his voice. "He's...Dad. He belongs here."

Cory buried deeper into her side. She could feel him shaking. "I don't want us to be separated," he said, his words small and muffled. "Ask Dad to come back."

"Oh, kids, it's not that simple."

"Sure it is," Justin said. "You can do it, Mom. You can do anything."

"Please, Mommy?" Bethany begged, arms tightening around Cathryn's neck. "Please make him come back?"

What could Cathryn say? She hated the distress this situation was causing her children, and this was only the beginning. How could she possibly not try to get Dylan back and make them a family again? It'd be difficult; she'd have to swallow a lot of pride and let go of a lot of hurt and anger. But the alternative was clearly unacceptable.

"All right. I'll try."

Three small bodies went still, and then, as if a switch had been flipped, infused with life. Justin sat up, alert. Beth and Cory giggled in nervous relief.

"Don't just try," Justin said. "Do it, Mom."

Cathryn hesitated. "I'll do my very best."

"Promise?"

She grumbled and mumbled, then finally said, "Oh, all right. Yes."

"Awright!"

"Now, how about catching some Zs? Morning'll be here before you know it."

Justin leapt into his own bed without another word of argument, and Cory and Beth burrowed under their covers. "G'night," they sang, their limbs already relaxed.

"Sleep tight," Cathryn responded, turning off the light. Ten minutes later, as she was shimmying into her night-gown, she heard Cory, her allergy sufferer, snoring.

In all likelihood her children *would* sleep tight tonight. In their minds, the separation was as good as over. But would she? Oh, God, oh, God. What had she gotten herself into? She sat on the edge of her bed, feeling more fragile than ever.

She couldn't imagine life without Dylan, so she supposed she'd only expressed her own desire when she'd promised the kids she'd get him back. But she shouldn't have. She'd raised their hopes, and now they'd hold her responsible, and maybe even hate her, if she failed.

Expelling all her breath, she flopped onto her back and gazed up at the softly lit ceiling. *I'll find a way,* she thought.

Yeah, right, responded a mental image of Zoe Anderson in all her slender, stylish, sneering beauty.

Cathryn rebutted, *Twelve years has to count for something.*

Zoe disappeared and Dylan took her place, reciting his list of complaints, all the hurtful things he found wrong with her, from her weight to her wardrobe, her boring hobbies to her lack of imagination in bed. This time she had no rebuttal because she knew he was right. She was a frump, a bore, and apparently, a loser in bed.

What am I going to do? Cathryn asked the ceiling. She had never had to worry about competition before, not even when she and Dylan were first dating. And now, when she felt least able to compete, here it was in overwhelming proportions—36-26-38 would be her guess. How could she fight that?

Unexpectedly Tucker Lang popped into her thoughts—Tucker, who'd had women competing for his attention most of his life. He'd know what made a woman attractive. He'd know the qualities men sought most in the opposite sex, what lure they couldn't resist. Maybe she could pick up some pointers from him.

Sure, she could do that. What did she have to lose? The worst he could do was laugh or say he had no time for her foolishness. And after last night, how much pride could she have left, anyway?

She had already planned to see her parents tomorrow to tell them about her and Dylan. After her visit she'd go next door to Tucker's, maybe take him something homemade to thank him for his kindness. He was bound to ask how she'd made out with the kids, and from there it'd be an easy slide into telling him about her promise to them.

Feeling infinitely cheered, Cathryn slipped between the sheets and turned off the bedside light. Within very little time, sleep was stealing over her, making her limbs heavy, her thoughts thick. She suspected she was playing the same mind game her children had played when they'd placed their hopes in her, but frankly she didn't care. Although placing her hopes in Tucker was a slim lifeline, she'd take it. She needed something to get her through the night.

CHAPTER FIVE

"SON OF A BITCH!"

After bumping his head on the bedroom's low slanted ceiling for the third time that morning, Tucker decided he'd had enough of sorting through Walter's belongings. He'd worked at it all last evening, had already put in three hours today, and the only thing he'd accomplished was to create a mess of biblical proportions. Everywhere he looked there were mountains of clothes, bedding and miscellaneous junk. And this was just the front bedroom. Where had he ever gotten the idea he'd be off the island by week's end? It was definitely time for a break, preferably one that was strongly alcoholic.

At least he didn't have any legal or clerical matters to face today. After leaving Cathryn's, he'd spent all of yesterday dealing with red tape at Town Hall, calling utility and insurance companies, and paying bills. Inheriting a house didn't come without its headaches. There were still some loose ends to tie up, but he'd tackle them another day.

Tucker descended the narrow boxed-in stairs at a trot, slapping the wall overhead as he approached the bottom— an old habit that used to drive Winnie nuts since it usually left handprints she had to clean.

He was just opening the refrigerator, hoping he had enough leftovers from the funeral brunch to make an early lunch, or late breakfast as the clock would have it, when the phone rang. Sighing, he answered, and then wished he hadn't. It was a patron of Walter's garage, asking what he was supposed to do about his car. It seemed old Walt had up and died before he'd finished working on it.

After running through a few possibilities, none of which overjoyed the customer, Tucker surrendered. "Okay. First chance I get I'll look at it myself." That was just what the customer had been waiting for.

After hanging up, Tucker opened the fridge again, stared into the dank interior, and wondered just how many unfinished jobs were sitting out there in the garage. After grabbing an apple, he shut the door with his heel and headed outside.

The garage wasn't far from the house, about a hundred feet away along the road. Behind the long wooden structure, a fenced-in yard for auto parts kept the outside neat. In summer, Walter had even grown flowers—lots of morning glories, Tucker seemed to recall—to pretty things up. Inside, though, it was a typical garage, cluttered, dirty, and redolent of oil, gasoline and rubber.

It was also fully occupied. Three cars and one truck waiting to be repaired.

Tucker swore, "Damn, damn, damn," all the way back to the house. There was no way around it. He was going to be on Harmony at least another week, probably two. Which meant he was going to miss his next scheduled race. Which meant he had to call the track and withdraw his name from the lineup. And while he was at it...

Tucker glanced at the phone and thought of calling Jenny. In spite of the nonc-too-subtle heave-ho she'd given him, he'd been hoping to see her before his next race. He'd planned to go from Harmony to her, and from her, home to Montgomery to pack up. Now those plans would have to be scrapped, too. But he did want her to know he'd at least intended to visit.

Tucker lifted the heavy receiver and dialed. A moment later he was smiling and saying hello to the woman pregnant with his baby. His baby. God, he still couldn't believe it. Within a minute he realized Jen wasn't smiling back. Within two, he was slogging knee-deep through a familiar, frustrating quarrel.

FOR SEVERAL MINUTES after leaving her parents' house, Cathryn sat inside her van, trying to get her composure back. The visit had gone just as she'd envisioned. At first neither her mother nor her father, a semiretired electrician, had believed her announcement. When she at last succeeded in communicating that she and Dylan were indeed having problems and he'd moved out, her mother burst into tears and her father sagged like a broken old man.

Eventually, however, the optimism that Cathryn had inherited from them came to their rescue.

"Things'll turn out," they had said.

"Yes, I hope so," she had answered.

"Have faith," they had stated.

"I do."

"Would you like us to talk to him?"

"No. Give him the space he requested."

"Do you need any money to tide you over?"

"No, he'll be over once a week to go over bills."

"You know we'll help in any way we can."

"Yes, I know."

"Don't worry. It'll work out."

"That's what I'm hoping.

"It can't possibly be serious. That woman and Dylan? She's no doubt just having a fling."

"You think?"

"Yes, a fling. With the gardener."

"I never thought of it that way."

"It'll blow over. Have faith."

Even as they'd hugged and encouraged her, however, pain and shock had remained in their faces. Sitting in her van, Cathryn couldn't shake the image.

And I still have to go through this with Lauren and Julia, she thought, remembering her lunch date with them today.

All the more reason to talk to Tucker and get herself on the road to rectifying matters with Dylan. After dabbing her eyes with a tissue, she picked up the casserole dish from the seat beside her and slipped out of the van.

At least the sun was shining brightly, and the temperature had climbed into the forties, which made the day feel positively balmy. On the drive over, Cathryn had even noticed surfers riding the strong winter waves in their wetsuits, looking too comically like the seals that played in the swells nearby.

Out of habit she ignored the Lang's front entrance, went around back, carefully climbed the three saggy wooden steps and tapped at the kitchen-entry door. No one answered. Hmm. She knew Tucker was home because his car was out front. The inside door was open, too. Was he napping? Out for a walk?

She was about to leave when she heard a voice, distinctly Tucker's. Thinking he'd called out for her to come in, she opened the door and stepped into the entry where Walter's waders and fishing poles rested in a corner, as if waiting for him to return.

It didn't take more than a few seconds for Cathryn to realize Tucker hadn't answered her knock but was on the telephone. She froze on the doormat, uncertain what to do. Should she slip outside? Knock again, harder? Call out hello? Actually, the conversation Tucker was engaged in didn't sound like the sort he'd appreciate having interrupted.

In fact, it sounded fairly serious. Maybe she should just leave and...

Huh? What was that?

Ducking to one side of the entry, out of sight, Cathryn slowed her breathing in order to hear more clearly. She knew her behavior was reprehensible, but how could she *not* listen when every word she heard was so shocking and revealing of a Tucker Lang she never in a million years would've dreamed existed?

The phone call ended abruptly with a curse, the big one, repeated three times, each louder than its predecessor until the last was practically a yell. Cathryn surmised the woman he'd been talking to had hung up on him.

Oh-oh. Were those footsteps heading her way? Oh, Lordy, yes. With no time to think, she instinctively flattened herself against the wall, drawing her casserole in tight to her waist. Suddenly Tucker shot past her, rammed open the outer door with two hands and stomped outside. He hadn't even noticed her.

Frozen to the wall, she watched him light a cigarette and pace an agitated circle in the yard, uncaring that it was February and he was wearing only a T-shirt. Maybe, while he was facing away, she could slip into the house and out the front door?

He completed one circle, then another, this time letting his gaze swipe the house, specifically the entry with its two curtainless windows and wide-open door, and the cigarette he'd been sucking on dropped from his mouth.

Cathryn tried to smile but suspected she only looked nauseated. "Hi?" she said uncertainly.

He nodded fractionally without smiling back. Another long moment passed before he moved.

"What are you doing here?" he asked, stalking toward the porch.

Her answer was a chagrined shrug. Although he was scowling, she could see embarrassment entwined with his anger.

"Have you been standing there long?"

She swallowed. "Long enough."

"Shit." Tucker slung himself down onto the steps, took his pack of cigarettes out of his shirt pocket and lit up again.

"Got room for another person?" Cathryn asked. He didn't move, so she squeezed by and sat on the step below him. For a couple of minutes they stared at the gnarled old apple tree straight ahead. When she got tired of that, she said, "I'm sorry, Tucker. I didn't mean to eavesdrop. I was just coming by to give you this." She lifted the casserole off her knees.

He exhaled a long plume of smoke and continued to glare at the tree. "What is it?"

"Lasagna."

"Why?"

"Why?" Feeling more than a little foolish now, she said, "Just to say thanks for helping me the other night. It's already cooked. All you have to do is heat it. There's some broccoli in there, too. I know you've been busy and might appreciate having a home-cooked…" Her words dwindled to a whisper under the realization that she was babbling. "Want to talk about it?"

Tucker chuckled wryly. "No."

She didn't blame him. Nevertheless she said, "Talking helps. At least that's what a wise man once told me." She glanced over her shoulder to see if he recognized his own words, and noticed the barest of smiles throwing off the symmetry of his beard.

"It's a helluva predicament I've got myself into, Shortcake. Nothing you can help with."

"Maybe not, but…" She scratched her head, thinking. "How about we just go for a walk then, a long fast one?"

He took a meditative drag on his cigarette and studied the tips of his black shoes. Cathryn surmised he was going to say no again.

"It might clear your mind, give you a fresh outlook on things." Still no interest. "At the very least you'll get some exercise."

Just when she was about to give up, he flicked the cigarette away, got to his feet and drawled, "What the hell."

Cathryn's parents and the Langs lived on a long winding road typical of the interior of Harmony. Because the island had been farmed and grazed right into the early twentieth century, much of it was still open field crisscrossed by stone walls, terrain that bore a marked resemblance to an Irish landscape. Fields that weren't regularly mowed had grown over with bayberry, Rugosa roses and other wild shrubs. For the most part, the vegetation was squat, and views remained breathtaking no matter where one stood on the island.

Cathryn and Tucker had walked nearly a mile, soaking up the beauty of the sunlight filling the enormous sky and glittering on the encircling ocean, before Tucker said, "Funny, how you and I keep stumbling into each other's disasters."

That sounded like a cue if ever she heard one. "Mmm. Almost seems fated." She waited, one stride, two strides, three, four. "So, you're going to be a father?"

Tucker stubbed his toe on a frost heave. "Shit."

Maybe it hadn't been a cue.

But then he added, "A father? Uh, yeah. Yes."

"When?"

"About six months from now, we think."

"And by *we* you're referring to yourself and…?"

"Her name's Jenny. Jenny Reese. Like the peanut butter cup."

Humor. That was encouraging. "Where's she from?"

"St. Louis. We met last fall while I was racing the midwest circuit." He wasn't wearing a hat or gloves. His hands were jammed into his pockets and the tip of his nose was red.

"Obviously we didn't know each other long before she got knocked...pregnant."

Cathryn was struggling to keep pace with Tucker. Her heart was whomping her ribs and each breath was a white-hot knife to her lungs. Jeez, she was out of shape. Tucker, on the other hand, appeared to be just warming up. A smoker no less. Life just wasn't fair.

"What's she like?" she asked, trying not to gasp.

"Jenny? Oh, she's a bit on the young side. Twenty-six, I think. She has curly reddish-brown hair, green eyes and stands about so high." He indicated a height of about five-foot-three. "She has a nice figure, and I suppose you'd say she's pretty. Not a knockout but pretty."

"Yes, but what's she *like?*"

He had to think a moment. "Well, she works as a waitress."

"What kind? Diner? Cocktail?"

"It's an upscale restaurant. She does very well. Lives in a nice apartment." He paused again. He seemed to be struggling with his answer, trying to find something to latch on to. "I met her at a party one night during a big race week. The place was crawling with groupies, and..."

"Groupies? There are groupies in your line of work?"

He cast her a look that said: You *are* naive. "Anyway, there she was, at the party, looking and acting like all the rest of our...esteemed admirers. In other words, like a bimbo. I was attracted anyway. I usually am. I'm a pushover for tight leather skirts and little sweaters that ride up to here. So I asked her out, and she said yes. To everything. Just as I'd thought.''

"Oh, Tucker.'' Cathryn gripped her knitted tam and tugged it over her ears. "A bimbo?''

He grinned, his teeth remarkably white in contrast to his beard, another of his myriad contrasts. "That's the funny part. There turned out to be more to Jenny than I expected. When she stopped trying to show me what a fast-living city chick she was, I discovered a fairly decent person. Come to find out, she isn't a city chick at all. She was born and raised in the country, on a farm. She even has some 4H ribbons to prove it.''

Cathryn sighed in relief. "So, why did she put on the act?''

"Did. Does. The act comes and goes. As to why…'' Tucker shrugged his wide shoulders. "It might have something to do with her parents. From what I gather, they're conservative, church-going people who raised her strictly. She might be rebelling against them and her upbringing. Or, after years of suppression, she might honestly need to cut loose occasionally. Or maybe it's simply a case of her believing that's how sophisticated city folk behave.''

"Sounds like she's a bit mixed up.''

Tucker grunted in agreement. "Whatever the reason, I rode the roller coaster for six or seven weeks, whenever I was in town.''

Rode the roller coaster? Did he mean an emotional roller coaster? Or was that a new term for having sex? Jeez, she really was out of touch.

"Then one day I dropped by and found her throwing up.'' Tucker's lips twisted into a rueful smile. "Seems I do that a lot with women. You aren't pregnant, are you, Shortcake?''

"If only," Cathryn said before she'd censored her response. Feeling his eyes on her, she urged, "Go on. She was throwing up..."

"Yes. That's when I found out about her condition. It was a helluva shock, believe me. I'd enjoyed Jenny's company, but I'd never thought of her as anything but a temporary girlfriend."

"But now that she's pregnant, you're willing to marry her?"

"Of course. I've proposed until I'm blue in the face."

A car came toward them, slowed to a crawl as it approached, and Angie Perry, one of the hairdressers at the Shear Delight, waved to Cathryn and Tucker, but there was no question for whom her smile was meant.

"Trouble is," Tucker continued, ignoring the drive-by come-on, "Jen isn't interested in marriage." He squinted off toward the horizon, his long black hair blowing across his face. "Correction," he said, tucking the wayward locks into his collar. "She isn't interested in marrying *me*."

"Why not?" Cathryn panted.

He must've realized she was about to faint from lack of air, because he slowed his pace. "Lots of reasons, but they all boil down to one thing—her image of me. In her words, I'm not husband or father material."

Cathryn could understand that. He wasn't. "What does she base her criticism on?"

"Ha! Where to start?" He gazed up at the sky as if for guidance. "My livelihood, for one thing. She doesn't like me racing."

"I hate to admit this, Tucker, but I agree with her. Isn't it dangerous?"

"For some guys." He smirked, arrogance dancing in his dark eyes. "That's not her only complaint, though. She also resents my being gone so much. She says I *like* being on the road. I don't have roots and won't ever sink any, and that's no way to raise a kid. But, hell, if I want to make any sort of decent money at racing..."

Cathryn cast him a baleful look.

"I know, I know. I should quit and find a normal job. And I've *told* her I would." After a moment he admitted, "Maybe I wasn't convincing enough."

Or maybe you didn't mean it? "What else does she object to?"

"My smoking. If I really cared, she says, I'd stop and not expose her and the baby to my secondhand poison."

"I'm beginning to like this girl."

Tucker pouted, eyes averted. "Okay, she has a point. But all of a sudden she finds my grooming offensive, too, which makes no sense at all, because she liked me well enough when we first met. Now she says I don't look respectable. Do you believe it? Respectable. This, from a woman with rings through her nipples."

Cathryn flinched. So did her breasts.

Soon she and Tucker arrived at the bridge over Little Harbor inlet and stopped to lean on the rail and watch the water sliding under them with the tide.

Tucker murmured, subdued, "She also prefers marrying a man who knows kids, who's had experience with them." He sighed. "A man who'll be with her when she takes them to church on Sunday."

"Sounds like she held on to all those old-fashioned principles she was raised with, after all. Now that she's pregnant, they're all rising to the surface."

"And cutting me off at the knees."

They watched the water, the rockweed bending with the current, the occasional zigzagging fish.

"Question. If Jenny doesn't want to marry you, why do you keep asking her?"

Tucker lifted his chin as if Cathryn had tweaked his pride. "The baby, of course. It's mine, and I won't shirk my responsibility." He turned and braced his elbows on the top rail, his jacket pulling across his chest. "I don't want to shirk it, either. I *want* to be a father to this kid. I want to protect it and provide for it, nurture its talents and encourage its dreams, teach it all the things I learned the hard way..." He left the sentence open-ended, Cathryn noticed. Like his wishes. "I refuse to be shut out, Cath. A kid needs his father."

And if anyone should know, it's you, she thought.

"You don't trust Jenny to raise the baby without you?"

"Oh, she'll do her best." He pushed away from the railing, and they resumed walking.

"But you want to be there, too."

"Damn right."

"Have you told Jenny how you feel?"

"Yep. But she doesn't believe me. She thinks I'm just spouting what she wants to hear."

"Maybe what she wants to hear is that you love her."

Tucker plucked a dry milkweed pod from the side of the road and studied it intently.

Cathryn studied his profile. "You don't, do you?"

He looked pained, raw, vulnerable. "It doesn't matter. I never expected to...you know..."

"What?"

"Find love. Be in love," he mumbled.

"Why not? Everybody hopes for that."

He cast her a strange, sad smile. "Hope. Expect. They're two different words, Cathryn. One implies possibility, the other..." He went back to examining the seed pod, but his eyes were focused inward.

"What are you saying? You think it's impossible to love or to be in love?"

"Not for everybody. But for some people it is."

"People like you?"

He tipped his head in an oblique nod. "People whose early childhoods lacked love. Something's missing in their makeup."

"I'm not sure I agree with that. You weren't abused, just neglected. Right?"

Again, the halfhearted acquiescence.

"That had to have made a difference."

Tucker tossed the seed pod, squinted off to the watery horizon. "I'm thirty-five years old, Cath, and never been in love, never felt any deep connection with a woman. How do you explain it?"

"I don't know. Maybe the right girl hasn't come along yet?"

He smiled at her with fond affection. "Nice try."

A car approached, the same one that had passed them earlier. Cathryn wanted to hang on to the conversation they were having, but it slipped away as the hairdresser beeped. Her smile was seductive again, and again aimed at Tucker. Cathryn looked up at him when the car was gone. He tried hard not to meet her eyes or react in any way, but soon he was sputtering with laughter.

Reminded of his chronic appeal to women, she said, "What about the big issue, Tucker? Fidelity."

"Gulp."

They crossed the road and entered a conservation area of beach dunes and bluffs spanned by walking trails.

"Surely Jenny has brought up the subject."

"Oh, yeah. She's raked me over the coals for that, too—for my profligate ways. And I deserved it. I haven't exactly been a monk since I left Harmony."

"Weren't much of one when you were here, either."

"But I'd change once I was married."

"Ah, famous last words."

He actually appeared hurt. "I would."

"Are you telling me you could honestly remain faithful to one woman for the rest of your life?"

He nodded adamantly. "I have a lot of faults, Shortcake, but I try to be a man of my word. Once given, I wouldn't go back on it."

Call her crazy, but she believed him. Call her crazier, but she wanted to help. "In that case, the solution is simple."

"Solution? You have a solution?" His raven-dark hair gleamed in the sunlight as it tossed about his shoulders.

"Sure. In order to convince Jenny that you're father and husband material, you simply have to *become* father and husband material. You have to change."

He laughed. "Oh, is that all?"

"Uh-huh. As far as I can see, you already possess the most important quality—desire. You want to be a good husband and father, and with that attitude, success is just a matter of time."

They crested a rise that commanded a view of Harmony Harbor in the distance. The ferry was sitting at the pier waiting to make its afternoon run back to the mainland. Other than fishing boats, there was no traffic in the harbor. Along Water Street, shops and Victorian hotels dozed in the winter quiet.

Tucker huddled into his jacket collar and turned his shoulder toward the breeze. "Okay, just out of curiosity, how do you propose I change?"

"How do *you* think? You've already recited all of Jenny's complaints."

She watched him thinking through them, tallying them mentally. "Oh, man."

"Don't get discouraged. The trick is to take them one at a time. One day lose the earring. The next, cut the hair."

"Oh, man," he repeated, sounding as if she'd asked him to remove his spleen. "You really think that's necessary?"

"Only if you want to marry Jenny and be a father to your child." She patted his arm. "It'll be hard, but not impossible, and I'll gladly help. I just know there's a clean-cut, suburban type somewhere inside you waiting to pop out."

"Yeah. Like in the movie *Aliens*."

"Oh, stop," she said, laughing.

"By any chance, is there still such a thing as a barber on Harmony? Not that I've decided to take your advice…"

"There is, but Saturday is the only day Gordy opens his shop during the winter."

"Aw, hell. Gordy Welman's still in business?"

"Yes. Why?"

"He was always trying to get me into his chair when I was a teenager. Always used to stand in his doorway and call me girlie. He's gonna have one helluva laugh if I walk in there now."

Chewing on a smile, she said, "You could go to the Shear Delight. A lot of men do."

"No!"

"In that case, *I'm* pretty good with a pair of scissors. I do Dylan's and the kids' hair all the time."

"That right? Dylan's cut looks downright professional."

"Thanks. So, shall we assume we have an appointment?"

"I must be out of my freakin' mind," he muttered. "Sure. Why the hell not." Cathryn made a mental note to suggest he clean up his language. But not yet. As she'd said, one thing at a time.

They came to a fork in the trail and took the path that led out of the preserve.

He asked, "When's a good time for you?"

"I'll be free Saturday. Dylan's coming for the kids in the morning and keeping them overnight."

Finally reminded of her children, Tucker said, "Oh, I forgot. How did it go yesterday?"

"It wasn't fun."

"No, I never imagined it would be. Are they okay?" Before she could reply he added, "Dumb question. Of course, they're not okay."

"They want Dylan back."

Tucker shook his head. "Poor kids."

"No, you don't understand. They want Dylan back, and they expect me to get him back. In fact, they're counting on it."

Tucker stopped in his tracks. "How'd that come about?"

"I told them I would." Cathryn scrubbed her palms over her face. "I know. It was a mistake, and actually what I said was, I'd try."

"Why?" He stared at her as if she'd lost her mind.

"Why?" She resumed walking. "Because they begged me. And because he's their father, Tuck. Do you have any idea how devastating divorce can be on kids? I've seen too much of it—the anger, the behavior problems, the depression and regression. I don't want my kids to go through that. Not even a little of it."

Tucker nodded. "I never knew my own father and yet I missed him something fierce. I can't imagine losing a father you know and love and depend on. The sense of abandonment must be something you never get over."

"That's right. That's absolutely it. They need him, Tuck. I can only do so much. A father's input is unique and irreplaceable." Tucker's laughter was sardonic. "What?" She scowled. "Oh. That's precisely what you've been telling me."

They trudged on, through sand, over boardwalk, onto macadam, before Tucker spoke again. "Would you be able to take Dylan back?"

"Yes. I happen to consider marriage and the vows we exchanged twelve years ago sacred. You know, for better or worse, till death do us part? This just happens to be one of those worse times. Time to suck it up."

"Yeah, but would you be able to accept him back emotionally?"

She sighed, long and raggedly. "I won't deny it'll be difficult. But it's not impossible. I've read lots of articles in women's magazines about infidelity and moving past it to save a marriage. I know that couples do it all the time. If others can, so can Dylan and I. There's counseling, too. That'd be a crucial part of it, I'm sure."

"Yes, but..." Tucker hesitated, a frown pinching his brow.

"No 'buts.' I'm totally convinced that's the way to go." *I just don't have a clue how I'm supposed to convince Dylan of that,* she thought ruefully. Her husband would have to *want* to reconcile with her before they could move past anything. That was where Tucker came in.

However, now that the moment had arrived for her to ask for his advice, she felt reluctant. Presently Tucker had enough on his mind. Maybe some other time—Saturday, for instance—after he'd become adjusted to the idea of his own makeover...

"Well, best of luck to you," he said. "And I mean that."

When they arrived back at Tucker's, he invited her in to help him eat the lasagna she'd brought over.

"Thanks, but I already have plans for lunch. I'm going to Lauren's. Julia will be there, too."

She didn't realize she was frowning until Tucker stroked her jacketed arm and said, "Hang in. They're your best friends. Sure, they're going to be shocked and sad and full of questions, but after that they'll be your strongest support. Remember that."

Tucker was right, she thought, backing her van out of the driveway. He was so right.

TUCKER WALKED into the bathroom feeling uncharacteristically hopeful. For the first time in ages, he and Jenny seemed to have a chance. He wasn't crazy about the idea of changing his appearance, but Cathryn was probably right. He didn't look like the sort of father any kid would want to claim on parents' night at school. Nor did he resemble the sort of husband any woman would want to take home to her old-fashioned parents.

Tucker studied his chin, turning his head from one side to the other, then opened the medicine cabinet and got out his shaving cream. He'd better jump in before he had time to think about it.

He was lathering up when his thoughts turned to Cathryn and her promise to her kids to reconcile with Dylan. An uneasy feeling slid through him. Convincing Dylan to return home was going to be no small task, given that the jerk had been so eager to move out. Something awfully strong, namely Zoe Anderson, was pulling him away.

Obviously Cathryn had made the promise because she wanted Dylan back, too. Moreover, from the way she'd phrased certain statements, Tucker got the feeling she believed she could…and would; reconciliation was possible.

Tucker hoped she was right, but he had a sneaking suspicion she underestimated the seriousness of Dylan's affair. She was living in denial, as the pop psychologists would say.

His razor stroked off the last of his whiskers, and studying his face in the mirror, Tucker felt a period of mourning coming on. But Jenny would be pleased, and that was all that mattered. In fact, he should've done this long ago. "Thanks for the boot in the rear, Shortcake," he murmured. "I owe ya."

CHAPTER SIX

"YOU DID IT!" Cathryn exclaimed, as Tucker shuffled from one foot to the other on her front doorstep.

Feeling naked, he rubbed his smooth-shaven jaw and wondered why he'd listened to her. "What do you think?" he asked.

"I love it," she said on a genuinely pleased laugh.

He began to feel better.

"It's incredible what a difference it makes," she continued. "Your mouth isn't all crowded and boxed in anymore. In fact, your whole face looks more open and natural. What do you think?"

"I'll...get used to it."

"Oh, come in, come in." She waved her hands in apology.

Tucker was just stepping into the foyer when footsteps pounded down the stairs and a young voice called, "Is that Dad?" It came from a lanky, good-looking boy wearing green sweatpants and a basketball jersey. He leapt the last three stairs, landed with a thud and noticed Tucker. "Oh." His voice dropped along with his face.

Tucker hadn't expected to see the boy, either, although *his* reaction was radically different. "Hey, I bet you're Justin."

"Who are you?"

"Justin!" Cathryn was appalled by her son's rudeness. "This is Tucker Lang, an old neighbor. He used to live next door to Nana and Grampa Hill, with the Langs. He was their nephew.''

Still smiling, Tucker held out his hand, but the boy took it only reluctantly. Speculation wizened his Dylan-blue eyes. Aw, hell. Did the kid suspect him of playing a part in his parents' troubles?

''Where's Dad?'' Justin asked his mother.

''He's running late.''

''Hi. I'm Bethany.''

Tucker's attention shifted to the top of the staircase, where the cutest little girl he'd ever seen began sliding down on her behind.

''Nice to meet you, Bethany,'' Tucker said when she landed.

She giggled and scrambled to her feet. ''We're going to sleep at my Grammie McGrath's tonight. She and Grampa have a farm. No animals, though,'' she explained with sudden regret. ''Just vegetables.''

''I know.''

''You do?'' She scrunched her Cathryn-short nose.

A horn tooted in the driveway, and from the eager tension that took hold of the children, Tucker knew it must be Dylan.

''Cory!'' Cathryn hollered up the stairs. ''Daddy's here. Don't forget your backpack.''

Tucker was eager to meet the last member of Cathryn's tribe, but Justin and Beth already had their coats on before he even heard any movement upstairs.

Dylan knocked at the door, then opened it and leaned in, doing a slight double-take when he noticed Tucker. ''Are the kids ready?'' he asked his wife.

''Almost. Cory! Oh, there you are.''

''Hurry up, slowpoke,'' Justin urged impatiently.

Tucker didn't get introduced to Cory. Forgotten in the

avalanche of last-minute instructions, admonitions and searches for stray mittens, he decided not to feel slighted. Obviously this wasn't the right time or place. He and the boy did check each other out, though.

"Sorry 'bout that." Cathryn said, closing the door.

"About what?" Tucker thought she was sorry for too many mysterious things.

"The mayhem. Running into Dylan. Oh, I don't know." She pressed her fingertips against her eyes and let out a shuddery sigh. A post-Dylan reaction, no doubt.

"Are you okay?"

She nodded, then shook her head. "He didn't even ask why you were here."

Tucker had noticed. To make her feel better, he stumbled through a few half-ass excuses for Dylan's behavior, until Cathryn raised a hand and said, "I'm fine. Really." She even smiled to prove it.

"Your kids are great, Shortcake," he said, shrugging off his jacket.

Her smile became genuine. "I kinda think so, too. Would you like some coffee?"

"No, thanks. I'd rather just get down to business before I change my mind."

"Right. The haircut."

"Yeah. The haircut."

Cathryn was ready for him. She'd clipped a dozen or so pictures out of catalogues and arranged them on the coffee table. Tucker sat beside her on the couch and studied her selections. Every single model wore his hair short, traditional and preppie, or whatever the current lingo was for that sort of look. "Oh, man," he mumbled, feeling he was making a grave mistake.

"I think all of these men have attractive cuts, but if you'd like to keep looking…'' She gestured toward a stack of catalogues to one side.

He reached for one of them and began to flip through. He'd worn his hair long for so many years, if he went from one extreme to the other, he'd get the bends for sure. ''There,'' he said, pointing. ''There's a happy medium. Short, but not too short.''

Cathryn tilted her head, scowling at the picture. But then she surprised him by chirping, ''Okay.''

Still feeling he was making a mistake, Tucker got to his feet and said, ''Let's do it, then.''

CATHRYN GRIPPED a hank of Tucker's long black hair and wondered what on earth she was doing. Not with his hair. She really was proficient in that department. What bothered her was the amount of time she was spending with Tucker. He was the most unlikely candidate for a friend she'd ever known, yet, weirdly, his was the only company she seemed able to tolerate these days.

Her visit with Lauren and Julia had gone about as well as her visit with her parents. Which was to say, it had left her close to tears. Not that her friends had disappointed her. As Tucker had said, although they'd been shocked and aggrieved and full of questions, they'd also offered her boundless support. ''Anything you need, anytime you need it, we're here for you,'' they'd said. Like her parents, they'd also lent encouragement. Things would work out, they said. The affair was just an aberration. Still, Cathryn hadn't been able to get away fast enough. She'd felt contemptible, dropping her stink bomb into her friends' fragrant lives.

Cathryn positioned her hair clippers and snipped. Tucker winced. She snipped again. He moaned. ''It's going to be all right, Tucker. Trust me.'' He tried to turn toward the bathroom mirror, but she grabbed his head, almost stabbing him with the scissors. "No, don't look yet." She'd been lopping off the bulk, cutting straight across, and at the moment he shared an uncanny resemblance to Buster Brown. If he saw himself now, he'd likely hyperventilate.

"Tell me about your house. Are you making any progress cleaning it out?"

Tucker answered in tense monosyllables for a while, but before long he was into his subject, asking her where he could unload used clothing, laughing over the stash of risque calendars he'd found—and forgetting entirely what was happening to his hair, which was exactly what Cathryn had hoped.

"There. I think that does it." Cathryn ruffled the hair at the crown of his head, then finger-brushed it across his brow.

He came to with a start. "We're done?"

"Uh-huh." She stepped back, eyeing her work. "Wow," she said softly. Even she couldn't believe the improvement.

He turned to the mirror with caution and his eyes widened. He said nothing, simply stared.

Cathryn's heart dropped. "You don't like it?"

"Nuh-no. I just…I barely recognize myself. It's a good cut. A great cut. I just have to get used to *me* in it."

"You're sure?"

"Positive." He unfastened the sheet from around his neck, folded it carefully and said, "Thanks."

"You're most welcome."

"How can I repay you?" Tucker asked, ambling down the hall toward the kitchen. "Can I take you to lunch?"

"Actually, no. I already have lunch prepared. But as long as you're feeling indebted, I do have a favor to ask."

"Fire away."

Cathryn could feel heat climbing up her neck into her cheeks. "Wait a sec," she said, ducking into the laundry room. When she felt more poised she returned, carrying a basket of clothes from the dryer. "I'm thinking of changing some things about myself, too," she admitted, while she folded one of Cory's shirts on the kitchen table. "And I'm wondering if you…can help." She peeked up.

Tucker's dark, seductively winged eyebrows squiggled into a shape that spoke volumes about his reluctance to do any such thing. "This is to charm Dylan into coming back, I take it?"

"Yes."

"Cath, there's nothing wrong with you."

"Ha!"

"Why me?"

Did he really have to ask? "You've had women chasing you all your life. If you don't know what makes a woman attractive, nobody does."

He sighed, still reluctant, but she sensed his attitude was starting to turn. "I don't give haircuts," he cautioned.

"That's okay." She smiled. "All I need is your advice."

He let out a slow breath, hooked his hands on his unfairly slim hips and studied her assessingly. "What do you want to change?"

Her spirits zoomed. "I have a list." She dropped the socks she was matching and dashed to a drawer. "Mostly these are details Dylan brought to my attention, but I've added some things myself." She turned in time to catch Tucker's expression of dread. "The list's shorter than it looks."

Resigned, he said, "Okay, what's first?"

"Well, the most obvious. My weight. I want to lose approximately thirty pounds." She returned to the table, placed her list where she could read it, and resumed folding laundry. "I've already lost five this week. Do you believe it? All that vomiting and loss of appetite had its advantages.

But frankly I'd rather approach losing weight in a healthier way.''

Standing at the hutch, studying a photo of the three children taken at Christmas, Tucker shrugged. ''Diet and exercise. You don't need me to tell you that.''

Cathryn folded four T-shirts while trying to frame her response. In the end she simply said, ''Follow me. I have something to show you.'' She led Tucker into the family room to the entertainment center, then opened the side cabinet and pointed. One entire shelf held nothing but exercise videos. ''I know I should exercise. I keep buying tapes, thinking the next one will be the charm, but, truth is, I *hate* to exercise and don't have the discipline to force myself. What I need is a personal trainer—a slave driver, actually— who'll make sure I'm exercising every day and doing it right.''

''Me?'' Tucker's eyebrows did that squiggly thing again.

''You wouldn't have to actually be here all the time. A phone call might be effective enough, if you were stern. But if you wanted to be here...'' She bit her lip, then stumbled on, ''Harmony doesn't have anything like a health club, and you're probably used to working out...''

''And maybe you and I can work out together?''

''Hey, there's a thought.''

Tucker grinned, and the newly exposed creases around his mouth were simply delightful. ''You realize I won't be on Harmony very long.''

''Yes, I know. But once I'm in a groove, I'm more likely to continue on my own.''

He considered her proposal, his dark eyes moving over her slowly, assessing the challenge. ''Let me take these tapes home and review them. Okay?'

Shot through with excitement, Cathryn hurried to the

kitchen to get a shopping bag. When she returned, she found Tucker reading the text on one of the video cases.

"I'm already familiar with this one," he said, slipping the tape out of its case. "Someone I once dated swore by this program, and her figure was out of this world."

Glimpsing the title just before the VCR sucked it in, Cathryn muttered, "Oh, no."

"What?" Tucker asked distractedly.

"That's Tae-Bo."

"Yeah. Kickboxing exercise seems to be really popular lately."

"But...I can't do it."

Fast-forwarding through the preliminary footage, he asked, "Why not?"

"It goes too quickly. I get confused."

"Ah. A common complaint. The problem is, people get discouraged prematurely. They think they have to be perfect right off the bat and don't allow themselves any time to learn the routine. The trick is to give yourself some slack, Shortcake. Just do what you can, go through the motions. Sure, you'll mess up—everyone does—but before long you'll get the hang of it. It'll happen." He pressed the Play button and stepped back. "Ready?"

"What! You want to exercise *now*?"

"You aren't wimping out already, are ya?"

"No. No, that's not it. Just..." Just what? Wimping out was exactly what she was doing. "Let me change into more appropriate clothes."

Tucker pressed Pause. "I'll be waiting."

I MUST BE OUT OF MY FREAKIN' MIND, Tucker thought, ducking out of Cathryn's way as she punched and kicked with all the coordination of a rag doll on speed. Ostensibly, he was exercising *with* her. In reality he was just trying to protect himself.

"Auk!" He stifled a gasp when she connected. Oh, well. He'd never needed that kneecap anyway.

"Am I doing it right?" Cathryn panted, the T-shirt and shorts she'd changed into already damp.

"Yeah. You're doing great."

"It doesn't feel great. It feels awful."

"Naturally. You're just learning the routine."

"If you say so."

She continued. Right hook. Undercut. Left jab. Everything looked the same. Like spaghetti-arms flailing. She turned unexpectedly and backhanded Tucker across the throat.

"Oops. Sorry."

Yeah. Me too, he thought, struggling to draw breath.

Somehow they made it through twenty minutes of the routine before she collapsed on the sofa and declared herself unable to go on. She did look exhausted, so he didn't push her. Rather, he praised her efforts and said she'd done better than most beginners. And although she gave him a skeptical look, she did seem pleased deep down. Funny how far that went toward persuading him to repeat the ordeal tomorrow.

"Mind if I take a quick shower?" she asked.

"No, of course not." He hadn't even broken a bead of sweat.

"While I'm gone, you can look through my catalogues of men's clothes."

"Why?" As if he didn't know.

"Don't you want to continue, you know, with your transformation? Or shall we leave it for another day?"

He had to hand it to her; she had a way of phrasing things that left him little choice.

Cathryn was a catalogue junkie. A washtub-size basket in

the family room was chock-full of the damn things. Most sold housewares and gifts, but enough were devoted to men's clothing to keep him turning pages for hours if he was so inclined. He wasn't. Clothes had never fazed him. He wore certain things he liked and replaced them when they wore out. Button-fly jeans. T-shirts without logos. Plain sweatshirts for warmth. He also owned a couple of dress shirts and a sports jacket. What more did a guy need?

"A lot," Cathryn told him when she returned, smelling of a fragrance he couldn't quite pinpoint but associated with spring.

"I don't do stripes, Shortcake," he protested after they'd been "shopping" for a while.

"What's wrong with stripes?"

He didn't answer. "I don't do polo shirts, either."

Obviously a fan of polo shirts, she opened her mouth to protest again.

"No," he said firmly, cutting her off. "And I think pants with pleats are ridiculous. They make a person look as wide as a rowboat. They take inches off his height, too."

Cathryn seemed offended, or at least subdued, and he realized belatedly that she was wearing pleated pants.

"When we finish your order," she said, eyes downcast, "maybe we can look through my wardrobe and weed out some things. Clothing is the next item on my list, anyway."

Oh, swell.

"I'd really appreciate your input, Tuck. And if you're worried about the time you're wasting, not working on your house, I'll help you. How's that?"

Trapped again. "Thanks." What else could he say?

Her shoulders relaxed. "Now, what kind of underwear do you use?"

"What!"

Her cheeks glowed like polished apples. "Underwear. Boxers or briefs? Believe me, it makes a difference."

Deciding she'd finally gone too far, he left the room and poured himself some coffee from the pot she'd prepared with lunch.

"Briefs," he answered, returning to the family room where she waited patiently, catalogue in hand. "Black mostly."

"Wrong answer."

"Why? What the *hell* is wrong with briefs?"

"Nothing. Boxers are just…the underwear of choice in suburbia. Besides, it's a proven fact that briefs, because they bind, decrease a man's sperm count," she said, mustering a prim dignity he had to admire. "You wouldn't want that, would you?"

No. But he didn't want boxers, either. "I'll think about it," he replied.

That afternoon Cathryn somehow convinced him to call in an order to L.L. Bean. Khakis, suede Hush Puppies, oxford cloth shirts, crewneck sweaters, something called a barn jacket and, yes, even some boxer shorts. He held his ground on the polos and pleats, though.

In turn, Cathryn modeled the contents of her closet for him, and he convinced her to chuck most of what she normally wore. The big, blah, shapeless things. The old, out-of-style things. The plaids and ruffles and horizontal stripes that did nothing for her figure. He also pointed out the outfits he did find attractive. There were few of those, though, making it obvious she needed to replenish her wardrobe, too.

She was averse to spending money on clothes that would only be transitional, though. "Fortunately I can sew," she said. "And what I can't sew I'll buy at a resale shop."

Tucker thought she deserved to buy new. It'd give her

self-image a boost. But he was uncertain about her finances, and so kept the thought to himself. "Just avoid froufrou, Cath."

"Froufrou," she repeated so seriously he wanted to laugh.

"Yeah. Look for clean lines," he advised her. "I also noticed that when you wear different colored tops and bottoms, you look cut in half, sort of. Definitely shorter. If I were you I'd put together outfits in solid colors. Then again I don't know jack sh—" he paused, " —anything about fashion. Maybe you should go to one of those image consultants who can tell you what to wear."

"You certainly do know—" her lips twitched "—something about fashion. But I'll stop by the library anyway. I'm sure I can find books that do the same thing as a consultant, free."

Neither of them mentioned ladies' underwear.

Tucker inched back the sleeve of his sweatshirt and glanced at his watch—discreetly, he thought.

Cathryn noticed. "Do you want to continue another time?"

He was dying for a smoke, but cigarettes were forbidden in her house. "Yeah, I do. We've inflicted enough damage for one day. Besides, how much more can there be?"

Her laugh gave him the willies.

TUCKER HAD DRIVEN to his house scrunched down in his seat and with his hand shading his face. Cathryn, following in her van, was more observant than he'd thought. "You look fine, Tucker," she assured him when they got out of their respective vehicles. "You do," she insisted.

He hurried inside anyway.

They worked well and steadily together, and when his great-aunt's little anniversary clock chimed eight, the front

bedroom was done. Organization, apparently Cathryn's
forte, was the key. She'd made four signs and tacked them
to the walls. One said, Dump, another, School Trash and
Treasure sale, a third, Church clothing drive, and the last,
Tucker, to indicate items he wanted to keep, mementos of
his great-aunt and uncle mostly.

He couldn't believe it. What had been mayhem was now
boxed, bagged, labeled and ready to go. Before anything
left the house, though, Cathryn suggested he invite Winnie's
sister over to collect whatever she wanted. After that he
planned to sell the furniture to a store that dealt in antiques
and used goods. And after that?

"Who would you recommend I list the house with?" he
asked. He was sitting with Cathryn in the living room, sharing a pizza and listening to one of his uncle's scratchy Mitch
Miller albums.

"Either Ann MacDougal or Jack Sutter. They're both
competent." Cathryn's gaze circled the room. He knew
what she was thinking. The house was what a real estate
agent would call cozy and quaint—which was another way
of saying it was small and in dire need of renovation.

"You know," she said slowly, "before you try selling it,
a little cosmetic work might be to your advantage. Spiffed
up, it'd sell faster and fetch a better price."

"I don't want to spend the time."

"You wouldn't have to do it yourself."

"Don't want to spend the money."

She took another slice of pizza from the box, but then,
sighing mournfully, put it back and reached for her glass of
water. "I don't mean to get personal or anything, Tuck, but
have you considered keeping it? Can you afford to?"

"Yes, I can afford to. The question is why would I want
to?" he countered, although he'd begun to feel awfully proprietary since inheriting the place. He'd never owned a

house before. He sat back, trying to ignore the couch spring screwing into his left shoulder.

"Why?" She stared at him as if he'd just landed from Mars. "Harmony's a great place to own a second home..." Her voice faded to silence. Tucker waited. Suddenly she leapt right out of her seat. "Tucker!"

"What!" he mocked, matching her enthusiasm.

"I've got an idea."

"What?" he said, less flip, more curious.

Slowly, she lowered herself back to the sofa. "This house is a great opportunity for you to further prove yourself to Jenny."

"What?"

"You could tell her you're keeping it for the benefit of your family."

"My family?"

"You and Jenny and the baby. And any other kids you might have."

Oh. Right. That family.

"You could describe the wonderful vacations you'll take here with her. Or you could hype the extra income you'll earn if you rent it out. Summer rents are incredible, Tuck. And property values on Harmony have nowhere to go but up...if you decide to sell the house some day. You might even argue it's a retirement nest egg. Just think of all the family values you'd be communicating to her with this line of reasoning."

Family values? Tucker was still stuck on the word *retirement*. His poor stomach was doing back flips as he considered all the years ahead, a lifetime of them, spent with the same woman, one he hardly knew. *That'll change,* he told himself. *Time will make us close.*

Cathryn laughed lightly, apparently pleased with another emerging idea. "Actually, if you keep the house and fix it up, you'll also be showing Jenny what a caring person you are, what a sentimental person." She sat on the edge of the cushion, upright with excitement. Her eyes danced, her cheeks glowed, and Tucker began to think Dylan was the biggest fool who'd ever lived. "What a *rooted* person you are."

"Rooted?" he repeated skeptically.

"Sure. One of Jenny's complaints is your wanderlust, right? Your lack of roots? So, show her she's wrong. You've got roots. They just happen to be here, not in Missouri. But," Cathryn added, raising a finger for emphasis, "you'll carry your appreciation for roots and show her your willingness to sink new ones wherever she wants to settle."

The urge to argue swelled in Tucker's chest again, and then mysteriously subsided. Maybe Cathryn was onto something.

"Okay, let's see if I have this right. You've got me keeping the house, fixing it up, and telling her I'm doing it all for the sake of my family." He glanced at Cathryn for confirmation.

"Right."

"One question. How do you propose I convince her this house even exists and I'm really working on it and not off gallivanting somewhere else?"

"You could send her snapshots. Or..." Cathryn's hazel eyes brightened by about a thousand watts. "Or a videotape. I have a camcorder you can borrow. Sure. That'd be even better. You could walk her through, add commentary, update progress every couple of days." Suddenly she clutched his wrist and gave it an enthusiastic squeeze. "Oh, oh, oh! You could include footage of yourself, too, to show her how your appearance has changed and how hard you're working to better yourself to please her. It could be a combination makeover, you *and* the house."

Tucker couldn't help laughing. "Know something? You're certifiable, lady."

"Yeah, well, that makes two of us, because you're listening to me." Her lips twitched with a self conscious grin she tried to suppress. "That's one of your best traits, you know. You really listen."

"That's not why the ladies usually praise me." He slanted Cathryn a cocky glance and then caught himself. Something about it didn't sit right. It felt too much like flirting.

She took an uneasy sip of water—damn—and said, "All kidding aside, I do think the house would work to your advantage. I realize I sprang the notion on you unexpectedly, but maybe you could think about it?"

"Okay." He nodded and waited two heartbeats. "Finc. I'm keeping it."

Cathryn choked on the water she was sipping. When she finally caught her breath, she said, "Just like that?"

He shrugged. "What's to decide? So, did you bring your list with you, by any chance? Not that I want to throw you off my case, or anything." He grinned.

"I did," she said, returning his grin. She dug into her pocket. Leaning toward her to read, Tucker picked up her scent again. Spring.

"What is that?"

"What?"

"That perfume you're wearing?"

Her color deepened. "Um, lily of the valley."

"Ah. Nice."

She fixed her attention on the paper. "Diet. That's next."

"Can't help you there. I know nothing about special diet plans, Cath."

"You don't need to. Along with the exercise videos, I've collected an awesome number of books on nutrition. As I said, I just need an overseer, someone to report my progress to.''

"Groan. What else is there?''

"Hair.''

Tucker leaned back and studied her hair. It was long, straight and, as usual, tied back—featureless except for too-long bangs. And the color was indeterminate, a shade between brown and dishwater blond.

"Help,'' she cried.

He stroked his hand over his jaw and studied her some more. "You might play around with the color.''

"How? Lighter? Darker?''

"Either way, as long as you get out of wishy-washy.'' He raked aside her bangs, bared her forehead and nodded at the improvement. "You're not twelve anymore, Shortcake. Get rid of the curtain. Show off those pretty eyes of yours.'' They truly were pretty, he realized. More green than brown, and shaped like a cat's. Yes, they were cat eyes. Eyes made for seduction. Eyes so incongruous with the rest of her...or was the rest of her just waiting to catch up?

"Length?'' she questioned, jerking his attention back to where it should be.

She slipped off the elastic that bound her hair and it spilled free about her shoulders.

"Hmm. A little shorter, I think.''

"Is there a style you like in particular? A style you consider especially...'' In a small voice she finished, "...sexy?''

Chuckling, Tucker reached under the sofa and came up with a fistful of his uncle's *Playboy* magazines. "Ta-da!''

"Oh, God.''

He flipped through one of the magazines. "I like that. And that, too.''

Before long Cathryn was approaching an alarming shade of magenta. "Enough. I've got the idea."

Shrugging, Tucker stuffed the magazines back under the sofa. "What's next?" He nodded toward her list.

"Oh." Her tone sank. "Things get more involved now."

Tucker leaned closer and read, "Hobbies and Interests."

"What I think I need to do in this area is bring my interests more in line with Dylan's. That might involve my dropping some activities that are time-guzzlers. But that's okay. I hadn't realized how widely we'd diverged until he brought it to my attention."

"What are...his interests?" Tucker had almost said, *the jerk's interests.*

Cathryn twirled a lock of her hair, her head tilted piquantly. "Well, his work. Landscaping is his primary interest. I've always supported him, of course, but I can't keep up. Correction. I *haven't* kept up."

"And Zoe Anderson has? I don't think so, Cath."

Her spirits dropped like a rock off a skyscraper. Tucker berated himself. Why'd he have to introduce that name into the conversation? "What else?" he went on quickly.

"Dylan enjoys boating. We even have our own boat. But I don't go out much. I get seasick even in a pond."

"Well, f—hell with that. Something else," he urged.

"Football. He loves football. He even belongs to a group that travels to Foxboro a few times a season to see the Patriots. Maybe, if I tried, I could get into that." She looked about as enthusiastic as someone heading into a bat cave.

"Let's take this from another angle. What are *your* interests, Shortcake? What's a time-guzzler you could drop?"

"The PTO probably. This year I'm vice-president, which means I'm involved in a major fund-raiser almost every month. I also volunteer at the school library."

"Anything else?"

Cathryn scrunched her nose much the way her daughter had. "My interests are pretty dull. That's something else I'd like to work on—dropping the really boring activities and picking up more exciting ones."

"Let me be the judge of what's boring. Isn't that why you hired me?"

She smiled a soft, close-lipped smile and said, "Oh, right." She smoothed her hands over her thighs. "Well, I sing in the Ecumenical Choir."

"Okay," Tucker said noncommittally.

"Another activity I've gotten into is square dancing."

Tucker tried to keep his bland expression in place, but it was hard. "Square dancing?"

"Yes. Practice is the highlight of my week, actually."

"What do you mean, practice?"

"I belong to a club. The Harmony Squares. We get together once a week to practice and learn new steps and help each other sew outfits."

Outfits? Tucker's mind filled with images of petticoats, a plethora of them, and garishly colored ruffles.

"I know I should quit. I look like a hippo out there when we perform."

They performed? Oh man. The pictures in his head were getting more painful by the second.

"I'm a little uncoordinated, too," she admitted, scrunching her nose again. "Now I can see why Dylan was so embarrassed."

Suddenly Tucker's barometer swung around. He was going to kill the jerk.

"Do you have any other hobbies?"

"Oh, sure. I sew and do crafts—obsessively, Dylan says, and again he's right. Every bed in the house now has at least three comforter sets and window treatments to match."

"*You* sewed those?"

"Uh-huh."

"Amazing."

"Yes, well, Dylan doesn't think so. He'd prefer I..." Her face lit with color.

"What?"

"Nothing."

Tucker chuckled softly. "It must have something to do with sex. You only get that look when the topic is sex."

"Okay. Yes. If you have to know. Dylan happened to mention that our marriage might be healthier if I'd spend less time sewing curtains and more on reading about sex." She shut her eyes tight and winced. "I can't believe I told you that."

"Why did you?"

"I don't know." Her eyelids fluttered open, but she wouldn't look at him. "Maybe I'm going crazy on top of everything else."

Tucker didn't feel comfortable prying any further into her love life. Whatever her shortcomings, he didn't want to hear them. He was sure she didn't want to divulge them, either— *if* she had any, and the jury was still out on that. And even if she did, Dylan should have said something years ago. He should have helped her shed her innocence and inhibitions, not betrayed her with another woman.

"Anyway," she said, "that's what Interests and Hobbies mean."

Tucker slipped down in his seat with a sigh. "Darlin', I don't have a clue what you should do. To be honest, I don't see anything wrong with your interests. My gut is saying you should just be yourself, do what you enjoy. There's nothing more attractive in a woman than that." They were sitting close enough for him to see the minute variations of green and brown in her eyes, the starburst of gold around the black irises. Yes, those were definitely eyes a man could get lost in for a few dozen years.

She put some distance between them, cleared her throat and ran her hands over her thighs again. "You're very kind, but what's wrong with my interests is that I've been hiding behind them. Scared or not, I need to come out of hiding, Tuck."

He reached over, his hand spanning her two and stilling them. "I'll do what I can. It's going to take some thinking, though."

"Of course." She smiled her soft smile again, and again his attention focused on the curve of her lips. "Likewise, I'll think about how I might help you." She got to her feet. "But right now I'd better go home."

Tucker was surprised by a desire to ask her to stay.

She continued, "It's Saturday night and I suggest you go out somewhere like the Brass Anchor or Old Harbor Lounge, and give your new look a test run."

"Nah, I'm pretty bushed."

"Bushed or afraid?" she needled, slipping on her jacket.

"Hey! If you're cool, you're cool, no matter what you look like."

"Right. And you have the double advantage of being cool *and* looking great." She buttoned up and pulled her hat out of a pocket. "Go out and sit on a barstool somewhere, Tuck. I think you're going to be pleasantly surprised."

He did. He was.

CHAPTER SEVEN

CATHRYN PLUMPED HER bed pillow, uncapped her pen and wrote *Sunday, February 20* on the first page of her notebook. This was Tucker's idea. He said he always kept a journal to chart his workout performance—the weight he'd lifted, the number of reps he'd done, the miles he'd jogged and the time it had taken. He suggested she do something similar, charting her weight loss and her measurements as well. Seeing her progress recorded on paper would encourage her to keep working toward her goals.

Of course, that assumed there would *be* progress, and at the moment Cathryn looked on that with a very cynical eye. She hurt everywhere, and today was only the second day she'd exercised. Nevertheless she logged her weight and measurements, along with the fact that she'd endured thirty minutes of Tae-Bo that morning, then placed the notebook on the night table and turned off the light.

She lay in the dark for twenty minutes, eyes shut, but sleep eluded her. Her thoughts were like a swarm of gnats. With a huff of frustration, she snapped on the light and picked up the notebook again.

Dylan moved his office equipment out of the house today, she wrote, recalling how writing in a diary when she was a girl used to put an end to the day and help her sleep.

He brought the kids home too early, barely midafternoon, especially considering this is school vacation

week. They were bummed, a mood that only deepened
when he started packing up his PC and files. I assured
him I didn't mind if he came home to work, it's still
his house, but he said it'd be easier if he had his stuff
at the farm. I also invited him to stay for supper. (I
wasn't too desperate, was I?) But he said he had to
leave. Didn't give a reason, didn't notice the makeup
I'd put on, nor the outfit, and was gone in forty
minutes, taking everything of importance with him. He
left his pictures of me.

Cathryn reached for a tissue, studied the paragraph she'd
just penned and realized she was doing more than simply
unburdening thoughts. She was starting a second kind of
journal, one to parallel the first.

So this is where Dylan and I stand on this 20th day
of February. This is where I begin my journey of bringing him home...

She considered closing—what more was there?—but then
stuffed another pillow behind her and continued writing.

Tucker showed up for my daily dose of torture a
short time later. He wasn't too eager, but when he saw
how mopey the kids were in the aftermath of Dylan's
leaving, his attitude changed dramatically. Their sadness really seemed to resonate with him.
At first the kids were standoffish, especially Justin.
I think he suspected Tucker of coming between me
and Dylan. Tucker was very sweet and patient, though,
explaining again who he was and why he was here.
The kids found that intriguing—that he'd come over
to help me exercise. We never explained why I was

exercising or that it was part of a larger plan, but they seemed heartened anyway. As if they understood implicitly we're on our way somewhere. Moreover, we aren't walking alone any longer.

Of course, Justin wanted to know why he was bothering to help me. Quite deftly Tucker answered, because *I* was helping *him*. It was a reciprocal favor. Then he told the kids about his problem with Jenny, including the pregnancy, which thoroughly freaked me out, until he made it clear to them that expecting a baby is wrong if two people aren't married, and he's striving to make it right. That confession, that he's trying to improve himself in order to win over another woman (and I'm just helping), eased Justin's suspicions more than anything, and it endeared Tucker to the other two. Weaned on fairy tales, Beth is a sucker for a romantic underdog anyway. Before long she was sitting in his lap and the boys were suggesting ways in which *they* might help.

Unfortunately (for me) Tucker deflected their enthusiasm by announcing it was time to get down to business. Beth begged to work out with us. Cory joined in, too. Justin abstained. But later while I was setting the table—yes Tucker stayed—Tucker challenged Jus to a one-on-one basketball game. They came in from the driveway red, sweaty and laughing over a joke they refused to share.

During supper, conversation returned to methods of helping Tucker win his lady, and I mentioned my idea of a videotape. The kids loved it and insisted on helping. We got out the camcorder, and in very high spirits began plotting our documentary, which hopefully Tuck will send to Jenny in a couple of weeks. We start taping tomorrow.

The kids dropped off to sleep almost as soon as their heads hit their pillows. And quite frankly, I'm mighty sleepy, too. I can't forget the vision of Dylan carrying his office equipment out of the house, but maybe it wasn't such a bad day after all.

STANDING BESIDE his aunt's pressed-oak rocking chair, Tucker combed his hand through his hair and cleared his throat. "Can this be edited?"

Cathryn squinted through the viewfinder. "Yes. We have a two-deck VCR in our basement. The work is tedious, but I've done it before."

Sitting on the old plaid couch with his siblings, Justin rolled his eyes. "Mom, there are computer programs now that make that sort of thing a snap. We have 'em at school."

"Great." Tucker smoothed the collar of his maroon dress shirt. "You're in charge, then, sport."

Cathryn raised the camera again. "Ready, Tuck?"

"As ready as I'll ever be."

The date, February 21, appeared in red glowing letters, and taping began.

"Hi, Jen. Tuck here. You'll probably have trouble recognizing me. As you can see I've cut my hair and shaved my beard. The earring's gone, too. I hope you like the new look...." He paused a second to glance down at his notes. "But there's more to come. This is just the beginning of a process that I hope will turn me into the type of man you always wanted to marry, or at least someone you can accept as a husband and a father to our baby.

"But before we go any further you've got to meet an old friend of mine. Excuse me while I take the camera." He snatched the camcorder from Cathryn, who sputtered in embarrassed surprise, and aimed it at her. "This is Cathryn McGrath and those are her three children. They're going to be helping me, so you'll be seeing a lot of them on this tape, too. Everybody, wave. Thank you.'' He handed back the camera and continued his monologue.

''It was Cathryn's idea to make this video. She figures, if a picture's worth a thousand words, then a video's worth a few million, and it might take a few million to show you who I am, who I'm becoming, and that I'm worth taking a chance on. I'm not sure it'll work, but I'm gonna give it my best shot.''

Tucker paused, withdrew a cigarette from his shirt pocket and lit up. Cathryn lowered the camera, owl-eyed with stunned disbelief. ''Keep rolling, Cath.'' He took a couple of drags, and a couple more, then crushed the cigarette in an ashtray. ''That was my last smoke, darlin','' he said to the camera. He heard Cathryn gasp, and was glad her reaction was captured on tape. What better testimony to the difficulty of the step he'd just taken. ''There. As of today, cigarettes and I are done. One more reason to marry me.'' He winked into the camera and said, ''Cut.''

Feb. 22

Exercising was difficult again. I have no strength. My muscles go into spasms of exhaustion so fast. And I'm SORE! Still, I got through it somehow. (Tucker's taunting was how.)

After showering, we went over to his place—the kids too, even though it's vacation week and they could've been playing with friends. They helped us organize and bundle some more of the Langs' things. I taped about fifteen minutes for Tuck's documentary, which Cory has brilliantly dubbed ''Opus for Jenny.'' Where does the kid pick up this stuff?

Later Tucker took over the camera and walked Jenny through the house and around the yard, explaining what he hopes to do with the property. I was happy to hear that his ideas echo those I proposed the other day. Shows he's thinking in terms of family and future.

Winnie's sister popped by while we were there. The old girl was highly confused about what was going on, but she added a nice "rootsy" touch to the video.

We stayed for dinner—pizza again. (The man has got to broaden his culinary repertoire.) He didn't smoke in our presence and swears he hasn't yet, and I believe him. He's a man of his word. But where does he get his discipline? Going cold turkey can't be easy. I could take a lesson from him.

Maybe I will.

Feb. 23

The kids and I went to the library this morning. I checked out some jazz tapes, hoping to cultivate a more interesting musical palate. So far, so good.

Tucker's new clothes arrived. Wow. I knew there'd be an improvement, but I was still stunned. He does for a crewneck sweater what Baryshnikov does for ballet.

I think Beth has a crush on Tuck. He's taken to calling her Peanut. She loves it. She's never had a nickname before.

Feb. 24

I'll never get the hang of that Tae-Bo tape. I fell today. Got twisted up in my own limbs and just toppled. Still, I finished the whole routine and am thankful for that. It was a first.

Dylan took the kids today and after working out, Tucker went home to repair a car—which left me alone with the opportunity to dye my hair. Or try to. I even got as far as the hair-products aisle at the drugstore, but as I was looking over the various brands and colors, along came Jackie Truman from choir, and I pretended to be looking for shampoo instead. Bad enough the woman's heard about me and Dylan. (Yes, word's out.) If she ever saw me buying hair color, it'd be all over town that I'm reacting like a fool, trying to compete with the Anderson woman. Which is exactly what I'm doing, of course. I left without the dye.

I wish I hadn't already told Tucker what I intended to do. He came by after supper to see how the color turned out. He wasn't pleased with me. Said I shouldn't care what people think, it's my life and about time I lived it on my own terms. Easy for him to say. He's swum against the tide from day one. People here expect it of him.

I think he's going through nicotine withdrawal.

Feb. 25

Yesterday I bought a new pattern and material, and started cutting it out today, but with the kids underfoot I didn't accomplish much. Bethany wanted to bake, and Cory was hungry for everything but what I had on hand, and then Tucker barged in for my daily torture session. Fortunately Justin came up with the suggestion that we give Tucker a cooking lesson. It was brilliant. One stone killed three birds.

I wasn't sure Tuck would stay. He's turned into such a bear since he quit smoking. But he did. He's aware Jenny will need his help in the kitchen, especially with a new baby to take care of. But what convinced him, I think, was my arguing that women love men who can cook. "Hey, I cook," he protested, his eyes dancing with the double entendre. That's when I knew it'd be okay, he'd comply. And he did, even though superficially he continued to give me a hard time.

We spent the entire afternoon in the kitchen. Made four simple but nutritious entrees, one of which Cory immediately dived into. We also baked the cake that Bethany had been clamoring for. Tucker had never made a cake before, and wasn't keen to make one today. That's what the bakery is for, he said.

I thought his first attempt came out great even though it left him, me, the kids and the kitchen all in a royal mess. Spilled flour everywhere. Broken eggs. Spattered batter.

I managed to catch a lot of his bumbling on tape, too, which didn't exactly thrill him, but I thought it was cute. "Cute, my ass," he said. Bethany giggled, Cory gasped, and Justin mentally filed away the phrase as one more cool Tuckerism to imitate.

Later I had a talk with Tucker about his language. He's agreed to curb it—not just because of my kids, but for his own as well.

He left in a grumpy mood. But what else is new?

One last item—and I'm blushing even admitting this on paper—I sent away for a set of instructional tapes that I saw advertised in a catalogue. It's called Better Sex for Loving Partners. I had a zillion qualms, but if it helps bring Dylan home....

Feb. 26

It's Saturday, and again Dylan took the kids overnight. Alone, I sewed all day. Completed my new burgundy, trim-lined, non-froufrou outfit. Will wear it tomorrow when Dylan returns the kids. I've been watching for signs that he's noticing me and the little changes I've made in my life—things like cutting down on fussing with the house and crafts. (Tucker says men feel uncomfortable when a house is too neat or full of dainty things.) But so far, Dylan seems oblivious. It's disheartening, but I must remember to be patient and persevere. It's only been a week.

Tuck worked in his great-uncle's garage all day. Didn't come over to exercise. But he did call. What a bear! He threatened to start smoking again. Post haste, I went to the library, then to the garage and presented him with the grossest pictures of rotted lungs I could find. He tore them to shreds. I told him to go to the clinic for a patch. He told me to mind my own business. I congratulated him on not saying "freakin' business," and he escorted me to my van.

It wasn't a good day.

THE NEXT AFTERNOON Tucker was removing the muffler from a '78 Buick—cars lasted forever on Harmony if they were garaged—when a knock and a melodious "hello-o" drew him out of his concentration.

"Hey! Lauren!"

The redhead stepped farther into the cluttered old garage. "You remembered me."

"I never forget a pretty face." He removed his work gloves and they shook hands. She had a firm grip, a confident gaze and a polished appearance that reflected her years of living and working in Boston.

After she'd extended her condolences to Tucker on the loss of his great-uncle and he'd congratulated her on her recent marriage, he asked, "What can I do for you?" Through the half-open garage door he glimpsed her car, an almost-new Prelude.

"No, it isn't a mechanical problem."

"Good, because I'm supposed to be on the air shuttle in two hours."

"Not leaving us already, are you?"

"Only temporarily. I'm going to Alabama to check on my house and get my car. I'm tired of driving a rental. I should be back in four, five days."

Lauren cocked her head. "You're getting your car?"

"Mmm. Looks like I'll be here longer than I expected. The house needs some renovation and repair."

Lauren's eyes sparkled with interest. "Do you plan to rent it out?"

"Don't know yet."

"I hope you realize I'm a professional property manager. If I can be of any help…"

"You'll be the first person I call. Now, if you're not here about a car repair…"

"It's Cathryn."

"Let's go sit in the office."

Tucker admired Lauren. For as long as he'd known her, she'd been a hard worker, making money to help her family. She was a proud little scrapper, too, which had come in handy when she got pregnant at the age of fifteen and had all that trouble with the baby's father and his parents. Tucker had always thought it odd that she and Cathryn had been best friends growing up, but maybe they'd needed each other to round themselves out. Or maybe they were more alike than he thought. Cathryn was surprising him these days.

Lauren didn't beat around the bush, but laid the situation out as quickly as possible. She was aware that, for whatever reason, Cathryn had gravitated to him for companionship while simultaneously withdrawing from her and Julia, and she wanted to know what was going on.

"Nothing sexual, if that's what you're wondering," he answered without offense. "I know I'm supposed to be a reprobate—" he grinned amiably "—but I wouldn't take advantage of a woman when she's vulnerable." He reached into his shirt pocket and then remembered his cigarettes weren't there anymore. He pulled out a toothpick instead. "Besides, this is Shortcake we're talking about."

Lauren nodded as if he was only saying what she already suspected. "I always figured your reputation was overblown, Lang."

Tucker accepted the teasing with a chuckle, but he didn't meet Lauren's eyes. She was too sharp, and truth was, he *had* caught himself flirting with Cathryn lately. He *did* find her attractive, and *had* been getting an inappropriate rise out of being with her. However, he refused to make anything of it. It'd simply been too long since he'd had sex and he missed it. That was all.

"So what *is* happening with you two?" Lauren asked, unbuttoning her white wool jacket.

Tucker was glad to tell her. He was tired of carrying the weight of Cathryn's confidences and hopes alone, and since she'd never actually sworn him to secrecy, he didn't feel guilty sharing them.

"Ah!" Lauren exclaimed, enlightened. "That's why she quit choir."

"Yep. It's part of her overall strategy, dropping dull activities in favor of more exciting ones."

"Well!" Lauren pretended to be insulted.

"You belong to choir, I take it?"

"Yes. Cameron does, too." She shook her head, mouth pinched at the edges. "I'm glad Cath wants to lose weight and improve her life generally, but I can't say I'm too thrilled with Dylan, making her feel she has to. What a nerve!"

"I agree." Tucker tossed the frayed toothpick into the wastebasket. "And I wouldn't be helping her except that hope is keeping her afloat, and who knows, maybe a little change *will* make a difference. In a way, I hope it does. It kills me to see the kids confused and scared, and if Dylan doesn't come back, it'll only get worse.''

Tucker and Lauren fell silent, the only noise a Beethoven tape playing in the background as part of his own self-improvement program.

''I'm worried about her, Tuck.''

''It's not time to worry yet.''

Lauren gave a series of quick pensive nods. ''How's she doing, anyway?''

Tucker made a see-sawing motion with his hand. ''It's only been a week. She's sore as hell from exercising, and not feeling any benefits yet. But at least she's stopped punching out lamps and tripping over her own feet.''

Lauren got a laugh out of that. Sobering, she studied Tucker a long moment. ''Why you, Tuck? Why is she turning to you and not me or Julia?''

Tucker spread his hands. ''Sometimes it's just easier to face your imperfections with a person who isn't so close—or so perfect himself.''

Lauren smiled.

''Oh, well. I guess it doesn't matter, as long as she's turning to somebody. But I do want to help.''

''Jump in anytime. Julia, too.''

''How? What can we do?''

Tucker grinned. ''Do you have a pen? You might want to take notes.''

Feb. 28

Lauren dropped by quite unexpectedly this morning after the kids left for school and suggested we go have our hair done at the Shear Delight. I was embarrassed and angry, to say the least, realizing that Tucker must've talked to her about me. But then I realized how immature I was acting, so we went and I had a great time.

I intended to have my hair dyed chestnut or auburn, mainly because Zoe Anderson is so conspicuously blond. But Angie said it'd be a sin to go that route, and convinced me to go lighter, simply with highlights. I'm grateful she did. They blend with my natural color, and yet make such a difference. I glow! The cut she gave me is flattering, too. More up-to-date. Dare I say sexier? I should've done this years ago.

My only regret is that Tucker is in Montgomery and I'm unable to flaunt my new look.

March 1

I found a patch of snowdrops blossoming on the south side of the house today. Amazing what that did for my winter-weary spirits. Or maybe, as Tucker said when he called to see if I'd exercised, my lifted mood's come from the endorphins now flooding my bloodstream. Whatever the reason, it was a pretty nice day.

P.S. I never realized what a sensual phone voice he has. Deep, slow, intimate, it's a voice that says he's paying absolute attention to you. Jenny Reese doesn't know how lucky she is.

March 2

Tucker returned from Alabama this afternoon. Must've broken every speed limit along the way. When I lectured him on the dangers of speeding, he laughed and reminded me what he does for a living.

I think he must do it very well. He arrived in a beautifully restored, vintage Mustang. A 1965 Shelby GT-350, to be exact. (Not that I knew what a Shelby GT-350 was before today. After an hour of Tucker's expounding, however, I'm practically an expert.) It's white with a wide black racing stripe over the top and a red leather interior. Justin went bonkers when he got off the bus and saw it parked in our driveway. He recognized its value right away. I have to admit, it *is* a nice set of wheels.

Mar. 3

Not a good day.

Dylan was here to pay the past month's bills, and I blew it. I asked him how much longer he needed to think about us. Could we talk about it. All at once he got really cool and distant. Said he doesn't want to be rushed. Which leaves me in limbo again with only my hopes and fears for company.

Before he left he said he'd come by for the kids tomorrow, same as other Saturdays. But I asked if he'd mind leaving the kids with me. Had to remind him tomorrow's my birthday.

No, not a good day at all.

Mar. 4

I turned thirty-one today. Tucker took me and the kids on a magical mystery tour. We rode the ferry across the sound, then went clothes shopping at the Hyannis mall. On the ride over, he handed me a card with three hundred dollars' worth of gift certificates. I was speechless. Tried to give it back, but he said I'd earned it, putting up with him and his moods.

I bought a couple of attractive outfits. But secretly I can't forget Tuck's words about short leather skirts and tiny sweaters that ride up to here. Maybe someday....

Mar. 5

Dylan came by with flowers and an apology for forgetting my birthday, then took the kids horseback riding at the stable on Old Harbor Road.

With a few hours to myself I returned some Brazilian music I'd borrowed from Julia. She and Ben were re-arranging furniture, an activity I usually excel at, but the language they were speaking was all new to me. As I soon learned, Julia's into Feng Shui. But why am I surprised? Put a deejay with a philosophic bent on the west coast for two years, and how else would she return home?

Always on the lookout for new and interesting topics to add to my conversational skills, I asked Jules to explain Feng Shui. What a hoot. Two hours later I came home with one of her books, and spent the rest of the day rearranging things, especially in the Love and Marriage trigram (which, in this house, falls in the family room).

Will it help? Time will tell.

Mar. 6

It's been two weeks since Tucker stopped smoking and finally he's returning to the human race. He credits his more tranquil mood to finishing the bathroom ren-ovation. I credit it to the patch I noticed on his arm. Whatever the reason, he's been much more amenable to my self-improvement suggestions lately. Conse-quently 'Opus for Jenny' is bursting with great footage.

Most notably, tonight I took him to square dancing practice. (I didn't tell anyone I plan to quit, though.) I figure, if Jenny truly wants a husband with small-town values, she'll be floored by the sight of big bad Tucker Lang learning to do-si-do with his Harmony neighbors. He agreed, but still didn't like it.

He couldn't get over that we call ourselves the Squares, that we actually *admit* to our dorkiness. I said what *I* couldn't believe was that he was joining us, and he must be out of his freakin' mind. To which he answered I couldn't swear worth a damn, but he found it cute anyway. "Cute, my ass," I replied, which earned me an appalled "Cathryn!" Are Tuck and I trading personalities?

Tucker has a natural aptitude for dancing, and learned the steps and calls with little trouble. He had lots of willing teachers, too, all female, of course—another reason he was soon allamanding like a pro. But, I must say, he still looked pretty silly. And I captured most of it on tape! If Jenny doesn't love him after this...

Leaving the community center, several people expressed the hope he'll return next week. Under his breath he vowed to get even with me.

Mar. 7

Recently I brought Tucker's attention to the classes in baby care being offered at the clinic, but he wasn't keen on broadcasting to Harmony that he's an expectant father. He's even gotten the kids to keep quiet about it. But he did agree that learning basic baby care is of the utmost importance. So today we had a class— Tucker, myself and one of Bethany's dolls—right here at the house.

The very first thing Tuck did was drop the doll on its head. Not a propitious beginning. I decided maybe we should switch to book learning and ease into the practical stuff gradually.

I reviewed gestation, labor and birth with him, using my old books from when I was pregnant, and we followed that up with a film called "The Miracle of Birth" that I got out of the library. But I forgot he's a man. He didn't see much miracle, only pain and mess, so I quickly moved on to feeding. Discussed formulas and breast milk. Showed him my pump and explained how it works.

We were well into the practical stuff, changing diapers, giving baths and dropping dolls on their soft spots again, when out of the blue Tuck asked me why I'd kept my books and pump and other baby-related stuff. I told him I was simply a pack rat, but he knows me too well, and we both know he knows the answer.

Mar. 8

Today I borrowed Judy Williams's new baby for a couple of hours, and Tucker got to hear real baby crying and clean real baby poop. And I got to laugh. Despite the changes he's made to his appearance, Tuck is still one big macho guy, and to see him panicked by a twelve-pound infant cracked me up. He hung in, though I'm happy to say and I have every confidence he'll be a fine new father.

By the way, I'm doing quite well with Tae-Bo now. I finish the full routine every day with no trouble, and plan to start the advanced program tomorrow. I have more energy, more strength, and I've lost several inches from my waist and thighs. (Yay!)

Mar. 9

Today I discovered what Tucker meant when he promised to get even with me for dragging him to square dance practice. A couple of catalogues arrived in the mail. One was from Victoria's Secret, the other from Frederick's of Hollywood! *I* didn't order them. I was mortified. What must the mailman think!

Mar. 10

Julia hosted a makeup party, the kind where some-one comes to your house, demonstrates her products, gives free makeovers, and then expects you to buy, buy, buy. I didn't want to attend. Everyone knows about me and Dylan. But Lauren came by and insisted I go. I did. And I bought, bought, bought.

Mar. 11

"Better Sex," the video version, arrived in the mail today. (Plain brown package, thank God!) Hopefully, better sex, the true-life version, will follow shortly.

Mar. 12

Dylan came over to repair the dishwasher. It's been leaking. Having learned my lesson the other day, I steered clear of asking about us. Rather, I acted indif-ferent and unconcerned. Discussed Feng Shui and Joao Gilberto, and assured him the new sculpture in the fam-ily room wasn't expensive. 'What sculpture?' he asked. 'Oh, that one,' I answered innocently, pointing to the couple kissing, which I think is beautiful but grosses out the kids. As for Dylan, lately I swear I see a change in him. He seems more attentive to what I say and how I'm dressed. His gaze lingers...

Am I deluding myself?

Mar. 14

Nearly every night this week, my dreams have been sexual. It's probably the instructional videos I've been watching. The upsetting thing is, the man in my dreams is usually *Tucker*. Sometimes I only see eyes or a mouth or hands, but they're always his. Rationally I know it doesn't mean anything. He's simply the man I'm with most often and, therefore, the symbol my sub-conscious latches on to at night. But it sure makes for some uncomfortable moments during the day.

Yesterday, for instance, I was giving him a lesson in decorum, on how to behave around women after he's married. One point I wanted to make concerned dancing. If he danced with a woman other than his wife, I told him, he shouldn't hold her close. And I demonstrated proper dance form. I also warned him to look women straight in the eye, not to stare at their bosoms. And I began to turn red and couldn't stop, because we were still in dance position, and he smelled wonderful, and suddenly I was terribly aware of him. I think he knew it, too. Of course he did. Tucker can read a woman like nobody else on earth.

And, devil that he is, he only made my discomfort worse by following up my lesson with one of his own. And I couldn't protest, because I'd asked him to teach me how to dirty-dance. I'd practically begged him. Except, that was two weeks ago.

Mar. 16

I was right. Dylan came by tonight to balance the checkbook and discuss upcoming household expenses, and the subtle change I noticed in his attitude a few days ago was more pronounced. He looked at me more. Looked at the house more, too. Sitting at the kitchen table, I watched his eyes roaming, lingering on favorite objects. And throughout the visit, he seemed kind of sad. He even stayed for an extra cup of coffee.

Has he finally come to his senses? Realized how much he has here, how much he was walking away from? Are my patience and diligence finally paying off? I won't jump to conclusions. I'd hate to be disappointed. But he asked me to dinner Saturday night. I said yes.

CHAPTER EIGHT

CATHRYN SPENT the next two days warning herself not to jump to conclusions. For all she knew, Dylan might just be gearing up to tell her he wanted their separation to continue another month, or maybe two, or even become permanent. Wasn't that how the movies always handled it—one spouse lowered the boom on his partner at a nice restaurant where she was unlikely to cause a scene?

Still, it was hard not to be optimistic. After all, Dylan was taking her to the Surf Hotel, the very place where they'd held their wedding reception and celebrated numerous anniversaries since. In addition, when he came by on Saturday morning to pick up the children for youth basketball, he mentioned there was a Disney film playing at the Empire, and his parents wanted to take the kids to see it that night. "It'd probably be easier all around if they slept at the farm, too."

Which meant, after their date at their favorite restaurant, they'd be coming back to an empty house....

With the kids gone, Cathryn treated herself to a long fragrant bath and shampoo, then spent a couple of hours styling her hair, painting her nails, applying makeup, and choosing her outfit. It would definitely be the black dress she'd bought on the shopping trip she'd taken with Tucker on her birthday. But first...

Telling herself that desperate times called for desperate measures, Cathryn opened the top drawer of her bureau and dug under her neatly folded utilitarian underwear. She came up with a black satin underwire bra which she'd bought from Victoria's Secret during one of her recent, and increasingly frequent, lapses of sanity. She snipped off the tags with a nail clipper, looped the straps over her arms, fastened the front closure, and adjusted the cups. Oh, yes!

Next came matching bikini panties, followed by sheer black pantyhose. Both articles of clothing were lovely—but not when worn together. Noticing her quite visible panty line in the full-length mirror, Cathryn winced. Her soft knit dress would show every lump and bump.

Should she remove the panties? She always wore underwear with her panty hose. Always. Should she put on a girdle? Ha, that wasn't even an option tonight.

"Okay, so the panties go," she decided. These particular panty hose didn't require underwear anyway. Even the package said so. The stretch-lace top already formed a panty. A scandalous French-cut panty, to be exact.

Turning her darkly smooth, scantily-covered backside to the mirror, Cathryn muttered incredulously, "I must be out of my freakin' mind," and immediately thought of Tucker from whom she'd picked up the phrase. Wouldn't *he* be surprised if he knew what she was wearing! And *he'd* provided the catalogue!

She was grateful he had. She turned and studied her body. She hadn't yet reached the weight she eventually intended to be, but five weeks of diligent exercise and dieting had firmed her significantly and brought her down a full dress size. Not only did she feel desirable in this underwear, she *looked* desirable.

She reached for her dress, removed it carefully from its hanger and slipped it on. The plain, long-sleeved knit was perfectly appropriate for dinner at a nice restaurant, yet it had won an enthusiastic thumbs-up from the kids and an embarrassing wolf-whistle from Tucker. She had to admit it was flattering. Its side-wrap design and surplice neckline seemed to carve her body and accentuate all the right parts.

Four-inch heels added height, and simple gold jewelry added class. As a final touch, she spritzed on a new "pheromone" scent she'd bought with great skepticism.

Cathryn studied herself in the mirror, and a shiver of excited panic raced through her. Was she advertising more than she could deliver? Was Dylan even interested?

"You look great, Cath," he said a short time later, helping her into her coat. "New perfume?" He leaned in and took a sniff, his closeness sending tingles down her spine.

"And you look…" She was about to say wonderful, but then thought it wiser to temper her enthusiasm. "You do, too." To be alluring it wasn't enough to be physically pulled together. She planned to be alluring in manner, too. Which meant not crowding him. Rather, she'd be poised, casual, and even cheerfully indifferent to their relationship.

The hostess at the Surf greeted Cathryn and Dylan politely and led them to a table in the middle of the dining room. Cathryn would've preferred a table by the window overlooking the ocean, but on a Saturday night, those required reservations and apparently Dylan hadn't called ahead.

The cocktail waitress served them their drinks while they studied the menu.

"Since when do you drink martinis?" Dylan asked with an uncertain smile.

"Since I decided life was too short not to." Not a typical reply from the sensible Cathryn he knew. She lifted the delicately stemmed glass and saw his eyes follow it to her lips. Did he like their new fuller shape and richer color? she wondered. She really couldn't tell. Usually she could read his underlying mood, but not tonight.

"Are you ready to order?" asked their waiter, a young man Cathryn remembered baby-sitting.

"I believe so," Dylan replied, closing his menu.

With their choices made, they settled into an uncustomary conversation about sports—her doing. Dylan had begun talking about the children, but she wanted him to know her world had expanded. It hadn't really; Tucker had simply given her a crash course on the NFL, but Dylan seemed impressed anyway.

Watching the candlelight dance in his eyes, she wondered if he was watching it in her eyes, too. Was he noticing how it picked up the gold in her hair? How it warmed her complexion? Deepened her cleavage?

Again, she was at a loss.

Their dinner arrived and she deftly shifted the conversation to his work. Did he have many jobs lined up for spring? Had he started any yet? What did they involve? Did he have a large enough crew?

"I read a fascinating article last week about the gardens at Versailles," she said, breaking off a forkful of her low-fat, low-cal, low-flavor haddock. "I hadn't realized that French…formality…was…" Dylan had slipped into that familiar state of abstraction again. Two deep lines etched his brow. "Dylan?"

He blinked and looked up, but didn't actually focus. "Cath, the reason I asked you here…" he said out of the blue.

Her heart leapt and jammed her throat. *Yes? What?*

"Lately I can't help noticing how well you're doing. It's extraordinary, really. You're so much more pulled together than I ever expected."

Oh, this is good. Go on, go on.

"Your attitude seems to have spilled over on the kids,

too. Considering everything that's happened, they've been unbelievably resilient.''

"That's only because—'' She stopped abruptly.

"Because…?'' he prompted.

She gathered her courage and all her hopes and prayers. "Because they believe you're coming home.''

For an interminably taut moment he didn't say a word, but he didn't have to. The bleakness in his eyes spoke for him. "Cath…'' He reached across the table and took her hand. To strangers, she thought ruefully, it must appear as if he were proposing. "I think you realize by now that isn't going to happen.''

No. No. No! I realize no such thing!

He gazed down at her hand, tightening his grip so that her wedding and engagement rings bit into her fingers. "I've finally decided, Cath. I want a divorce.''

The increased pressure on her fingers registered only from a distance. In fact everything seemed distant to her, and quiet, and slow. So slow it felt stopped. All she heard was the thudding of her heart, and that was slow too.

"You want a divorce,'' she repeated dully.

Dylan drew in a breath, lips pressed tight, and nodded curtly. She tugged her hand from his and cradled it in her lap. "It's the movies, after all,'' she mumbled.

His brow lowered. "What?''

"Nothing.'' She shook her head. The slight movement made her dizzy, though, and she had to close her eyes. Heat built behind the lids, a prelude to tears. But she couldn't cry, not in the middle of a crowded restaurant where half the patrons recognized her and Dylan.

"Dylan, don't do this,'' she said, striving for a bland demeanor. "Think of the kids.''

He rested his forehead on his fingertips and stared at his

unfinished steak, his normally proud shoulders rounded. "I think about them all the time."

"Do you? Do you have any idea what this is going to do to them?"

Dylan blinked rapidly, gathering his composure. "I'll do whatever I can to help them get through it. I promise."

Cathryn felt she was clinging to a rope with all her strength, but it was all slipping anyway. "And what about us, Dylan? What about the twelve years we've shared as husband and wife? How can you destroy all that we mean to each other, everything we've worked so hard to build?"

"Believe me, it isn't easy."

Their young waiter came over and asked if they needed anything else. With a gargantuan effort, Cathryn smiled and replied, "No, thanks. Everything is great."

As soon as the waiter was gone, she leaned forward and in a hushed tone said, "Okay, so you've had an affair. But with love and effort we can get past it, Dylan. Marriages do survive infidelity, you know. We might not know how to go about it right now, but help is out there."

"I won't go to counseling, Cath."

"But if it means saving our marriage…"

He shook his head, a muscle jumping along his jaw.

A panicky tremor took hold of her and refused to let go. "But there are so many reasons why we *should* save our marriage," she said and proceeded to stammer more warnings regarding the children. Platitudes about the sacredness of marriage vows came next. She also brought up their extended family and how divorce would ripple out and destroy them, too. Finally she reminded him of the role they played in the community and how without them the community would suffer. And when none of her arguments made any headway, her reasoning powers dissolved and she fell into that most unalluring of mindsets—desperation.

In a voice that quavered she told him how much she still loved him, regardless of his affair, and how ready she was to forgive and forget and go on. He was her one and only, she reminded him. They were meant to be, and she could never see herself with another man.

But even as she made these claims, she already knew she was speaking out of something more than pure love. Fear had joined her arguments. Fear of being alone. Fear of having to fend for herself. And because she recognized it so readily, she suspected it had resided with her all along.

"Why?" she pleaded, surreptitiously dabbing her eyes with her napkin. "For the last five weeks I've done nothing but try to change myself for you. My looks, my habits, my interests. I've quit square dancing and fussing with the house, started buying *Cosmo* instead of *Good Housekeeping*. I've even been watching instructional videos on sex."

Dylan's eyes darted over the table as if tracking a fly.

"Isn't that what you wanted, Dylan?"

He sighed. "Cath, what I want...what I want is so beyond what you understand about me."

"Well, how am I supposed to know if you don't *tell* me?"

He looked at their half-eaten meals. "Maybe this wasn't such a good idea." He called the waiter and got the check.

Outside, the air was mild enough to invite a walk around the hotel's extensive grounds. Strolling along the sea wall, Dylan continued, "First of all, I want to say it isn't you."

Oh, man. She was really in trouble now. *It isn't you* was another staple of breakup scenes in movies.

"It's everything about my life here." Dylan spread his hands to encompass Harmony. "I have career dreams this island can't fulfill."

"Like what?" she challenged.

"Bigger jobs. Parks, estates, municipal projects. And I'm

not thinking just of the money, although God knows it'd be more than I make now. It'd also be the prestige, the respect I'd get. I want that, Cath. I want to be a name in my field. And Zoe is certain I can be.''

The name pierced Cathryn like a poisonous dart, its paralyzing effects racing from her heart to her brain cells to her toes. It took a long moment to say, ''What makes Zoe so certain of your abilities, when she's only known you for a year?''

''Three. I did work for her a couple of years before we became involved. And to answer your question, she's seen my work, we've talked about it, collaborated. She just...knows. She also has connections. She figures once she's recommended me to a few new clients and I've done those jobs, my reputation will be established and I'll be off and running.''

Cathryn's mouth was dry as the winter grass underfoot. ''And where exactly will you be doing this...running?''

''New York, Connecticut, Long Island.'' Dylan shrugged his shoulders. ''Who knows?''

''But what about your business here?''

''I intend to sell it. Jack Mendoza has already expressed interest in buying me out.''

''You told one of your employees you were planning to sell before you told *me?*''

''Well, I didn't see the point. It'd only upset you.''

''You got that right!''

They'd circled the large hotel, keeping to the shadows, and now came to a sweeping lawn where garden parties were held in summer. A white gazebo stood on a knoll in the moonlight like the lacy topper of a wedding cake. Cathryn gazed through shimmery tears at the structure, not knowing what to say, except, ''I had no idea you were so dissatisfied.''

Dylan sighed heavily. "It's been building."

Cathryn climbed into the gazebo, her steps echoing hollowly on the wooden floor-boards. "You'll have to pardon me but I'm still having trouble with the concept that you want to leave Harmony. That *is* what you're saying, right?" She turned and watched Dylan follow her up the steps.

"Yes." He paced restlessly, stopped at the rail and looked up at the star-strewn sky. "There's so much to do in this world, Cath. So many places to go, things to see. Sometimes I get so tired of the sameness here, the ordinariness, I feel as if I'm choking to death."

Cathryn pressed her hands over her solar plexus, where her tremors seemed to be originating. "We can do those things together, Dylan. I wouldn't mind traveling. In fact, I'd love to travel."

Dylan stepped closer and gripped her arms. "Cath…"

"I'm not as certain about moving off-island, but I will, if that'll make you…"

"Cath!" He gave her arms a squeeze and tiny shake.

She stopped rambling, gazed into his pitying eyes, and her heart splintered. "But we've been together forever, Dylan. What we have is so special."

"Maybe it was special once, but those days disappeared long ago."

"How can you say that?"

"Because it's true, only you've refused to admit it. You've insisted on living in a fantasy world. You're doing it now. I haven't *had* an affair, Cath. I'm having one. Present tense. What's more, this isn't even my first."

Cathryn felt as if she'd been hit by a bus. She was completely stunned.

Dylan sucked in a breath. "I…I didn't mean to say that."

She yanked away from his hold. "You've cheated on me

before?'' Even in the moonlight she could see his color deepen. "I don't believe this. When?''

He didn't answer.

"When?'' she shouted.

Dylan's embarrassed gaze darted around the cold moon-washed landscape. "You have to understand, Cath, a man has physical needs, and you had three not-so-easy pregnancies all within five years. That's an awful lot of sexual denial.''

"You cheated on me while I was *pregnant?*''

"Those affairs didn't mean anything. They were one-night stands. Pickups on the mainland.''

"Oh, blow it out your ear,'' she said, borrowing a favorite line from her strong, outspoken friend Lauren. She didn't feel like Lauren, though. She was coming unglued. "Tell me something, Dylan, does your affair with Zoe not mean anything, either?''

He ran his hand around the back of his neck. "Not really. Actually, the word *affair* isn't appropriate in her case.'' He dropped his arm, sighing. "I'm sorry, Cath. But Zoe and I...I've fallen in love with her. And I'd like...'' He swallowed. "I'd like to have my freedom so she and I can be married.''

Cathryn heard something like the groaning of an old tree about to keel over—only the creaking sound was coming from her.

"Take me home,'' she said in a voice whose calmness was remarkable considering how volatile she felt.

"But we haven't finished...''

"We most certainly have.''

AFTER CRUISING the up-island beach roads to fill time, Tucker drove to West Shore Road to check on Cathryn's house and see if she'd returned from her big date. It was the third time he'd checked tonight. He didn't know why, except that his instincts were telling him she might need him when she got home.

This time when he approached, Dylan's truck was sitting in the driveway and lights were on in rooms that had been dark before. Tucker slowed but couldn't see beyond the drawn shades. He drove away, drove back, then parked in the shadows at the top of the street, before, finally, Dylan's truck took off.

As Tucker's Mustang pulled into the driveway, he muttered, "I must be out of my mind."

He knocked on the front door, feeling caught within a fold in time. Would she be curled up on the couch, dull with shock, the way he'd found her five weeks ago? Would she be throwing up?

The door opened and the force of her pent-up anger nearly blew him off the stoop. Whoa! Not what he expected.

"What!" she demanded. He could see she'd been crying, but not for some time.

"Uh… How'd it go?"

She snickered, crossing her arms. "The makeover didn't work."

Tucker's gaze swept over her. "Could've fooled me."

Briefly, she seemed about to crumble, but then she squared her shoulders and threw back her head. "I was just pouring myself a cocktail. Want to join me?"

"Uh…" His eyes filled with uncertainty. "Sure."

He followed her to the couch where she poured straight gin into a glass and handed it to him. She picked up her own glass and took a healthy swallow.

Side by side, they sat without speaking.

"Divorce?" Tucker finally asked her.

"Yup." She took another hit of the gin.

"You married a fool."

"No. I'm the fool. The biggest one ever born." She grimaced after her next sip. "This stuff's awful," she said, and put the glass down. "Do you realize that Zoe isn't even Dylan's first affair?"

Tucker tried to appear shocked, but frankly he wasn't surprised.

"And all that time, while he was screwing around, I was *sooo* good," she said with bitter disdain. "I was so stinking *good*." Suddenly she exploded, "Dammit!" She sprang to her feet and glared down at Tucker as if *he* were the offending party. "I don't deserve this treatment."

Tucker looked her directly in the eye. "What did you say?"

She frowned, slightly confused. "I don't deserve this treatment?"

"Yes. Say it again."

"I don't deserve this treatment."

"Again. With conviction."

"I don't deserve this treatment! I don't, goddammit!"

Tucker smiled, raised his hands and applauded. Finally!

"Tell me what happened."

Cathryn hardly needed the nudge. She sailed into her narrative as if a hurricane were blowing her. Unfortunately for Tucker, her newfound anger interfered with her sense of coherence and linear reasoning. For the next fifteen minutes, her thoughts jumped here and there, back and forward, and often came out in fragments. Oddly, though he couldn't follow her linearly, he still understood her—enough to want to go find Dylan and break his kneecaps, as he'd threatened years ago.

Cathryn stopped ranting abruptly, cocked her head toward Tucker and announced, "I'm going out."

"What?"

"Out. I don't want to stay in tonight. I don't want to

be—'' she looked around her living room with the eyes of a hateful stranger ''—here.''

''Where are you going?'' Tucker expected her to say Lauren's or Julia's, but instead she just shrugged.

''Out,'' she repeated, heading for the bathroom. She returned a short while later with her makeup repaired. ''It's Saturday night, and I'm tired of playing by the rules. Why should I? No one else has.''

Uh-oh. Tucker's eyes swept over her for about the thirty-seventh time, and a premonition of disaster hit him. ''Maybe that's not such a good idea, Shortcake.''

She tossed back her long, satiny hair. ''Don't call me Shortcake. Okay? Don't call me Cathryn, either. Or Cath. Definitely not Cath.'' She pivoted on her extra-high heels, searching for her purse. ''Know what I've always wanted to be called, Tuck?''

Tucker held his breath. Seemed she was causing him to do that a lot tonight.

''Cat,'' she answered.

''Cat?'' His eyebrows lifted.

''Yes. Call me Cat. Now where did I leave my coat? Have you seen a black…oh, here it is.''

Tucker shot to his feet, ''Cath—I mean Cat—wait.''

''Don't try to stop me, Tuck.'' She slipped her arms into the wool coat and draped a white silk scarf around its raised collar.

Tucker knew she was angry and in a destructive, hell-raising mood. But then, why shouldn't she be? She had a right to rage for a night. And actually, a bit of rage might do her some good. Like scream therapy. As long as she had someone to watch over her.

He lifted his hands in surrender. ''No, I wouldn't do that. I just want to go with you.''

She paused with her hand on the doorknob, turned slowly and looked him over. He started framing arguments, expecting her to say she preferred going out alone. But she didn't. All she said was, "Cool."

CHAPTER NINE

IF YOU HAD to make up for thirty years of lost time in a single night, there was no better companion to do it with than Tucker Lang. He'd made an art of rebellion, from breaking trivial school rules to defying the very laws of nature.

"Where to?" he asked. Even the way his wrist draped over the steering wheel seemed audacious to Cathryn, and she felt "bad" just riding with him.

"I'm not sure." She glanced at the limitless, moonlit world ahead. "How about the Brass Anchor?"

Tucker's response was an exaggerated yawn.

"Now see? That's why I need you along. Where would you suggest?"

"How about the Old Town Tap?"

"Isn't that kind of a dive?"

"Nah. It's just honest."

"Well…" Cathryn's pulse fluttered. "I'm all for honesty. Let's go."

The Old Town Tap really wasn't such a bad place, she decided, walking in. It was simply a local bar that didn't cater to tourists or try to be more than it was. The low-slung building occupied a featureless paved lot far enough away from the harbor that if the noise level rose too high or the police had to be called in, not too many feathers got ruffled.

Its best feature, however, was its dim lighting, Cathryn thought. She was in a mood to cut loose—or maybe just drink more than she usually did—and a little darkness would be to her advantage when she wobbled out of here later on.

Tucker helped her off with her coat and hung it on the hook outside their padded vinyl booth. They'd barely settled in when a small fortyish waitress, still writing an order in her palm-size pad, came trotting over. "What can I get you folks?"

"What've you got on draft?"

She glanced up as if her head were on a jerked string. "Tucker Lang, my God, how *are* you?"

"I'm just fine, Lois. And how are you?"

Cathryn sat through the mild flirtation, ignored.

"And you, miss?" the woman asked at last. "Oh, Mrs. McGrath!" She was only slightly surprised to see Cathryn with Tucker. That should've relieved Cathryn, but it annoyed her instead. She'd been spending an excessive amount of time with Tucker, yet no one on Harmony had even raised an eyebrow. Why? Did they think he couldn't possibly find her attractive? Was her reputation as a good girl so ensconced that they couldn't imagine her doing anything wrong, even with the island's most notorious lover?

"I'll have a glass of champagne," Cathryn answered. "On second thought, bring the whole bottle." The waitress's quick speculative glance from her to Tucker pleased her inordinately.

"The whole bottle. You got it," the waitress said and trotted off to the bar.

Tucker's slouch was eloquent, as he batted an ashtray back and forth, one hand to the other. Cathryn reached across the heavy pine table and gripped his hands in hers.

"I just needed to get out of the house tonight. I can't explain why. I just felt…choked there. The air smelled as if it'd gone toxic on me."

He nodded. "I know, I understand."

"Great. So stop fidgeting. I'm not planning to do anything stupid. The worst that'll happen is I'll get wasted and you'll have to carry me out."

He didn't appear amused. "Is that what you want to do, get wasted?"

"You betcha. I've never done that before. Do you believe it?"

"No great loss, in my estimation."

"Sure, because you've been there."

"More times than I care to remember."

The waitress returned with their order. Placing a plastic flute and a bottle of inexpensive champagne in front of Cathryn, she said, "Whatever you're celebrating, have a good one."

"Thanks." Cathryn dredged up a smile, which faded a moment later as she held her glass poised and searched for an appropriate toast. "This is to all the Saturday nights I spent sitting home knitting, while my beloved was over on the mainland trolling for bimbos to boink." While Tucker was still sputtering with stunned laughter, she clicked her flute against his beer mug and with wry lightheartedness and said, "Cheers."

After savoring a long, nose-tickling sip, she set the flute down and twisted in her seat to study the room. Along the bar sat a mixed bag of locals, from a wind-dried old fisherman to a nubile young woman. In one lighted corner two middle-aged men were playing pool. A jukebox spewed colored light and country blues, but seemed ignored by all except the three couples out on the dance floor. At every table and booth, groups talked, laughed, drank and ate. Of the fifty or so people in the joint, Cathryn knew or recognized at least two-thirds.

Tucker had been watching her. "Does it bother you to be seen here without Dylan?"

Cathryn ran her index finger down the stem of the glass. "You mean, am I embarrassed or self-conscious? Sure. But only a little. I don't seem to have much tolerance for those feelings tonight, and I'll be damned if they're going to get in my way. It's about time Harmony realized I'm human, too. Don't you think?"

Human, too. Tucker tacked the phrase on a mental corkboard where he was collecting clues. He was fairly certain he already knew what was fueling Cathryn's engine tonight, but she had a way of surprising him.

She lifted the green champagne bottle and topped off her glass. He didn't try to slow her down. If she was determined to drink the entire bottle, so be it. The less interruption, the faster they'd be out of here.

"You know what I resent most, Tuck?" Her speech was beginning to thicken.

"What's that…Cat?"

She paused, frowned, then laughed. "I don't know. I resent so freakin' much." She massaged her temples. "Dylan's assumption that I had no dreams of my own, no yearnings, that it was easy for me to economize and forgo activities that weren't in the best interests of our family." Her eyebrows lifted in quiet surprise. "That it was easy for me to be *happy.*" She raised her glass and drained half its contents.

"I would've loved to travel, Tucker," she continued so earnestly, the statement was nearly an entreaty. "In my early twenties, I would've given anything for a trip to Paris. How I fantasized. But I didn't travel, didn't even mention it, because there were other responsibilities."

Her brow knit and her eyes darkened as she traveled backward through her memories. "It wasn't easy watching friends leave the island, go places, do things and grow past me." She dipped her head to her champagne glass and sipped. "My teachers wanted me to go to college. Did you know that?"

Tucker shook his head.

"I even applied to a couple of schools."

"Were you accepted?"

She nodded. "But I was planning to marry Dylan after graduation, so..." She shrugged one shoulder, lifted her eyebrows again, sighed. "What I miss most, though, I think, are the romantic opportunities I passed up when I was young, all the falling in and out of infatuations that teenagers go through, all the flirting and anticipation of dating. I squashed every urge."

Tucker wondered if she limited those urges to high school.

She moved her flute aside, stacked her forearms on the table and leaned in, that heartrending sincerity in her expression again. "Why did I do it? I don't know. But I'm sure as hell mad at somebody—my parents, as much as I love them. Harmony in general." Her gaze swept the bar. "Or just myself, me, for buying into their assumptions that I'm Cathryn the Good, just an old-fashioned girl and a paragon of virtue. What a burden. What a *trap!*"

Her eyes returned to Tucker. "That's what I resent." But he could see she was rising out of the seriousness of her thoughts. Her mood was lightening. "Sorry for unloading on you like that, Tucker." Her smile was slightly self-effacing, slightly impish and totally delightful.

"No problem, darlin'. Happens all the time in bars."

Just then, the manager of the establishment unplugged the jukebox and startled unaware patrons with an overamplified, "Good evening, folks." His microphone whistled, hitting a pitch that almost peeled the paneling off the walls. A moment of tapping here and there seemed to correct the problem. "Sorry 'bout that," he mumbled.

With a sinking heart, Tucker realized the guy was standing on a small makeshift stage. Overhead, multicolored Christmas lights blinked in a blinding running pattern, and behind him more lights throbbed from a machine that Tucker recognized only too well from his misspent time in bars.

"Good evening, folks," the manager began again. "And welcome to karaoke night at the Old Town Tap."

Tucker leaned toward Cathryn and said in an undertone, "Do you want to leave?"

She tucked in her chin and stared at him as if he'd grown another nose. "No. Why?" Then she returned to watching the stage, her eyes bright with anticipation. "It looks like the fun is just getting started."

"Tonight," the emcee continued, "thanks to the generosity of several local merchants, we have an extra-large number of prizes to give away. So don't be shy." He lifted and waved a sheet of paper. "Five people've already signed up. Don't let them walk off with everything. Give 'em some competition. If you look in the menu holder on your tables, you should find a list of songs to pick from. If something strikes your fancy, come on up. What've you got to lose but your pride?" He laughed at his own joke. "Okay, without further ado…"

Tucker slouched in his seat, Cathryn perked up in hers, and the first contestant mounted the stage.

If Cathryn had expected Las Vegas quality performances, reality soon readjusted those expectations. But it didn't make any difference to her. She was in Tucker's direct line of vision, and it was obvious to him she was having a great time listening, laughing, cheering. Forgetting her troubles. Maybe karaoke wasn't so bad after all. It all depended on who you were with.

Some of the singers were just plain awful and intentionally hammed up their numbers, but because everyone in the place knew everyone else, it sort of became an inside joke and the humor was all the funnier. Likewise, when someone made a serious effort, support was unquestioned.

A sixty-something woman with a shaky voice was warbling her way through what felt like the twenty-eighth verse of "Blowin' in the Wind" when Tucker noticed Cathryn reach for the song list. He also noticed her bottle of champagne was half empty and her cheeks were glowing. She leaned toward him, crunching the list, and winced prettily. "Should I try?"

Tucker was caught unawares by an urge to lean in, too, meet her halfway across the table and kiss her. "Darlin', I think you should do whatever you want."

She caught her lower lip in her teeth, studied the chart again. "I think I'll do..." She looked up, wincing in that special way of hers that went straight to his heart. "'I Will Always Love You'? You know, the Whitney Houston song?"

Tucker didn't overanalyze her choice, just gave her a casual thumbs-up and said, "Go for it."

She slid out of the booth, took two unsteady steps in her high heels, then trotted back and gave him a peck on the cheek. "Thanks."

"For what?"

"Going along with this. With me."

"Hey..." He shrugged dismissively and waved her toward the stage.

She began her number like a little girl at her first recital—carefully, squeezing the mike, her voice soft and tentative. But she seemed to be enjoying the experience anyway, and Tucker reminded himself that was all that mattered. She'd never done anything like this before, and while singing ka-

raoke might be run-of-the mill to some folks, to her it was
the equivalent of a trip to the moon.

The emcee had given her an enthusiastic introduction—
standing close and looking down her V-necked dress,
Tucker had noticed. And because he'd announced this was
her first appearance on the Tap's karaoke stage, and also
because she was Cathryn, the audience was with her all the
way, even when she didn't quite reach a couple of the
song's more difficult notes. That support went a long way
toward relaxing her, and before long she was in her zone,
if not quite belting out the tune, at least doing a commendable job.

She looked like a stick of dynamite, too. Tucker had
known she was pulling herself together a little more each
day, but somehow the cumulative effect had escaped him.
There it was now, the full package, and he was over-
whelmed—by her, and by his sudden proprietary feeling
toward her.

When she was done, the audience applauded spiritedly,
with a few whistles thrown in for good measure. She bowed
deeply, came up beaming and hurried back to the booth.

"Ahh!" She sighed, falling into her seat. Tucker topped
off her champagne and handed it to her—a mistake. She
had worked up a thirst and downed the entire glass in a few
gulps. Plunking the flute on the table, she sighed again and
smiled at him with such drowsy self-satisfaction, he couldn't
help but smile back.

The emcee called a brief intermission, a smart ploy to
keep customers hanging on and drinking longer. He turned
on the jukebox again, and a few couples shuffled out to the
dance floor. Just when Tucker was getting the uneasy feeling Cathryn wanted to join them, a couple she knew came
over to their booth and complimented her on her singing.

"By the way, you're looking wonderful, Cathryn," the

woman said with a congratulatory smile before she and her husband drifted off. Neither one had mentioned Dylan or asked where he was. They knew. Five weeks had thoroughly broadcast the news of the McGraths' separation.

"Well, I guess *they* won't be saying 'poor Cathryn' when they discuss me at breakfast tomorrow."

Poor Cathryn. Tucker pinned that on to his mental corkboard, too.

Suddenly she sprang to her feet. "Let's dance, Tucker."

Tucker took a quick sip of his beer, uncoiled from the booth and led her forward with a hand at her back. The number was fast, to his immense relief, and Cathryn danced in her habitual fashion, which was modestly unobtrusive.

By the second number, however, it had seeped through her champagne-soaked brain that she knew another way to move, Tucker's way. She called it dirty dancing, but it really had no name. It was just his natural style.

Tucker's response to her sinuous moves was added caution. He knew from experience that the liquid courage that had gotten her up on stage could turn on a dime into liquid foolhardiness, and it was his job tonight to make sure that didn't happen, that she walked the fine line between just right and too much.

"What's the matter?" She stopped dancing, planted her hands on her oh-so-nicely-rounded hips and pouted.

"I'm kind of tired," he said. "Let's sit this one out."

"I don't feel like sitting just yet. But you can go back, if that's what you want." She peered past him and around the room, searching for another unattached male. With a sinking heart, Tucker saw her find one, a guy with the unlikely name of Chucky Norris. He'd gone to school with Tucker. And he was peering back.

Not a wise choice, Cat, he thought, his hand shooting out and catching her by the elbow.

"What?" she said, whirling in surprise.

"I changed my mind. You want to prove something, you prove it with me."

"Oh." Her O-shaped lips eased into a smile, which worked its way up to her eyes. "Great. Because quite frankly, Tucker, you've still got it all over these other guys."

Cathryn hooked her left arm around Tucker's neck and, hanging on, let her head fall back to view the swirly colored lights over the dance floor. She felt so much better being out tonight than she would have, sitting home brooding over Dylan. The champagne had gone to her head, of course—but nicely. She wasn't intoxicated, nor was she queasy. She was just floating along, enjoying the ride. And what a ride it was.

Tucker was right, she *was* out to prove something tonight. Lots of somethings, she was quickly discovering. And one of those somethings was that she was not an object of pity. She didn't want people saying, "Poor Cathryn. Did you hear? Dylan's left her for good." Or, "Poor Cathryn. Have you seen the other woman?" Or, "Poor Cathryn, all alone now. We hear she's falling apart."

Cathryn righted her tipped-back head and gazed appreciatively at her partner, the wickedly exciting, wickedly handsome Tucker Lang. "Oh, no. Cathryn is not to be pitied," folks would say tomorrow. "Dylan may have that Anderson woman, but did you see who Cathryn was out with last night? Dancing, no less. Dancing and getting on with her life. That girl's not the fool we thought."

"What's the matter?" Tucker's deep watchful eyes narrowed on her.

She smiled. "Nothing. I'm just admiring my handiwork."

He pulled up straighter. "Me?"

"Hmm." Her advice had made a remarkable difference

in his appearance, but, loath though she was to admit it, most of his appeal was beyond anyone's doing. It was simply Tucker's essence to be, as Justin would say, "a babe magnet," although at present he didn't appear too comfortable in his essence. He was wearing such a grim expression and his bearing was so ballroom stiff, she had to laugh. Especially because the record they were dancing to was a dark and simmery blues number. Oh, this wouldn't do. Then people would be saying, "Did you see what Cathryn did to Tucker Lang? She even managed to turn *him* off. No wonder her husband left her."

Cathryn closed the space between them, but when their bodies met, he flinched and gritted his teeth. Her heart dropped to her knees. "Just for tonight," she said, her brow pinched and achy, "Could you pretend I'm someone you find attractive, please? Someone, say, like Jenny?"

Tucker tipped up her chin, making her meet his eyes. Their dark fiery depths contrasted confusingly with his rigid demeanor. "And who will you pretend I am?"

"You?" Cathryn gazed at him awhile. "You'll be every young man I never flirted with, Tucker. Every opportunity I let slip by. Every dangerous leap I never took, every misdemeanor I avoided, every sin. You'll be my walk in the rain down the Champs-Elysees. The Grand Canyon seen from a white-water raft. Times Square on New Year's Eve…"

Cathryn wasn't quite sure when she'd stopped verbalizing her thoughts and started speaking with her eyes. She only became aware of it sometime after the fact. "Sorry," she murmured, dropping her gaze. "I seem to be wearing my self-pity on my sleeve."

"No. There'll be no sorrys tonight. Let's just dance."

"I was under the impression we already were."

One corner of his mouth lifted. "Then you were mistaken.'' Before she could catch his meaning, Tucker snaked his very proper leading arm around her back and dipped her. It wasn't such a dramatic move that it drew a lot of attention, but it changed everything about the way Cathryn clung to him. Desperately. At his mercy.

As he lifted her, though, her fear of being dropped vanished and turned to trust. And when he slid his knee between her legs and she found herself riding up his thigh, the grin she wore was as wicked as his.

Intuitively Cathryn linked her arms around Tucker's neck, freeing his hands to do whatever they pleased, whatever was necessary to guide her. What they did was span her ribs and pull her against him, causing their bodies to meld and move as one, rhythmically, sinuously, erotically. *Oh, what a scene we must be creating!* she thought. But frankly, she didn't care. And anyway, wasn't that the point?

''You're not wearing your lily-of-the-valley tonight.'' Tucker spoke with his lips against her ear, the hot vibrations of his voice sending shivers down her back. ''What is it?''

''Oh, just something different.''

''I like it, whatever it is.'' With a quick pivot, he dipped her again. She came up dizzy and laughing.

After that, not much of anything existed beyond Tucker. Tucker and his bedroom eyes. Tucker and his grinding pelvis. Tucker and his muscular thighs. After three more numbers, Cathryn dropped into their booth breathless, shaky and aroused. It was mortifying…and marvelous; despicable…yet empowering, because, although she couldn't be absolutely certain, she thought Tucker was turned on, too.

She poured fresh champagne into her flute, but instead of drinking it, held it to her red-hot cheeks, then to her forehead, her neck, and finally the area at the vee of her dress. Across the table Tucker watched her with avid interest and, when caught, didn't even try to make excuses. Rather, he

touched the tips of his fingers to his tongue, tapped her arm
and hissed in a credible imitation of steam.

He was a very kind man.

Not long afterward, the manager of the bar turned off the
dance music and resumed the karaoke contest.

"Ready to go?" Tucker asked hopefully.

"Not yet," she replied and reached for the song list once
again.

CATHRYN GOT a warm round of applause when the emcee
announced she wanted to do another number. It was getting
late and the crowd had loosened up significantly. So, apparently, had Cathryn, Tucker thought, watching her wobble
into the spotlight. And little wonder. Her champagne was
almost gone. Hell. Had he let her go too far?

Tucker held his breath as the music started. From the
hard-driving, gunshot-style of drumming, he immediately
recognized the recording as something by Robert Palmer.
Which one precisely, he didn't know until Cathryn began
to sing. It was "Some Like It Hot." Tucker dropped his
head back against the padded booth and half laughed, half
groaned. He'd created a monster.

The waitress paused on her way by the booth. "Is that
Mrs. McGrath?" she gasped.

"No, that there is Cat. Just Cat. You know, like Cher?"

Lois glanced at him as if he'd lost his mind. Which often
happened when a night was on the cusp of turning wild.

Where on earth had Cathryn picked up that provocative
bump-bump thing she did with her hips? And when had she
learned to toss her hair over her eyes and glance like a
seductress over her shoulder? And how was her choir voice
capable of making that sexy growl? And, oh God, what was
she doing with that chair?

The waitress standing beside Tucker laughed and clapped

as Cathryn swung one of her long black-stockinged legs
over a straight-backed chair—all that kickboxing came in
handy for something—and planted her high-heeled foot on
the rest of the crowd reacted similarly, adding
hoots and whistles to the overall noise.

But all of a sudden Tucker noticed her tense and tug her
dress between her legs. Was she afraid her underwear was
showing? The audience had also noticed, but it was such a
"Cathryn" thing to do, and a reminder of who she was, that
her moment of instinctive prudishness and three missed
notes only endeared her to them further. Tonight Cathryn
could do no wrong.

She sure could be bad, though. Tucker whistled softly as
she pressed one hand low on her belly and with the other
mussed her hair forward, all the while thrusting her hips
back and forth in perfect syncopation with the heavy drum
whacks. Well, almost perfect syncopation. But that was cute
too. What Tucker especially enjoyed was how her little
black dress stayed with her, clinging to her voluptuous
curves and riding up her thighs to show just so much leg
and no more.

He had to admit he was relieved, however, when she
purred the final "...some like it ho-ot" and the number
ended. The applause was fierce. There were catcalls and
foot-stomping and clamors of "Encore." But Cathryn simply bowed and returned to the booth where Tucker waited,
cautiously eyeing the joint.

True, it wasn't a bad place, and most of the patrons were
just ordinary respectable people. But there was also an element here that could go either way, a group who might
interpret Cathryn's performance as an announcement of her
new availability.

Glowing with the satisfaction of accomplishment, she

took a moment to catch her breath, then asked Tucker if he thought she had a chance of winning a prize.

Great. If he said yes, she'd want to stick around. If he said no, she'd be crushed. But Chucky Norris had already moved to a closer table and was eyeing Cathryn as if she were fair game. Tucker covertly scanned the bar. Oh yeah, it was open season on the McGrath woman, all right, and the hunters were closing in.

"Darlin', if you don't come in first, the contest is rigged. But, heck, you don't need a prize. Actually it'd be way more cool, as the kids'd say, if you just walked out now."

Her brows knit as she tried to follow his reasoning. "I think I'm drunk, Tucker."

"And I think we oughta leave," he said. But she still seemed reluctant, so he added, "There's so much more we have to do yet tonight."

"There is?"

"Uh-huh." Tucker got up and unhooked their coats, just as Chucky got up and started over. "Come on, darlin'. On your feet."

"But..." she glanced toward the stage where a young guy was belting out a recent rock ballad.

"They'll call you if you win."

"Oh."

Chucky's beefy shoulders suddenly cast a shadow over the coat Tucker was trying to get Cathryn's arms into. "Hey, where ya going?"

"Oh, hello, Chuck." Cathryn greeted him politely, speaking with the slow care of inebriation. "How are you?"

He answered with a question of his own. "Are you and your old man split for good, or what?"

"We're on our way out, Norris," Tucker interrupted as unantagonistically as he could.

"Ah, hell. You can't leave now."

"We have to. She's…got to get home to her kids."

A set of teeth as wide as a Buick flashed Chucky's disbelief that Cathryn was going home to anything but a roll between the sheets and, given her condition, it could be with him as easily as with Tucker.

Tucker took Cathryn by the arm and started toward the exit. A viselike hand gripped his shoulder.

"Maybe the lady wants to stay." Chucky said, spewing ignitable fumes with his words.

Tucker calculated how long it had been since he'd been involved in a bar fight. Oh, man. He was in trouble. But if he remembered anything from the bad old days, it was the necessity of putting up a strong bluff. He let go of Cathryn and leaned into Chucky nice and slow, giving him a direct, steady stare. "We can take this outside if you want, but maybe you forgot what happened the last time you and I danced."

"I didn't forget. This is what they call payback, Sucker. Oh, sor-ry." Chucky continued to smile. "I mean Tucker."

Tucker's name had been a bane during his youth, giving rise to taunts like Sucker—and worse. He'd hated those taunts, but he thought he'd outgrown his juvenile reaction to them. Apparently not. He butted Chucky's chest with his shoulder. "Let's go." This time he meant it.

They left the bar without making a fuss. But as soon as they reached the parking lot, they squared off. Tucker took a hard punch to the side of the head, but he landed a hard one, too, to Chucky's softer-than-expected stomach. Then, as suddenly as the fight had begun, it was over. Hands raised, Chucky shook his head and backed away as he fought to catch his breath.

"Ah, Chucky," Tucker commiserated, clapping him on the back. "We're getting old." He waited until his adversary was able to draw enough breath to curse, then Tucker slapped him on the back again and strode away, calling, "Take care of yourself, old man."

Cathryn was waiting by the car, her arms wrapped tightly around her waist, her shoulders trembling, and in her eyes hung two huge tears.

Tucker suddenly felt like a jerk. "Aw, darlin', I'm sorry." He stroked her arms. "It was a stupid thing to do. I should've known better."

She laughed softly and shook her head. "No, you misunderstand." She blotted her eyes on her coat sleeve. "Nobody's ever fought over me before."

Tucker's brow crunched as he glanced back toward the scene of the scuffle. "That was a good thing?"

She laughed again, sniffling. "Yeah. Very good."

"I-yi-yi."

He handed her into the car and came around to his side. "How are you feeling?"

"Surprisingly well, considering."

"Great. So where to now?"

She shrugged. "Let's just cruise. Something'll strike me. I'll know it when I see it."

Cathryn "knew it" when they passed Zoe Anderson's place, a two-million-dollar shingle-style cottage on the Point. Dylan's truck was in the driveway.

"Whoa, stop!" she said abruptly.

Tucker hit the brakes and skidded. "What's the matter?"

"Nothing. I…" Was she out of her mind? she wondered. "I just want to pay my husband and his lovely a visit."

The Mustang idled. Conflict warred in Tucker's features. "Confrontation might not be such a good idea."

"No, I'm not planning to confront them or even go to the door. I just want…to do something."

The lines of caution in Tucker's demeanor deepened. "This isn't going to get us arrested, I hope."

Cathryn widened her eyes. "Oooo, I've never been arrested before."

"Cat!"

"No. We won't be arrested."

"Okay. So what is it?"

Cathryn grimaced. Within the safety of her mind, her idea had seemed reasonable enough, but when pressed to reveal it, she didn't have the nerve. Her idea wasn't reasonable. It was immature and lewd and totally unlike her...and that was precisely why it so appealed to her tonight. Not only would her little act of rebellion stick it to Dylan and Zoe, it would also help her triumph over the inhibitions of her youth.

One Labor Day when she was a young teenager, her fun-loving friend Amber had suggested walking out onto the harbor's breakwater and mooning the last official ferry of summer. Amber had seen it as a splendid way to say good-bye to the hoards of tourists who crowded Harmony during that season. Her friends and classmates had agreed and all had participated in and thoroughly enjoyed the prank. All but Cathryn. She hadn't dared, not then nor the next year nor any year since, although it had become an accepted tradition on Harmony and scores of people now took part.

Well, it was high time she got over her qualms, and tonight she certainly had good reason.

"Trust me, Tucker. Just trust me. Okay?"

Tucker sighed heavily, shifted into reverse and backed up. Cathryn freed herself of her safety harness, took off her coat and tossed it into the back.

Turning into the moonlit circular drive, he glanced over and asked, "What are you doing?"

"Don't look at me. Don't watch," she said. "Please?"

He sighed again and turned away. By the time they reached the top of the driveway she had rolled down the window and was kneeling up in the seat.

"Stop here, in front of the porch."

"What the hell?"

"Beep your horn," she instructed, raising up her dress and holding it bunched high on her thighs.

"Oh, no. Cathryn, you're not…"

"I am. Now beep the damn horn."

Tucker stared at the windshield, frozen in disbelief, so she reached for the horn and did the job herself.

When the door opened she was ready, head tucked, forehead on the gearshift panel, her derriere raised to the window and proudly bared. From the porch came sharp exclamations, first of confusion, then of astonishment, and finally of disgust and anger.

"Okay, step on it, Tuck!"

Tucker was more than happy to oblige. As the car swerved toward the entrance gate, kicking up gravel and disdain, he caught a glimpse of Cathryn in his peripheral vision wiggling back into her panty hose and righting her dress. They were several yards down the road when he finally looked over. She was sitting secure in her seat belt, hands folded neatly in her lap, as prim as any schoolmarm on a Sunday outing.

When he at last stopped laughing, Tucker asked her what else she wanted to do, but Cathryn had had enough adventure for one night. "Home," she said. "I'm ready to go home now."

Tucker hoped so, but he doubted it. And sadly he was right.

Their night on the town had raised her above her pain for a while, but the intoxication didn't last. The pain returned as soon she arrived back at the house where she and Dylan had spent most of their married years together. In spite of all the cutting loose she'd done to prove she was strong and getting on with her life, the fact remained, Dylan was with Zoe and she was alone.

After shedding her coat, she quietly built a fire in the family room. Tucker helped, assuming she was trying to bring some warmth, some life, into the house. But when the logs had caught, she startled him by tossing in an armful of her exercise tapes.

"What did you do that for?" he demanded, rising from his crouch and hanging the tongs in their wrought-iron stand. She said nothing, just stood there watching the plastic melt, and before he could gather his thoughts on self-destructive behavior, she'd marched off to the kitchen.

Tucker grabbed the fireplace tools again and raked the tapes out of the flames to prevent the plastic from raising a stench or creating a hard-to-clean mess. That done, he joined Cathryn in the kitchen.

She had a half-gallon tub of Rocky Road on the counter and a jar of chocolate sauce warming in the microwave. She opened the refrigerator, poked around a bit and returned to the counter with a jar of maraschino cherries and whipped cream in a can. "Want some?" she asked grumpily, scooping ice cream into a soup bowl.

"No." Tucker leaned against the counter and crossed his arms. "And neither do you."

"Yes I do." She removed the chocolate sauce from the microwave and drizzled it over the ice cream.

"Cath, you don't *need* that. Think of all the effort it took to…"

"What difference does it make?" she challenged sullenly, squirting a twirly mound of cream and topping it with a cherry. "Perfect." She carried the sundae into the family room and sat in front of the blazing fire.

With a frustrated sigh, Tucker sat next to her. She scooped up some ice cream, swirled it around her mouth as if it were a precious vintage wine, swallowed, then licked the chocolate off the spoon. She repeated the ritual, but this time with less enthusiasm. Little wonder, considering what she already had in her stomach.

Losing interest, she placed the spoon in the bowl and stared at the fire. After a while Tucker moved the bowl to the coffee table. She surrendered it without even being aware.

He watched her face, her transfixed eyes. She sat so still that the subtle shifts in her expression might've gone unnoticed by someone who didn't know her. But Tucker did, and his heart was breaking for her. He stroked her back, reminded of the first time he'd walked into her house and found her in emotional shambles. He'd done the same thing then. But this was different. Five weeks ago, hope had still been an option.

Cathryn turned her head slowly, her hazel cat-eyes holding a mixture of gratitude and grief, embarrassment and…something else he couldn't quite define…until he lifted his hand from her shoulder and she protested. "Oh, don't stop. That felt so good."

His throat closed as if it had been stoppered. Was Cathryn headed where he *thought* she was headed?

Her brows lowered with caution, as she tried to read his hesitation. "What?"

"Nothing."

But it wasn't nothing. In that split second she'd sensed his shock and withdrawal from her, and it had resonated within her as another rejection, another reminder of her ineptness, her undesirability, her failure as a woman.

"Cath." He drew her to him and cradled her close. "Don't. Stop worrying. It's going to be all right."

She gripped his shirt in her fists and huddled against his chest, shivering but dry-eyed. "Is it?"

He held her closer, wanting to absorb everything she was suffering, all the shock waves of fear and grief and failure. "Yes. Trust me. Maybe not for a while. I'd be lying if I said you're going to wake up tomorrow feeling ready to take on the world. But eventually. You're stronger than you think, darlin'. More intelligent and talented, too. And beautiful. God! You may not feel like a million bucks right now, but you sure look like it."

Cathryn put a little distance between them, her eyes slowly moving over him—hair, eyes, mouth, chest, hands—coming back to his mouth. The room was absolutely quiet except for the hiss and crackle of the fire and the thudding of his heart.

Oh no. Oh no. She was determined to go ahead with this?

Slowly she raised one hand and traced his lips with the tips of her fingers. Such a light touch, but his mouth became sensitized beyond all reasoning, and he unintentionally opened it and nipped one of her knuckles. He was instantly mortified.

"Oh, Cath, I'm sorry."

"No." She crossed his lips with her fingers. "No sorrys tonight. Remember?"

Tucker's head swam as if he were the one who'd consumed all that champagne. She threaded her fingers through his hair, her nails combing his scalp, her scent drawing him closer. Slowly she closed the distance between them and touched his lips with hers. The kiss was confusing in its chasteness. It was like a kiss that one friend gave another when they said hello. Or maybe goodbye?

"Cathryn, think this through carefully."

"No. Thinking has always been my downfall. Too much thinking." She shook her head, her silky hair tickling his neck and provoking a tightness in his groin. She leaned closer. "Make love to me, Tucker."

He wanted to protest, *intended* to protest. But he knew what that would do to her. He'd already gotten a preview. And he couldn't hurt her that way.

Oh, man. He'd never been more stumped by the ethics of a situation. It was clear she was running on anger. Dylan had devastated her, and now she wanted to exact some revenge by having a fling of her own. Affection was the furthest thing from her mind. He doubted even lust was involved. She simply needed someone to use, someone she could seduce and who'd reassure her of her worth.

How could he not oblige her? She needed him, now more than ever. Her ego was extraordinarily fragile at this juncture, and it was resting in his hands. To turn away now might even be construed as a sin, quite literally.

Of course, there was still the matter of Jenny and the loyalty he owed her. But they weren't married yet. And she was far away and needn't ever hear about this. And if he was honest with himself, they'd probably never be married. The woman simply wasn't interested.

Only one fear remained…

But if heaven's lightning had passed through him and left him unscathed, surely he could handle whatever Cathryn dished out.

At last Tucker relaxed, feeling at peace with himself. He eased back into the plush pillows piled in the corner of the couch, flung one arm overhead and grinned. "I have a better idea, darlin'. *You* make love to *me*."

CHAPTER TEN

CATHRYN TEMPERED her sense of triumph with caution. Tucker was undoubtedly complying just to be a kind. He might even pity her. Oh, she hoped not. She couldn't imagine anything worse in this situation than pity. But even if he did, she was determined that he wouldn't when she was done with him.

She uncoiled from the sofa and walked to the stereo, moving as gracefully as she could, given the height of her heels and the amount of champagne fizzing through her bloodstream. After a hasty, hazy search through her CD collection, she put on what she hoped was appropriate mood music and switched off the lamps. Firelight was more than enough to see by, and the shadows would conceal a multitude of flaws—stretch marks and cellulite in particular. And all the while, Tucker lay there, one arm flung over his head, a gorgeous male in submission.

Unexpectedly, Cathryn hesitated. This wasn't just a gorgeous male. This was Tucker, who, for the past five weeks, had worked very hard trying to improve himself to become an exemplary father and husband. What was she doing? What about Jenny?

Cathryn momentarily felt sick. But maybe that was just the champagne backfiring on her, because Jenny really didn't factor into this scenario. Tucker hadn't talked to the young woman in weeks. He'd phoned, but she hadn't answered any of his calls, and Cathryn was beginning to think he was as blind as she'd been with Dylan. Jenny wasn't ever going to marry him.

As for Tucker, Cathryn was under no delusions that their lovemaking would mean anything to him. Considering all the women he'd known, she'd be just one more notch on his belt, and a small one at that. This sort of thing happened to him all the time.

Feeling a bit more sanguine about what she was about to do, she got on with it.

When her shins bumped the couch, however, she hesitated again, wondering what to do next, where to start. Tucker was clearly letting her take the lead. She tried to recall the "Better Sex" videos she'd watched so avidly, the hints they'd given and techniques they'd demonstrated, but everything was a blur, and so she just prayed for instinct to carry her through.

She perched on the edge of the cushion, angling herself to face Tucker, and lightly stroked his chest. Even fully clothed he was a tactile feast, all hard muscle and warm sinew under his chambray shirt. She didn't want to make comparisons with Dylan, but since Dylan was the only man she'd ever been with until now, not making them was impossible. Both men were well-built, but the novelty of Tucker's body fascinated her and made her ultra-aware of everything about him. It also made her slow down and take her time. Her overly alert senses seemed to demand it.

Or maybe her slowness was really just tentativeness and insecurity, she thought. After all, the man she was hoping to seduce was Tucker Lang! She wasn't at all sure she could do it.

Before rationality could spoil the mood, she leaned forward, bracing her hands on his chest, and kissed him. It was another getting-acquainted kiss like the first, a kiss to familiarize herself with his lips, their extraordinary softness, their warmth, their taste.

She pulled back to enjoy again the astonishment of realizing she was doing this with him. But more than that, she needed to touch base with a friend and be reassured that she was safe.

Tucker didn't let her down. He smiled just enough to calm her uneasiness and invite her back. This time she didn't hesitate. She angled her mouth over his, seduced and made love to it. Before long, she felt a recognizable tautness in his muscles and heard a quickening in his breathing that made her almost giddy with relief. Still, a part of her remained aloof and objective, as if monitoring her moves from above.

Several very long kisses later, she sat up again. Tucker's heart raced under her palm, but it was his eyes that told her what he was feeling. They blazed. Looking into them sent an unexpected and frightening shaft of heat straight through her.

Until now he'd continued to lie back, not touching her, but finally he made an overture. He raised a hand, lightly traced her jaw to her ear, circled the ear, then combed his long fingers through her hair, watching the firelight glisten in the tumbling strands. "Come here," he whispered, applying a slight pressure to the nape of her neck. "Come here."

TUCKER STROKED Cathryn's neck with his fingertips as gently as if he were petting a kitten. She *was* a kitten in a sense. Nothing she could do would be new to him, and that was precisely why his quick arousal so surprised him.

She draped herself across his chest again, bringing with her all those warm, solid curves that were provoking him, and he wrapped her in his arms—loosely, though, so she'd

think she was still in control—and as she kissed him, ran
his hands over her back. The soft knit dress she wore withheld very little from his sense of touch. He had intended to
let her do all the leading, but after a very short while he
couldn't help but join in. He was programmed to react in a
certain way, and if he didn't, he'd probably implode.

Cathryn sat up, the corners of her glistening lips curled
in a faint smile of satisfaction.

"Are you having fun?" he teased. The coarseness of his
breathing left no doubt what he was referring to.

She nodded slowly, her smile widening just a little. "Uh-
huh." She took hold of his hands and guided them up the
sides of her ribs to her breasts. Tucker drew in a hiss of
surprise.

"Oh, yes," he murmured, sounding husky with need even
to himself. She arched upward, giving his hands more purchase. Her head lolled to one side, her long shimmering hair
cascading over her shoulder. She closed her eyes, thoroughly enjoying the eroticism of the moment, although
Tucker suspected what she was enjoying was beyond eroticism. But that was all right.

She rose from the couch unexpectedly, moved aside the
coffee table and, limned in firelight, unfastened a tie at the
side of her dress. She did it slowly, swaying to the saxo-
phone music that drifted from the stereo, letting the soft
fabric fall and sway with her a few beats before she unfastened another tie inside the garment. The entire dress fell
free, like an open coat, giving him an enticing glimpse of
white skin and black lingerie. Inch by slow inch, she
stripped one long sleeve down her arm, then she stripped
the other. The garment slid off her and puddled on the floor.

Tucker gasped. She was beautiful. Far more beautiful
than he'd ever imagined. Backlit with firelight, she almost
seemed a primitive goddess, come to torture him in his

dreams. His eyes feasted on her breasts, cupped high and rounded by a sexy little bra, and he came strongly alive.

Still swaying to the music, she took a sinuous step closer, and in a move that stunned him speechless, swung her high-heeled foot over him and hooked it on the back of the couch. To draw out the pleasure, his gaze meandered slowly from her hair to her smokey alley-cat eyes, from her seductively parted lips to her succulent breasts, from her concave belly button to her...

Tucker nearly swallowed his tongue. She wasn't wearing underwear, just sexy-as-hell panty hose. He groaned and reached for her, but she captured his wrists and wouldn't let him touch her. Instead, she pinned his arms to his sides and straddled him.

She has no underwear on, he thought. Cathryn. No underwear. Everything in his overheated brain was obliterated by that one image...until he realized she was sitting directly over the button-fly closure of his jeans, and then *that* image consumed him. She slid forward, eased back, did it again, and again, eyes closed in a rapturous expression, and he of the iron control came very close to losing it.

He'd experienced it all, he'd thought, but he was wrong. He'd never experienced Cathryn, and that made all the difference.

"Wait, slow down, darlin'." He freed his hands from her grip and clamped them on her hips, stilling her undulating movements.

Her grin was that of a she-devil. "What's the matter, Tucker. Am I going too fast for you, or too slow?" She didn't wait for an answer, and a good thing, because he didn't have one. She went straight to work unbuttoning his shirt, making each unfastening an exercise in provocation. Parting the fabric bit by bit, she stroked his chest, circled the area of his nipples with her polished fingernails and occasionally leaned forward to tease him with a nip of her teeth or a flick of her tongue.

By the time the damn shirt was fully unbuttoned he'd worked so hard at control his eyes were practically rolled back in his head. Afraid that she might be getting ideas about the buttons at his cuffs, he whipped the garment off and flung it across the room.

"If you want to play with my clothes, let's move on to something more interesting." With that he fit his hands under her bottom, lifted her and settled her lower, over his thighs.

She gazed down at the ridge she'd been straddling, and self-consciousness flickered across her expression. She glanced up at him, shadows of uncertainty darkening her eyes. Tucker smiled softly, concerned for her comfort, and after a moment she smiled back and resumed her seduction.

Where she'd picked up her moves, Tucker didn't know, but he was beginning to believe her husband was the biggest fool on earth. She undid his belt gracefully, lingeringly, just as she did the buttons of his jeans. Trying to bank his impatience, he raised his hips, which allowed her to peel the denim away.

Lightly straddling his shins, she gazed up the length of his nearly naked body, then leaned forward like a stretching cat, and slid her hands up his thighs right into his shorts. His breath escaped in an abrupt gasp. *So that* was the advantage of boxers.

His back arched off the sofa as she found him, encircled him, inflamed him into a rhythmic thrusting long before he'd intended it. He groped for her, but she evaded his capture by sliding back and stripping him of his shorts. *Whoosh!* Just like that. He'd lost more than his shorts with that move, though. He'd also lost his control of the situation, completely.

She sheathed him in her hands again and stroked him into mindlessness. As if that weren't enough, she repeated the torment with her mouth. Tucker gritted his teeth and gripped the upholstery until he was sure he was tearing holes in it. He would've preferred gripping *her,* but whenever he'd tried, she'd brushed his hands away. She allowed him only her breasts, and even then she insisted the bra remain. Somehow that seemed to give her more confidence.

"Enough. Darlin', enough," he gasped.

In a matter of seconds, she'd shed her panty hose and straddled him again. Hair mussed, lips wet and swollen— the perfect temptress. But when she began to guide him inside her, he remembered he wasn't wearing a condom. With the last shred of rational thought left to him, he lifted and repositioned her, and immediately climaxed against her. It was a massive orgasm, shaking him from his hair roots to his toes, and when he finally fell back to earth it was to an amazement at how far up he'd been.

Slowly, he opened his heavy-lidded eyes and caught sight of Cathryn, leaning on an elbow, watching him.

"Was that all right?" A slight pucker on her brow betrayed her lingering insecurity.

He could barely catch his breath. He nodded, laughed, whispered, "Yes. Fine."

"Are you sure. You didn't…I mean, I meant to…"

"I know what you meant to do." Tucker raised one hip, tipping her off him into the crook of the couch. He reached for his jeans on the floor and dug into one of the pockets for his wallet. "I didn't have one of these, though." He flashed a condom, then dropped it on the floor within easy reach. Pulling a handkerchief from another pocket, he cleaned the slick mess he'd made, then went to the bathroom and returned with a towel for her.

She sat up, clutching a toss pillow in front of her. Self-consciousness had returned, although Tucker was fairly certain he'd noticed her smiling a little, too. He stood over her, looking down, sensing he was at a crossroads. He'd done what was needed. Now he could put on his pants and they could both go have a cup of coffee.

Instead, he snatched the pillow from her and threw it on the floor. All he'd done was the bare minimum, and with friends it wasn't his way to be stingy.

She shot him a startled glance. "What are you doing?"

He didn't give her an answer, just proceeded to divest the sofa of the rest of its pillows and arrange them into a nest by the fire.

"Uh…" She eyed her dress, in a heap under the coffee table. "We're done, right?"

Tucker gripped her under the arms, hoisted her to her feet and kissed her with all the aggression he'd been dreaming about during her seduction of him. He trailed his hands to her breasts where they lingered awhile, enjoying the tautness that betrayed her. Moving over her belly to her thighs, his fingers slid into her easily. She whimpered, arching into his hand, tight as a bow.

"Done?" He laughed, amazed at his own return to arousal. "Hardly."

CATHRYN HAD BEEN feeling fairly astonished with her success. She'd done it. She'd seduced the legendary Tucker Lang. But her sense of triumph dissolved with his announcement. "Wh-what do you mean?" Most of her question lacked sound, however, because Tucker had scooped her off her feet, swung her around and was lowering her gently to the pillows by the fire. She landed dizzy and disoriented.

"It's your turn," he said. Buck naked and consummately comfortable in his nakedness, he lay down alongside her and braced up on one forearm. "I take pride in being a gentleman when I make love, and the cardinal rule is to never leave a woman hanging.''

She shook her head. "But I'm not. I'm fine, Tucker. Really.''

He cupped the side of her face with one large hand, arresting the negative movement. ''Don't ever settle for less than a gentleman, Cathryn.'' And while she was still grappling with the ramifications of his message, he parted her lips with his thumb, lowered his head and invaded her mouth, his tongue swirling and mating with hers. Within milliseconds she was reeling. Memories of being on a wild amusement park ride whirled through her brain.

He was right. She *was* still hanging. Her own satisfaction had been the furthest thing from her mind when she'd begun. Her only goal had been making love to Tucker, pleasing *him*. But unintentionally she'd caught fire, too—which was probably unavoidable when you stepped that close to a flame.

Through half-closed lids and mounting pleasure, she watched fire shadows flash and leap over the familiar walls of her family room...over the chairs where her kids usually sat watching TV, over family photos and items that had been gifts, and on a bookcase in one corner the stylized sculpture of a couple kissing, meant to reignite her marriage.

For a moment, sadness crept over Cathryn, and she thought she might cry or at least sit up and stop what she and Tucker were doing. But then Tucker lifted his mouth off hers, eased away slightly and released his breath in a soft whistle. ''You're really hot. Are you aware of that, woman?'' He spoke with just enough teasing to coax a smile from her.

''Really,'' he argued in a lazy, intimate drawl while his index finger slowly traced the strap of her bra from her shoulder down to the satin cup.

Watching the firelight glitter in Tucker's dark, long-lashed admiring eyes, she packed up her sadness and slid it to a chamber of her heart marked Later.

"If I had realized just how hot," he continued, his eyes as intimate as his voice, "I would've made a move on you a long time ago." Now he traced the outline of the bra over the swell of her breasts.

"How long ago?" Cathryn asked, her body lifting and turning toward his feathery touch the way a flower reaches for the sun.

"Fishing for compliments, darlin'?"

She loved his voice, its deep vibrations. "Tonight, I'll fish for anything I can get."

The outer corners of his eyes crinkled upward, and shadow filled the indentation he refused to admit was a dimple. "Oh, I think you'll catch something more interesting than compliments. In fact I can almost guarantee it."

He nuzzled the valley between her breasts. "I love the way you smell tonight." His fingers followed her curves from waist to thigh. "I love the way you feel. So silky."

Impatient to get back to what they'd been doing, she sighed volubly.

"Sorry. I talk while I make love. Not always. Just when the mood strikes me." He returned to outlining her bra with his index finger. "I'll try to contain myself."

Cathryn bit her lower lip, studying this man who had the ability to read her slightest shift of thought or mood. "I don't mind," she said, feeling her breasts straining against their satin encasement. He'd stopped outlining the cup and begun a spiraling journey toward the center.

"I also keep my eyes open so I don't miss anything."

"I don't…ah…m-mind that either," she said shudderingly as he reached his destination. "Are there any more announcements you need to make?"

His grin broadened into a hearty laugh, and he clutched her to him with gruff affection. Cathryn was discombobulated, to say the least. What discombobulated her was Tucker's ability to so personalize this carnal act they were engaged in. He left no room for doubt who she was with, no room to imagine anyone else.

He relaxed his hold, easing her back into the pillows, and they gazed at each other in the firelight. Gradually their smiles faded, and serious intent darkened their eyes. He lowered himself to her and seared her with a kiss so formidable, it drew a helpless wanting sound from her. And he followed that up with another, and another still.

Finally he released her, lifting his head slightly and dragging his scalding lips across her cheek. "Is there anything in particular I can do for you?" he asked, punctuating the query with a tongue-flick over an erogenous zone inside her ear she hadn't even known she possessed.

"N-no." She'd never been asked that before. "I can't th-think of anything."

"Okay. I'll wing it, then." And that, he punctuated with an expert twist of the hook that fastened her bra.

Cathryn had likened Tucker's effect on her to that of an amusement park ride, but that was before he'd become serious. Serious, Tucker was the spin of a fearsome tornado, a faster-than-light rocket to the moon. Oh, the things he did!

And Cathryn clung to him desperately, because although he was the source of the wildness gripping her, he was also her release from it. Except that he wouldn't allow her that release. Moving over her with his hands and his mouth and his body, murmuring words of endearment and praise, he only took her higher.

Under him, Cathryn writhed, the pleasure-ache between her legs growing hotter, wetter, more urgent by the second. Tucker's arousal was apparent, too, and she strained for it, but always, he managed to pull away. "Not yet, darlin'," he growled. "For what you put me through, you'll have to suffer a little longer."

And suffer she did. He pulled all the way back, sat on his heels between her legs, and studied her a moment, abject debauchery on his mind.

"What?" she croaked, helpless.

"What we need here," he said consideringly, glancing from her around the room, "is...this." He reached for the bowl she'd abandoned on the coffee table. The ice cream had melted to a soup that drizzled perfectly when he tipped it over her breasts. Cathryn flinched. The ice cream wasn't cold, but it did tickle.

I can't believe I'm doing this, she thought in that very small part of her brain that was still working. *It's depraved.*

Tucker set the bowl down on the hearth and grinned, and even through the depravity and passion, she recognized Tucker, the friend. Tucker, the playmate. She returned his grin, and then they both laughed.

Why? Is it because I'm drunk? I don't feel drunk.

Tucker lowered his head, and his tongue swirled over the tip of her breast. Then he kissed her and the chocolate and cream taste on his tongue swirled into her mouth. He returned to her breasts, and soon even the tiny part of her brain that had been working a moment ago shut down, too. All that remained was feeling. Feeling attractive and wanted and even adored. Feeling free and wicked and oh-so-high.

"Tucker..." she begged, her back arched off the floor. "Tucker, please. I'm going to...I can't..."

"Yes you can," he said, holding apart the petals of flesh that covered the apex of all that was twisting and tightening inside her. "Just like this." A few more soft flickers of his tongue, and she did.

Her orgasm was cataclysmic, shaking high keening cries

out of her. After what seemed an interminable wave-upon-wave battering, the cataclysm ebbed. Her fingers loosened from their death grip in Tucker's hair and she collapsed into a sweet lethargic satiation.

But then Tucker started in on her again. Her eyes flew open. "Tucker, what...? Wait. I'm done. It was wonderful, but...really..."

Really, what? she wondered as she caught fire again. This couldn't be happening. This was impossible. Wasn't it?

It wasn't. Before long she was convulsing with another release, and a short while after that, with one more.

"Stop. No more. I'll die. I'll surely die." Her chest, slick with perspiration, rose and fell hard, laboring to bring oxygen to her exhausted flesh.

Tucker sat back on his heels, his hands on his thighs, a smile of pure satisfaction warming his eyes. Then he turned his attention to the dying fire. He reached for a log, grabbed the tongs. Depleted though Cathryn was, she still could appreciate the picture he created. What a magnificent male animal, not just in physique, but also in spirit. Kneeling there, tending the fire without a stitch of clothing on, he was perfectly at ease with himself, and with her, and with this mystery of sex they were engaged in tonight.

He rested the tongs on the hearth, reached for the condom he'd taken from his pocket an eon ago, and deftly slipped it over his erection. Then he nudged apart her legs with his knees and, holding himself high, spent an enlightening several minutes teasing her back to arousal.

Eventually, impossible though it seemed to her, she could take the teasing no longer and guided him to her center.

He tipped his head to one side. "Yes?"

"Please," she replied. He entered slowly, his mouth grim, eyes shut, fighting for control. Veins in his neck stood out like steel cords. He held himself deep inside her a moment, then withdrew and slid into her again, withdrew and slid, withdrew and slid, the sweet abrasion bringing her own primitive drives to vibrant life.

She hoped he was unaware of it, though. She didn't want him to stall his own pleasure in favor of hers anymore. But of course he knew. If Tucker knew anything, it was a woman's body. And when he at last exploded within her, she was with him, shudder for shudder.

"Oh God!" He collapsed heavily, his face nuzzling her neck. "Oh God, oh God, oh…God!" He laughed, his shoulders jerking under her softly stroking palms. "That was off the scale."

Suddenly tears filled Cathryn's eyes, because she knew Tucker meant what he said. No one was playing a game for the other's benefit. There was no agenda or artifice.

Tucker pulled an afghan off a nearby chair and drew it over them. "Come here, darlin'. I think you could use some sleep."

After adjusting the coverlet around her shoulders, he wrapped her in his arms. She snuggled close, burying herself in his warmth, and sighed. Safe. Sated. Avenged. What more could a woman ask for?

WHEN CATHRYN WOKE three hours later it was raining. Not a gentle spring shower to coax flowers into bloom, this was one of winter's cruel parting shots. Lying in the thin light that seeped into the family room from the night-light in the kitchen, she heard the icy sleet ticking against the window panes and the wind snapping the new daffodil flag she'd hung by the front door. Inside, the atmosphere was little better. The fire had died, the room was cool, and her feet, poking out from beneath the coverlet, were freezing.

Tucker still held her in his arms, one leg flung over her in a protective drape, but not even his body heat could fight the chill that had settled into her. Nor, she feared, would his company chase the sadness that had crept into her house while she'd been sleeping.

She circled the room with her wide-awake eyes, looking for remnants of the previous night, but the object of her search eluded her. Where was the boldness she'd felt onstage? Where was the elation of the singing and applause? What happened to the joy of dancing? The thrill of her drive by Zoe's house? Even her champagne-high was gone, leaving her merely with a headache.

But mostly what Cathryn searched for was evidence of her outrageously uninhibited, embarrassingly debauched and totally magical lovemaking with Tucker. But sadness infused her memories of even that. She didn't understand it. Where had this powerful thief come from?

Carefully, she lifted Tucker's arm off her waist and laid it between them, then wiggled until she was free of his leg. She sat up, shivering, and searched the predawn shadows for something to put on. Her dress lay within reach. She found the sleeves, turned them right-side-out and slipped them over her goose-bumped arms.

How she longed for her warm flannel robe, but it was upstairs in her bedroom, and suddenly she didn't feel much like entering that particular room. She tipped her head forward, pushed her fingers into her hair to hold it back, and heard herself thinking, *Welcome back to reality*.

Outside, the wind toppled a metal trash can and sent it rolling into the wall of the garage. Rain hit the windows in gusts. Inside, Cathryn dragged her hands out of her hair, wincing a little as some strands caught on her diamond. She pulled the broken hairs from the prongs, then held her hand out, gazed at the two rings encircling her fourth finger, and the sadness pervading her house took sharper form.

It didn't matter that Dylan had left her and wanted a di-

vorce. She was still married. It didn't even matter that he'd
cheated on her unconscionably. Two wrongs didn't make a
right. What she'd done with Tucker only proved she could
stoop to her husband's level.

Maybe she'd stooped even lower. *Oh, Tucker. What have
I done to you?* The hand that wore the rings pressed over
her tremulous lips. Remorse enveloped her far worse than
when she'd remembered her marriage vows.

She'd *used* him, one of the best friends she had—maybe
the very best. She'd thought more of her selfish needs than
she had of Tucker's altruistic ones. She'd provoked him into
a night of indulgence, and in so doing had forced him to
betray his commitment to Jenny and the virtues he was trying to cultivate—loyalty to one woman, in particular. She
was no better than Zoe herself. An interloper. A Jezebel.
She certainly was no friend.

Who was she to say that Jenny would never marry him?
For all she knew, Jenny was playing coy, or maybe she just
needed time to think about her decision? Although, after
sleeping with Tuck, one would think Jenny would be able
to make up her mind a little faster.

Mostly, though, Cathryn was angry at herself for the effect this would have on Tucker. He wasn't going to like
himself when he had time to think about what he'd done.
He wasn't going to like her either. How could she have
rationalized that their lovemaking would mean nothing to
him?

A hand touched her back. She jumped in surprise, turning
to glance at Tucker, his bare broad shoulders lying above
the blanket. Had he just awakened, or had he been lying
there watching her? One corner of his mouth lifted—a faint
smile to say "Good morning."

"What time is it?" he asked in a sleep-hoarse voice.

"Four-thirty."

He grunted, rubbed his eyes with the hand that wasn't resting on her back. They said nothing for a while.

"It might be best if I got out of here before your neighbors realize my car's still here."

His car had been here until morning before, the night when Dylan had first moved out, Cathryn thought. But everything was different now, wasn't it? She'd offered him the apple, he'd bitten, and now they were sitting outside the garden, knowledge sitting between them.

"Yes," she said. "I hadn't thought of that." She tied her dress with unnecessary care. "Do you mind using the downstairs bathroom?"

He shook his head, his mouth sober, his brow slightly pinched.

She got to her feet, aching in places she'd never ached before. "Okay, I'll, um, just, you know, go upstairs then." Feeling his eyes on her, she quickly padded out of the room.

She couldn't bring herself to use the bathroom in her bedroom. That would mean passing in front of her wedding portrait, and if God didn't strike her dead, then remorse would. She used the kids' bathroom instead.

Flicking on the light, she decided a mirror could be crueler than any sleet storm winter could devise. She looked awful. She was pale, and there were smudges of mascara under her bloodshot eyes, and an abrasion along her jaw from Tucker's stubble. Turning from the mirror with a moan, she quickly shed her rumpled dress and stepped into the shower. There, with the hot water streaming over her, she broke down and cried.

She was angry and melancholy and fearful…so many different feelings had taken up residence within her this morning-after. But there was one she'd overlooked until now. It was the feeling that something important and precious had ended, and it wasn't her marriage.

By the time Cathryn pulled herself together and came downstairs, Tucker had a pot of coffee made and was picking up the family room, setting it to rights. She poured a cup and held it in two hands, blowing on the steam, watching the dark eastern sky from the rain-spattered window over the sink.

Tucker's reflection joined hers in the window. "Lousy day ahead," he murmured.

"Hmm."

He turned and leaned his backside against the counter. She cast him a quick sideways glance. How she wanted him to smile, but the sadness weighing her down seemed to weigh him down, too.

"Cath, I did some heavy thinking while you were upstairs, and I've decided it'd be best if I didn't come around anymore."

She nodded, unsurprised. "I can't see us continuing as friends, either, no matter how I look at it."

Tucker swallowed with difficulty. "It's been great, though. I want you to know that."

"Yes, it has."

"And I wouldn't change a minute of the past five weeks, including last night. Even though it ended our friendship, what a way to go out." He attempted a smile, but it faded almost before it began.

"I'm sorry, Tucker." Cathryn knew she didn't have to explain what she was sorry about. He knew.

"Me, too. I'm sorry, too." He lifted her left hand off the rim of the sink and kissed the knuckles close to her rings. "All I wanted to do was prove there's nothing wrong with you—just the opposite. You're an incredible woman, Cathryn. And there *will* be life after Dylan." He held her hand against him high on his chest, his voice reverberating through her palm.

"In the meantime," he continued, "don't beat yourself up over what happened last night, okay?" He bent his knees to meet her reluctant gaze. "Okay?" he repeated. She nodded. "You're going to have enough of a fight on your hands in the months ahead. It'd be silly to add an unnecessary problem to the heap."

He released her hand. "Speaking of which, will you do yourself a favor and hire the best divorce lawyer you can afford? And will you do it soon?"

Cathryn drew in an enormous breath. "Yes."

"Another thing, stay close to your friends. They, better than anyone, will help you get through this."

Cathryn agreed again, although she'd felt herself pulling away from Lauren and Julia weeks ago, and she suspected the trend would only continue, if not worsen.

"And what'll you do, Tucker?"

"I'm not sure. Go home and sleep for a few days. You wore me out, woman," he joked, and she smiled, but it was all just for old times' sake.

"I guess this is it then," she said.

Tucker fit his hands around her waist, drew her toward him and pressed a long, tender kiss to her forehead. His eyes drifted closed and he inhaled as if trying to store her scent in his memory. "Be bad, darlin'," he whispered.

"And you be good."

They stepped apart, pretending neither of them had tears in their eyes, then he headed for the door...and walked out of her life.

CHAPTER ELEVEN

TUCKER SLEPT FITFULLY for a few hours after getting home from Cathryn's, and woke aroused. After a brisk shower, he ate an unappetizing breakfast, brewed some coffee, paced his semi-gutted kitchen and wished to God he hadn't quit smoking.

Usually he wasn't wrong when it came to women and what they wanted or needed. But last night he'd made one of his rare mistakes, and it was a big one. His objective had simply been to lift Cathryn out of her pain and make her feel better about herself. He'd succeeded only temporarily. This morning she hated herself and, to be honest, he wasn't too crazy about himself, either.

He'd consciously disregarded any commitment he owed to the woman he'd made pregnant. Granted, Jenny might never find out, but *he'd* know. And granted, they weren't married yet, but didn't the situation call for his loyalty anyway? His failure made him wonder about himself as a man of his word. As a man, period. Was there something innately wrong with him? Was he even capable of fidelity?

Then again, as he'd reasoned last night, Jenny had been avoiding his calls for quite a while, and he was quickly coming to accept that she didn't want to marry him and wasn't going to.

But, no, that was just a convenient rationalization. Jenny *might* marry him. Hell, he still had to send her the video

Cathryn and the kids had made. "Opus for Jenny" was bound to have an effect.

No two ways about it, when it came to being a man of his word, he'd screwed up.

He stopped pacing in the center of the kitchen, staring into space. The thing that bothered him most, though, was the way he'd made love with Cathryn. He'd gone too far, made love too often, too wildly, pushed her to her limits and beyond. And the reason had nothing to do with his wanting to make her feel better about herself. He'd been overwhelmed. What was *that* all about?

Tucker yanked open the drawer by the sink and rummaged under the towels until he found the cigarettes he'd hidden there as a test of his self-control. So far he'd won the contest. Big deal.

He clamped a cigarette between his lips, turned on a gas burner, bent to the flame and drew in a deep lungful of the biting smoke. He coughed but wasn't sorry. Sometimes a man just needed a little comfort.

With several good drags still left, however, he crushed the cigarette in the sink. Smoking was no more a cure for what ailed him than leaping in front of a train would be. He tossed the rest of the pack into the trash and gazed around the kitchen, feeling lost and wondering what to do about it.

For the first time in more than a month, he felt the need to get away from Harmony. He didn't know who he was anymore. So many aspects of him had been tampered with and contorted, from the way he shaved to the very things he dreamed about. He needed to find out what was phoney, what was real. What he needed, he suddenly realized, was to get back to racing.

There was nothing like it on earth to clear his mind of unnecessary clutter. The concentration it required was what did it. When you were driving two hundred mph and surrounded by a pack of cowboys also going that speed, concentration was everything. A guy had to know the track intimately, know how fast he could take the curves, and he had to be utterly aware of his vehicle—vibrations, smells, the sound of the engine. The slightest lapse could mean the difference between winning and losing—or worse.

As tense as that state of concentration was, Tucker loved it. When he was racing, he shut everything else out and became as one with his work as a person could get. The car became an extension of him...and life became extraordinarily simple. It was a track, a single one-way track, and all he had to do was go forward and try not to bump into anything.

Tucker paced to the threshold of the living room and visually tallied up the work that still remained to be done in that room. It could wait. All the work could wait. He had nothing more to do than lock up, drop a key next door with Cathryn's parents in case an emergency arose and hop the next ferry. In a few days he'd be fifteen hundred miles away.

And Cathryn? She'd be all right. She had her family and her friends to help her. She didn't need him. He'd only complicate her life if he stayed.

As fast as that it was settled. Tucker yanked the phone off its wall cradle, dialed Jenny's number and heard her answering machine come on. "Jen, this is Tucker," he said with businesslike abruptness. "It's Sunday, and I'm still on Harmony, but I'll be leaving for my place in Montgomery in a couple of hours. I'll be driving, so give me about three days to get there, if you need to call. In case you've lost my number..." He recited it slowly and added the address for good measure. "I hope you and the baby are well and you've been keeping your appointments with the doctor. I'll call when I get there. Take care."

CATHRYN OPENED her notebook and uncapped her pen.

March 19

This had to be the worst day of my life. After Tucker went home I tried to sleep a bit but couldn't, so I called Mom and Dad and told them the news about me and Dylan. Not good. We all cried. Even Dad got choked up. Then, before I could regroup, Dylan returned the kids and it was time to tell them. They didn't take it well. (I'm so exhausted right now—physically, emotionally and spiritually—that's all I'm able to say on the matter.) When I think of everything that's happened in the last twenty-some hours, starting with my dinner with Dylan, I reel. To top it all off, Mom and Dad informed me Tucker has left Harmony indefinitely. Although rationally I can see I'm still sitting here in my familiar bed, healthy and whole, I feel as if I've exploded and all the tiny pieces of me are shooting off into black space. I wish I could stop shaking.

LATE THE FOLLOWING afternoon, tired and hungry, Tucker pulled into a rest area with a food service and a gas station. He'd been gone from Harmony for twenty-seven hours and forty-eight minutes. But who was counting?

He bought a tray full of food and sat in a booth by a window where he could watch his Mustang. Before long, however, he realized he was staring more at the phone on the nearby wall than he was at his car. All day, every phone booth he'd passed, he'd been tempted to pull over and call Cathryn. He was curious to know how she was, if she'd suffered any repercussions from their night of carousing, if the kids knew about Dylan's decision to divorce and how they were taking it. Damn, he wasn't just curious. He was worried. So far, though, his better sense had won out.

Tucker hadn't quite finished his meal when his better sense deserted him. He slid out of the booth, digging into his wallet for his phone card, and crossed the room. He knew Cathryn's number by heart, pressed it in when the automated voice instructed him to and waited, growing hot with guilt. He shouldn't be doing this. He'd already cut her from his life. He had other priorities.

Her phone began to ring. Once, twice. But what if she needed him? What if…?

On the third ring someone picked up. He didn't wait to find out who. He slammed the receiver down, grabbed his jacket from the booth where his unfinished meal sat, and hurried out the door. The more miles he put between him and Harmony the better off he'd be.

March 21

I had lunch with Lauren and Julia today and told them the news. Taking a cue from Dylan, I suggested we meet at the Brass Anchor. I figured the setting would minimize any possible show of emotion. After telling the kids and Mom and Dad on Sunday, I couldn't take much more.

I waited until L. and J. had almost finished eating— no sense in spoiling their appetites, too—but I must've looked ill throughout because they both asked if I was all right. I said yes both times, and whether they believed me or not, they dropped the subject in favor of more lively ones. Pregnancy. Their work. Their husbands. Home renovations.

I'm afraid I didn't add much to the conversation. I couldn't. Everything they said was a reminder that their lives are moving forward. They're prospering in every way and I'm not. I'm going nowhere. In retrospect, I can see I've been going nowhere for years. My life has been stagnant.

When I finally got around to telling them, they were stunned. Divorce? The McGraths? At first they didn't believe it and kept saying, "This is a joke, right?" But once they accepted it as fact, shock took over. I expected that. What I didn't expect was the fear I saw in their eyes. But of course, they had to be thinking, if Dylan and I couldn't make a go of it, could they?

I spoke in fast-forward. There was a lot to cover and time was limited. I had to get home for the school bus. I also just wanted to get the ordeal over and done with. I couldn't bear being with them anymore, looking into their grief-stricken eyes.

Outside in the parking lot, Julia asked me if I was okay and we all had a good laugh over that. Of course I'm not okay, but I assured them I'd get through it somehow. They agreed wholeheartedly and said they'd help any way they could, but I sensed some doubt. I've never had to "get through" anything, certainly nothing like the problems and heartaches they've suffered. Compared to Julia and Lauren, I've lived a charmed existence. I went straight from a safe loving home with Mom and Dad to a safe loving home with Dylan. Except for a couple of summer jobs in high school, I've never even worked, never known career reversals or the stress of having to survive on my own.

I cried all the way home. I've let my friends down. Sunday it was Mom and Dad and the kids. Today Lauren and Julia. Soon, all of Harmony will know what a phoney I am.

I'm supposed to be the model of marital contentment and domestic wisdom. Even when I was young, everyone assumed that was who I'd be. Unlike Julia and Lauren and so many others, I saw no reason to flee the island. I had no interest in a career or desire to shun marriage.

Just the opposite. I was happy to stay on Harmony and hold down the fort. I saw myself as home base, the person who organized reunions, kept friends informed about what others were doing and nagged them mercilessly to move back. I was the glue of the group. Always had been, always would be—or so I thought.

Have Lauren and Julia finally come home only to find our circle unraveling at my end? And there's no question it is unraveling. Because I'm not the glue of the group. I'm not a model of marital contentment or domestic wisdom. I'm not any of those things anymore. And I find myself crying again, dammit, not for my friends or family, but for myself. Because if I'm not who I and everyone else believed I was, who am I then? Who the hell am I?

TUCKER LIVED in suburban Montgomery in a rented bungalow that came with a long, low building once used as a professional garage. There he parked his T-Bird and Mustang stock cars, along with the flatbed truck that hauled them. Beside those vehicles were his Harley, his Honda for everyday use, and now his Shelby Mustang. That still left room for tools, tires, car parts, a grease pit and a lift.

He knew he was lucky to have found such a tailor-made spot, especially since it was a rental, which meant he had none of the headaches of home ownership. He'd furnished the house with new inexpensive furniture, the three-rooms-for-one-low-price variety he'd found advertised in nearly every part of the country where he'd lived. And as in those other places, when he moved on he'd simply sell the furniture or donate it to charity. The only items he'd take would be his TV and stereo. He'd perfected the life of the bachelor on the move. Or was it bachelor on the run? he sometimes wondered.

In any case, he was glad to be back, and as soon as he'd restocked his refrigerator with beer and frozen dinners, and called a general contractor he sometimes worked for to supplement his uneven racing income, he headed for the speedway. Although it was short notice, he talked his way into the lineup, but only for Sunday and only a couple of events.

He spent the next two days tuning up the T-Bird and driving practice laps, but after a six-week hiatus, his skills were rusty. When he competed that Sunday, the results were abysmal. He wasn't concerned though. He wasn't called "Lightnin' Lang" for nothing.

During the following week he increased his practice time significantly, worked on a roofing job on the side, and when the weekend arrived he felt a lot more comfortable on the track. Over the two days' twenty-odd events, he consistently came in in the middle of the pack.

He felt better emotionally, too. Whole hours went by before he remembered to worry about Cathryn or her kids. He was sure she was faring better without him, too. Yep, separating himself from Harmony had been the right move all around.

April 4

Dylan and I met with our lawyers again this morning. It was long and stressful. Twelve hours later, I still have a headache. So many questions and papers. So many changes coming.

I took Cory to the clinic this afternoon to see about new allergy medication. Poor kid's suffering. Justin wasn't on the school bus again. Shuffled home on foot after five, even though I've threatened to ground him if he disobeyed me again. I...

I'm too tired to write any more. Beth hasn't been sleeping well, which means I haven't, either.

THAT WEEK Tucker returned to his habit of spending evenings with his racing buddies at their favorite sports bar, talking shop and jockeying for the women who sent them smiles and free beers. He didn't jockey too seriously, though. He found he simply wasn't interested.

He also added meditation to his routine and saw marked improvement when he raced the following weekend. He finished the two days in the top twenty percent.

He hadn't spoken directly to Jenny in several weeks by this time. When he called her that night and discovered her number had been discontinued, he almost felt relieved. *Not a proper response,* his conscience told him. So, first thing on Monday, he contacted the telephone company, and when that yielded no new number in Jenny's name, he called the manager of the building where she lived. She'd moved, he said, and left no forwarding address.

Hmm.

Tucker considered closing the book on Jenny then, but he knew she couldn't have simply vanished. She was somewhere, and he should find her. St. Louis was only six hundred miles away, but Tucker really couldn't spare the time. He'd promised to work on another job for his friend, the contractor. Plus, he had to get in his practice laps. To solve his dilemma he hired a private investigator.

That weekend Tucker saw his first win since returning. In fact, the worst he did was a fourth-place finish. He was in the money, in his zone, free at last, free at last.

You'd think a guy would be content. Quite mysteriously,

he wasn't. He felt restless instead. He seemed to have more time on his hands than he remembered, or maybe it was just that he took better care of himself now, didn't carouse or drink the way he used to and, therefore, didn't sleep as much trying to recuperate. Whatever the reason, he started dropping in at the Boys' and Girls' Club, volunteering his basketball coaching skills, meager as they were. He missed his games with Justin. Missed the McGrath kids, period. It had been nearly a month since he'd seen them and he was as curious as ever to know how they were. Cathryn, too. Cathryn, too.

The next Saturday began with a win, a prelude to how the day would go. ''Lightnin''' was back. That night the guys talked him into going out and knocking back a couple to celebrate.

While he was sitting at the bar, he heard a woman laugh somewhere behind him. She sounded so much like Cathryn that he whirled around, knocking over his beer. Helping the bartender mop up the mess, he decided his curiosity could be banked no longer.

He left the bar, went home and called Lauren. She wasn't surprised to hear from him, only that it had taken him so long.

''How's Cathryn?'' he finally asked after he and the red head had talked awhile, catching up.

''I wish I knew, but I don't see her half as much as I'd like. She's pulled into herself, Tucker. Whenever I invite her over, she has an excuse. She barely even talks on the phone.''

''Hell! I was afraid something like this'd happen. Do you at least know if she's hired a lawyer?''

''Oh, yes. And the divorce proceedings are well underway.''

''Not too rocky, I hope.''

"Not that I've heard. The only hitch she's told me about has been over the house. Dylan assumed they would sell it, but her lawyer negotiated it over to her side of the table."

"It's hers? Without buying Dylan out?"

"Uh-huh. Which is only fair, since he's getting the land-scaping business."

"That's great. For Cathryn, I mean."

"Yes, but it also means she now has the responsibility of paying the mortgage and taxes and utility bills."

"No alimony?"

"It seems unlikely. The kids aren't infants, and she isn't helpless—meaning, she's fully capable of going out to work. And she is. She's found herself a job."

"Cathryn? Where? What sort of job?"

"She's working for a housecleaning agency that mainly services summer cottages. During the winter the schedule's not too bad. It's mostly light maintenance. But right now, they're up to their armpits in work, preparing houses for summer. A lot of people start spending weekends here as early as May."

Tucker heard only one phrase of Lauren's declamation. "Housecleaning?" he repeated.

"My sentiments exactly. But she says it's what she knows."

"Hell! Not that there's anything wrong with housecleaning. It's an honorable profession. But she has so many other talents."

"Which she doesn't appreciate yet. I offered to explore them with her, see if there's a particular direction she'd like to take or an area she could develop into a home business. I even offered to back her financially, but she turned me down."

Tucker sighed. "It was probably too big a step for her."

"Probably. But if you ask me, she's developed a real

stubborn streak, Tucker. She's determined to get through this divorce and become independent all on her own.''

''Is she at least getting some satisfaction out of bringing home a paycheck?''

''I doubt it. Whenever I see her, she looks either tired or frazzled or depressed. I can't say I've ever seen her satisfied.''

Tucker needed to change the subject. He'd already worn a path in the rug with his pacing. ''How are the kids doing?''

''With a mother who's tired, frazzled and depressed, how do you think?''

Tucker dropped ''hell'' from his vocabulary and moved on to pithier expletives.

''Dylan sees them as often as he can, but they know the decision to divorce is final. Recently they found out why.''

''They know about Zoe Anderson?''

''Hmm. Dylan thought they could handle meeting her.''

''Stupid bastard.''

''I agree. Cameron and I took them to an Easter Egg hunt at Shipyard Park last week, just to get them out, and Bethany told me she's not doing well in school. Her teacher is giving her special tutoring so she won't be held back.''

Tucker crushed an empty beer can with his hand. ''How were the boys?''

Lauren's sigh wasn't encouraging. ''Cory was all stuffed up with allergies. He's been bothered all spring. And Justin…well…''

''What?''

''After he collected a few eggs, he moped off by himself and used them as missiles to throw at seagulls. When he ran out of eggs he used rocks. He cracked the windscreen of a fishing boat.''

Tucker tossed the crushed beer can against the wall. It

ricocheted into the wastebasket below. "Why the hell did he do that?"

"I don't know. I guess it's just his way of coping."

A way Tucker understood only too well. "If you see him, tell him…" He hesitated, realizing he had nothing to say, just the urge to help. "Tell him hi for me."

"I will." After a pause Lauren added, "And should I say hi to Cathryn, too?"

Tucker caught a trace of amusement in Lauren's voice. "Uh…" He stammered uncharacteristically, wondering what she knew or suspected. "Sure. Why not?"

"Why not, indeed?"

"Okay. What?"

She laughed. "I heard about the hell you and Cath raised the night before you left the island. *Everybody's* heard."

"Oh." Tucker grimaced. "And what's the verdict? Is Cath catching any flack because of it?"

"Nah. Most people think it's funny, especially the part about her mooning Zoe and Dylan."

Tucker groaned. "That got around, too?"

"Oh, yes, thanks to Zoe. And you know what, Tuck? If you were here, I'd give you a great big kiss right on the lips. Thank you for doing that for her."

He breathed easier. "Thanks for understanding. I didn't think anyone would—or could."

A long silence followed. "I don't understand quite as much as I'd like. Are you in any mood to enlighten me?"

Tension zinged through Tucker's nervous system. The lady was too damn sharp. "There's nothing more to say."

"Meaning, there's nothing more to say? Or, you don't kiss and tell?"

A chuckle rumbled deep in Tucker's chest. "Both."

"Okay, okay, I'll quit prying, but I want you to know that if there *was* more to say, I wouldn't mind. You did wonders for Cathryn in the short time you were here, and to be honest, I wish you didn't have other commitments and could return.''

''Thank you. It's nice to know I'm properly appreciated.''

They hung up soon after that, and Tucker tried to push the conversation to the back of his mind. He'd satisfied his curiosity, and now it was time to get some sleep. He had another full day of racing ahead, and while he'd done well today, he was determined to do even better tomorrow.

But as he lay in bed that night, running through an imaging exercise that always helped him before a race, he found his mind wandering, the exercise unraveling, and before long, instead of picturing tomorrow's track, he was picturing Harmony, and the three McGrath children, and their mother, sweet, sexy Cathryn. His curiosity—his concern—returned.

The next day Tucker placed third in the first event, second in the next two, and first in the one after that. But he knew his concentration wasn't what it should've been. His good performance resulted purely from disciplined skill, not from being in any sort of synchronicity with his car. Rather, he drove well *in spite* of himself.

The checkered flag waved, and the fifth race began. *Okay, concentrate now. Concentrate.* But he knew something was wrong. He shouldn't have to tell himself to concentrate; he should just be doing it naturally.

Three laps into the race, Tucker's gaze flicked to the crowds in the stands. *What are you doing, Tucker?* he asked himself angrily. *Focus, dammit!*

The next lap, his eyes strayed again. What was he doing here? he wondered. Why was he going round and round this track? Where was he going? Was this all there was?

Concentrate, Tucker!

But his mind wandered again on the fifth lap. He thought

about Harmony, its deep blue skies and endless views and the quiet within him when he was there. Was it possible that he'd been on the right track all along?

Sixth lap, Tucker took the south-corner curve too fast and grazed the guardrail, and although he told himself to concentrate, it was too late for that. He came away from the rail fishtailing, and before he could bring his car under control, the world was tumbling around him.

I'm having an accident, he thought with absurd detachment as he rolled like a runaway log and other cars screeched to avoid him. He'd had accidents before, but usually didn't fear them. Life had hit him with her best shots and he'd always pulled through. That did something to a person.

But suddenly it occurred to him that this might be it, this might be his time to die, and in that moment when his life passed before him, Tucker experienced a startling epiphany. The only thing he'd miss when he was burning in hell, which was where he was sure to end up, wasn't a thing at all, but a person. A person! He was amazed. He hadn't thought he was capable.

With a thud that jarred his teeth, his car bounced one last time and stopped. Tucker didn't breathe for several long seconds. Slowly he peeled away his gloved fingers from the steering wheel and stared at them. He wasn't dead? He flexed his fingers, moved his head, his shoulders, his legs, and finally unfastened his harness and climbed out of his car. The silent crowd broke into a cheer, a reaffirmation that, yes, he was indeed alive.

Medics and mechanics ran toward him and asked incomprehensible questions. Someone called him the luckiest son of a bitch he'd ever met, and Tucker said yes he was. Survived again, the same voice remarked, and again Tucker agreed.

But as he helped the crew push his car off the track, his vision whirled and his legs threatened to give out on him. Not that he hadn't climbed out of his car unscathed. He had. It was a different accident he hadn't survived. Her name was Cathryn.

May 3

Tucker's back. I heard the news from five different people, in addition to the kids who saw him in his yard while they were at Mom and Dad's after school. He was raking. They went over and helped. They planted pansies, too, and later played baseball with him. They haven't talked so much at supper since…well, since he went away. It ticked me off, and I don't even know why.

I asked the kids how he is—not that I care, I was just a little curious. They said he's great, he looks about the same and plans to continue fixing his house. (Okay, so I was more than a little curious). They also said he hasn't gotten Jenny to marry him yet, but as Justin explained defensively, Tuck only recently sent her the video we made.

Amazingly, he's quit racing, too. This I heard from Lauren, one of the many people who felt obliged to call and tell me he's returned. She also said he's moved all his worldly possessions to Harmony and is planning to take in cars for repair. I don't know what to make of that, except that he must be more committed than ever to convincing Jenny to marry him. Well, fine. That's only as it should be.

It's funny, though. I half expected him to drop by tonight for a visit. But of course, dropping by for visits isn't an option with us anymore. We put the kybosh on that sort of thing the night we crossed the line,

didn't we? Besides, now that I'm working, I really
don't have time for idle socializing anymore. I'm not
sure I even want to see Tucker again, or for him to
see me. There've been so many changes around
here—and in me—and not all of them have been for
the better. I'm trying. I'm really determined to get a
handle on this single, working-parent thing. But, I
have a long way to go.

Maybe he should've stayed in Alabama.

Maybe I should quit writing things I don't mean.

A WEEK PASSED before Cathryn actually saw Tucker herself.
She'd had an especially tiring day at work, her legs
throbbed, and the house she walked into hadn't seen a vacuum in two weeks.

"Justin?" she called, dropping her purse on the crumb-
covered kitchen table. She turned, took a step and almost
landed in a fresh spill of grape juice. Within the family
room, Cory and Beth sat in front of the TV, zombielike.

"Where's Justin?" Cathryn asked. Neither child responded. Cathryn strode into the room and snapped off the
TV.

"Hey!" Beth protested with that special irritability that
comes from watching too much TV.

"I repeat, where's Justin?"

Sneezing against his arm, Cory said, "We don't know.
He wasn't on the school bus."

"Again?" Cathryn wrapped her head in two arms and
emitted a strangled yell.

"We're okay without him, Mom," Beth said.

"Really? So why is there grape juice on the kitchen floor?
And why hasn't the trash been taken out yet?" Cory
sneezed again. "For heaven's sake, Cory, go get a tissue."

Just then Cathryn heard the front door open. She whirled,

dashed and intercepted Justin just as he was creeping up the staircase. "Hold it!" Reaching over the bannister, she caught him by the arm and, with a twist, brought him down. "Where have you been, young man? It's after five. School's been out for over two hours, and you were supposed to be home baby-sitting your sister and brother."

"Hey, take it easy!" came a deep familiar voice.

Cathryn released Justin's arm and pivoted to face the man standing on her doorstep.

Tucker stepped inside, scowling fiercely. "Justin's been with me, which he would've told you if you'd given him a chance."

She reddened under his none-too-subtle reprimand, her embarrassment vying with her righteous anger, and everything mixing with her pleasure at just seeing Tucker again. In all, it was a most confusing moment.

She smoothed her hands over the front of her green cleaning smock. "What was he doing with you?"

"He came by the garage to say hi and shoot the breeze." Tucker and Justin exchanged a suspiciously private glance. "He intended to be home earlier, but I put him to work patching a few tires. Before we knew it, it was four-thirty. It's my fault entirely."

"No, it is not." Cathryn glared at her son. "You knew you should've been on the bus. It was your responsibility to mind Cory and Beth this afternoon. You knew I was depending on you. Isn't that right?"

"Yeah, yeah." Justin's sullen boredom incensed her.

"Go wash up. We'll deal with this later."

Still sneering, Justin sauntered up the stairs at an I'll-do-it-my-way pace. Cathryn tried to compose herself before turning to face Tucker. He didn't look happy.

"He really shouldn't have gone to see you, Tucker. Now

that I'm working, he knows he has to pick up more responsibility around here."

Tucker's too observant eyes moved over her, making her aware how tightly she'd folded her arms. She made an effort to relax.

"It isn't as if I'm asking anything outrageous," she continued. "Two afternoons a week. That's all. A total of four, sometimes five, hours. Other days the bus drops the kids at my parents' house. But, heck, my mother has to have a break sometime, too."

His eyes continued to travel over her. "You've lost more weight. Still doing Tae-Bo?"

"No, it's a new exercise program I've discovered called Worry Those Pounds Away." She laughed, but heard no humor in the snigger. "It's funny, all those weeks I spent on self-improvement, that was just playing at change, wasn't it? I didn't have a clue what it really entailed."

Tucker opened his mouth but didn't say anything. He seemed at a loss.

She sighed. "Now, would you care to tell me what really happened with Justin?"

Tucker measured her awhile, as if debating whether or not to level with her. "I saw him floating on a makeshift raft on Cook Pond. It didn't look too safe, so I called him in. Then we went to the garage. I would've brought him home sooner if I'd known he was supposed to baby-sit. He didn't tell me."

Cathryn pressed a hand over her solar plexus, the spot that trembled worst when her familiar companion, panic, took up residence. "I'm going to strangle that boy. I've told him repeatedly to stay off that pond. Really, I'm going to strangle him."

"For heaven's sake, Cath, ease up on the kid. He's only

eleven, and there isn't a boy on this island that hasn't had a love affair with its ponds at some time or other.''

''Justin is *twelve*. He turned twelve. And quite frankly, I don't recall asking for your advice.''

''Well, maybe you should.''

Her heart was beating so fast she could barely breathe, and she didn't even know why. Anger? Fear? Exhaustion? Or was it simply seeing Tucker again and admitting what she'd refused to face since he'd left? She'd thoroughly enjoyed herself with him. Before their night together, she hadn't realized lovemaking could be that intense, that carnal and yet spiritual, that free and freeing. Why had it never been that way with Dylan? She felt gypped. All those years…she could've had a V8!

Breathe, you fool. Breathe.

''Sorry for snapping, Tucker. I appreciate your bringing Justin home. Thank you.''

''You're welcome,'' he scolded.

''But now, I hope you'll understand, I have supper to get started.'' She placed her hand on the door, crowding Tucker toward the threshold.

''Justin and I stopped at Mario's and picked up a couple of pizzas so you wouldn't have to cook.'' He stepped outside and lifted two pizza boxes from the wrought-iron bench on the stoop. ''It was his idea. He said you might be tired. He used the money I gave him for helping me at the garage.''

Cathryn felt like a graceless fool. Before she could mend the damage she'd inflicted, though, Beth and Cory came running from the family room. They had finally recognized Tucker's voice.

''Tucker!'' they chimed, breaking into matching smiles.

''Ooo, pizza!'' Beth hung on Tucker's arm, dancing on her toes. ''Are you staying for supper?''

"No, Peanut. These are for you guys."

"But why not?" She pirouetted toward Cathryn. "Mommy?"

"Oh, Beth, the house is such a mess." She felt her cheeks warming. Actually the house was a pig sty by her former standards.

"So? Tucker doesn't care."

Cathryn bit her lip. How could she tell Beth she and Tucker weren't friends anymore? The child would want to know why. Plus, not asking him to stay would only make her feel more graceless.

"Please stay. You brought the pizza."

"No, this…I wasn't searching for an invitation."

"I know. But you've found one. The kids will be disappointed if you don't stay."

"Well," He ran a hand around the back of his neck. "Since you put it that way."

They ate in the dining room because the table was large and could accommodate the pizza boxes comfortably. As usual, they did "Thanks" while they settled in. Cathryn was thankful she didn't have to cook. Tucker was thankful that Mario's was already open for the season. The kids bypassed the pizza and went straight for the pith. All three were thankful Tucker was back.

Cathryn was, too, although she'd never admit it to anyone. She kept conversation light throughout the meal and focused mainly on the children and what they were doing in school. She noticed Tucker did the same.

With the table cleared and the dishwasher loaded, Tucker said goodbye to the kids, and they went upstairs to do their homework. Thanking Cathryn again for her hospitality, he started for the door. They'd hardly talked, she realized.

"How are you doing with Jenny?" she asked, latching on to the first thing to cross her mind.

"Better than I was a month ago."

Cathryn's heart dipped stupidly. "How so?"

"She disappeared for a while. But it turned out she'd just moved back home with her folks."

"Really? I thought she didn't get along with them."

Tucker shrugged. "Seems being pregnant has changed her attitude."

"So you've talked to her?"

"Yes." He didn't elaborate. "How has it been going here?"

She forced a smile. "I'm doing okay." Her smile became rueful. "For someone working full-time and taking care of three active kids, an eight-room house, a huge yard, and an aging van." Hearing herself whine, she groaned and waved one hand like someone erasing a blackboard. "Really, I'm fine. I'm not going through anything that millions of women haven't experienced before me, and in most cases they've had it much worse. I'm really lucky. I have my family, my home, a job, my health. The only thing I don't have," she said, laughing ruefully again, "is a man, and there's no great loss there."

Tucker ran his teeth over his bottom lip—chomping at the bit to argue her insult. He let it go. "I noticed you didn't mention friends. Is there a reason for that?"

Cathryn stooped to pick up a few dried leaves that had fallen from a houseplant. "No. It was just an oversight." She placed the leaves on the saucer under the plant and plucked out a few more.

Tucker would never understand why she'd withdrawn from her friends. Lauren and Julia were married and she wasn't. And whenever she got together with them and their husbands, she felt like the proverbial fifth wheel.

Besides, what did she have in common with those women anyway? She was just *beginning* to grow into a life of independence, while they had been there more than a decade ago. Eons ahead of her, they probably found her progress boring, her small successes and frustrations ludicrous.

She didn't want their polite tolerance. Nor did she want their pity or their help. They'd struggled to get where they were all on their own. Now, quite simply, it was her turn.

"I called Lauren from Alabama a few weeks ago."

"Yes. She told me." Cathryn rubbed her hands together, dropping leaf crumbs on the carpet.

"She told me about Justin and his little rock-throwing adventure. What was that all about?"

Cathryn bristled. Lauren had no right. Then again, anger would only make matters worse. "Oh, who knows?"

"Has he been giving you trouble?"

She gave a sideways, halfhearted nod. "Nothing unusual, considering his parents are getting divorced." But Cathryn recognized a lie when she heard one. None of her kids had fared well during this cold spring of change. Beth was struggling in school, and Cory's allergies continued to plague him, exacerbated by stress. But Beth's and Cory's problems didn't really surprise her. Justin's did. He was her oldest and, until now, her most responsible.

He'd become defiant. No matter what law she laid down, he ignored it and did exactly as he pleased. She had tried talking to him, and when that failed, she'd tried punishment. She'd even attempted turning a blind eye. But his disobedience continued regardless of what approach she took. The next step, she feared, would be therapy, and for *that* she was furious at Dylan, because it was all his fault. He had done this to Justin. He'd caused all his children's problems.

"Speaking of the divorce, how are proceedings going?"

Cathryn squared her weary shoulders. "Smoothly. Quickly."

"Oh, great. I guess." Tucker's regard sharpened. "Uh…no?"

"No, it *is* good. If I look ambivalent, it's just that I'm tired of meetings with lawyers. 'Smoothly' is a relative term."

"No serious battles, I hope." Tucker paused. "Sorry. I don't mean to pry. I just got worried for a second—about the kids. Custody."

"Oh. That's no problem. No. What I've found stressful are the financial squabbles. I didn't realize we had so many assets to divvy up." She sighed. "It's been an eye-opener, believe me, seeing my marriage reduced to economics. Makes you realize that's all the institution is about, really. Always has been, right from caveman days."

Tucker's eyebrows hadn't moved out of their frowning mode since they'd started this conversation. Rather, they just kept lowering.

Okay, so it wasn't attractive to be bitter, but she had good reason.

"Lauren also told me about your job. How's that going?"

Was he hoping to find a subject she could be cheerful about so he could leave here whistling? Frankly, she begrudged her job. She begrudged leaving the house before the kids had even got on the bus. She begrudged coming home exhausted. Cleaning other people's houses was nothing like cleaning her own. She begrudged not being here for her kids after school, not cooking careful meals, not keeping up with clutter and dust and laundry. But since she was head of the household now, she forced herself out the door each morning, begrudging herself for not having stepped out years sooner.

"The job is fine."

Tucker sighed, looking unconvinced. "Listen, Cath, if you need any help, I know I said I wouldn't come around anymore, but this is an unusual situation and I have free time.''

''Thanks, but that's not necessary.''

''How about the kids? I can mind your kids occasionally…the afternoons they're not with your mother. Or weekends.''

''Thanks again, but I'd rather Justin learned to be more responsible.''

Tucker seemed to have more to say, but he swallowed whatever it was. ''Okay, if you change your mind you know where to find me.''

Yes, she did. But she wouldn't.

During the next three weeks Tucker saw Cathryn only in passing—at the market or coming to pick up the kids at her parents', and each time she looked tired, frazzled and depressed, just as Lauren had said. She also remained stubbornly aloof from him and her friends despite their continued offers of help. He wanted to throttle her. Pride was one thing, but determination to get through an ordeal alone—or die trying—was stupid.

At least he'd gotten her mother to go along with him regarding the kids. Meg had talked to Cathryn and insisted they spend every afternoon with her after school, and as far as he knew, Cathryn hadn't caught on that they spent half that time with him. The month of May saw him playing more hide-and-seek and Barbie-and-Ken and consuming more Kool-Aid and Popsicles than he cared to calculate.

He still wished he could talk to Cathryn. Not so much about Cory or Beth. He thought they'd be all right in time. It was Justin who worried him. Justin, the Angry. Justin, the Daredevil. Justin, the Trespasser, Shoplifter and Breaker of Windshields. Justin, who held everything tight inside.

But would Cathryn listen to what he had to say? Would she accept advice? Or would she tell him she was ''fine'' again, or accuse him of meddling or, worse, not knowing kids. Maybe she'd be right. Maybe he was totally out-to-lunch when it came to kids. Maybe he'd just use Justin as an excuse to be with her, because, God knew, being with Cathryn was on his mind all the time, night and day.

On Thursday of the first week in June, Tucker was putting the final coat of paint on his front porch and watching for the school bus, when Meg Hill came across the lawn to tell him the kids wouldn't be over that afternoon. Cathryn had taken the day off of work because her divorce was being finalized. She expected to be home from court when the kids got out of school.

"Isn't it too soon for the divorce to be final?" Tucker asked, dipping his brush into the paint again.

"I thought so too," Meg said. "But apparently not. As Cathryn explained it, a couple can be divorced just as soon as they get their papers together and presented to a judge, whether that takes them one month or ten years. After that there's always a six-month waiting period before the divorce is officially final, just in case one party or the other changes his mind. But for all intents and purposes, they are divorced as of that court date."

After Meg returned to her house Tucker continued with his painting, but he made a god-awful mess of it. He kept thinking about Cathryn and whether she was okay or needed company. He kept trying to imagine what it must feel like to be divorced. And then he started wondering if, now that she was a free woman, would she consider going out to dinner or a movie.

No, it was much too soon for that. Her message had come across loud and clear: all men were scum. It'd take her a while to get over that. But maybe he could call anyway and ask about the kids?

Tucker grappled with the temptation right through the

evening. Just when he thought he'd won the fight and would
watch some TV instead, the phone rang. It was Cathryn—
stubborn, determined-to-do-it-all-on-her-own Cathryn. She
said she was sorry for calling, she'd done what she could,
but now she needed help.

Justin had disappeared.

CHAPTER TWELVE

"WHEN DID YOU last see Justin?"

Cathryn couldn't stop the chattering of her teeth. "Around four this afternoon," she answered Ted Cuffy, the fire captain and leader of the Harmony rescue squad, who stood in her crowded kitchen gulping down coffee, preparing for the long night ahead. "He said he was going for a walk."

"Is that a habit with him?"

"Yes...well...I didn't find it unusual."

"Could you describe what he was wearing?" asked one of the three policemen present. Three policemen were the entire Harmony force.

Cathryn clutched her hands and held them tight in her lap. "Blue denim jeans, white-and-black running shoes, and a navy hooded sweatshirt." A half hour ago when Tucker had asked her that same question she'd been unable to answer, but she'd gone looking through Justin's closet to see what was missing.

She gazed at Tucker now, standing behind the other people gathered in her kitchen, and her heart ached with gratitude that he'd responded to her cry for help. He had calmed her with just his presence.

The side door opened and Julia's husband, Ben Grant, stepped in. He surveyed the group, assessed what was happening and, trying not to interrupt, simply explained that he was alone because Julia was still doing her radio show. Then he went to stand with Lauren and Cameron Hathaway, who'd raced over to help. Both of Cathryn's parents had also been among the first to arrive, but now just her father remained. She'd asked her mother to take Cory and Beth home overnight. They didn't need to experience this.

Cathryn had also called Dylan, who had officially become her ex-husband today. He stood by the hutch with some of his ex-neighbors. There was no doubt in Cathryn's mind that the finalization of the divorce had triggered this crisis.

"So, is it done?" Justin had demanded after school, and when she'd answered yes, he'd sworn a blue streak and gone stomping outside, kicking flowerpots and fence posts and anything else he could abuse. She'd gone after him and tried to reassure him he'd see his father often, he was still loved. But she'd been so emotionally drained herself that all she'd really wanted to do was lie down and sleep, and even she had heard the lack of care and sincerity in her platitudes.

A short time later Justin had announced he was going for a walk. She'd reminded him to avoid trouble and be home for supper. He'd grunted and let the door bang shut behind him.

At first when he didn't return, Cathryn had only been miffed, but by six-thirty she'd called his friends, concerned. No one had seen him. After that, her concern had grown to worry fairly quickly. Had he run to his father? she wondered. Would Justin do that, even though Dylan had moved in with Zoe? But if he had, Dylan would've called. Where could the boy be? Surely by now he was hungry. Nothing, including anger, kept him from his meals.

Packing Cory and Beth into the van, she'd driven around the island, checking out Justin's favorite haunts, thankful that it was early June and still light out. She drove for an hour, but Justin was nowhere to be found.

Cathryn had returned home and paced the living room

and prayed, battling panic with every step, every word. Finally, with the sun down and night deepening, Cory had sidled into the living room and gazed at her with eyes that reminded her of a moment last February. "Who'll take care of us?" he'd asked then, and she'd blithely replied, "I will." She felt like an utter phoney now, a failure.

That was when she'd decided to call for help. She'd surrendered, admitted she couldn't go it alone, and had phoned Tucker. Mysteriously, from that moment on, she'd begun to feel more in control. When Tucker arrived he had asked her what she wanted to do about Justin's disappearance, and she'd known immediately. No, she didn't want to assume he was all right and would show up in the morning. She wanted to act now.

While Tucker called the police on his cellular phone, she dialed Ted Cuffy, who assembled the Harmony Rescue Squad, a group of volunteers with training and experience in emergencies such as this. They'd also notified friends and immediate family. For the past twenty minutes, cars had been arriving at a nonstop pace.

"Do you have any idea where we should start our search?" the fire captain asked her while unfolding a map of the island on the kitchen table. "Any places where your son especially likes to play?"

As Cathryn named all the areas that came to mind, Ted Cuffy placed small red stick-on dots on the map. It was a discouraging sight. Stem to stern, Harmony was six miles long, three miles at its widest. A healthy twelve-year-old was capable of walking anywhere within that area, and the red dots showed that Justin could be anywhere.

Someone on the Rescue Squad asked, "Is there a chance your son could've left the island?"

Cathryn's heart jumped. "Oh, I doubt it."

Tucker pushed away from the wall. "Maybe someone could call the ferry service anyway."

One of the policemen nodded. "I'll take care of that."

While this exchange had been going on, Ted Cuffy had devised a strategy. He drew a long line east to west across the map, then two more that intersected it, dividing the island into six sectors. Everyone crowded around, studying the lines, imagining the topography within them.

"These two west sectors," Cuffy indicated with a wave of his pencil. "They aren't as large as some others, but you've got Cook Pond there, a lighthouse, lots of beach and dunes, and farther inland you've got the woods. I'll send in at least a third of my people there."

Tucker was standing close to Cathryn. She felt his nervous energy emanating from him palpably and knew he was thinking about the pond.

Impatient to get moving, Cameron Hathaway said, "I'll cover the harbor and the marina. While I'm at it, I'll talk to the harbor master to see if any boats are missing."

"I'll go with you," his wife said.

"Lauren!" he protested. "You're seven months pregnant."

"So?"

Cathryn came to Cameron's rescue. "So, stay here in case someone calls or Justin comes home."

Tucker frowned at Cathryn much as Cameron had frowned at his wife. "And where are you going to be?"

"Out searching like everyone else." Tucker appeared ready to challenge her, but her expression must've conveyed how desperately she needed to be an active part of the search. To sit here and wait while others were out looking would drive her mad. He gave in with a low growl.

Cathryn turned back to Lauren. "Would you mind staying?"

"No problem. But Cam should have help. The harbor is a complex area to cover."

"I'll go," Ben Grant said.

"Me, too," Cathryn's father chimed in.

The fire captain assigned a few more people to the top middle sector where the harbor was located, and then moved on to the eastern part of Harmony, with its dangerously high cliffs on the coast and, inland, acres of conservation lands and small ponds.

"The men who go into these two sectors will take the dogs," Cuffy decided. "I'm not sure how much we'll be able to accomplish in the dark, but we'll do our best." He smiled reassuringly at Cathryn, then at Dylan. "Don't worry. It's a mild night, and your boy evidently knows the island."

Which is exactly why he should already be home, Cathryn fretted silently. She felt a warm hand curl over her shoulder and leaned into it.

"What about Morgan's Hollow?" Tucker asked, referring to the bowl-shaped, heavily wooded ravine that occupied much of the middle-south sector on the map.

Cuffy sighed. "I'll send people in there first thing in the morning."

"I'll go in tonight," Tucker said. Heads swiveled in his direction.

"It's mighty dark in there at night," Cuffy warned.

"I know. I've been there before."

"Are you sure?"

"Yes," Tucker said decisively.

Cathryn glanced at Dylan, wishing he would volunteer to go with Tucker. Morgan's Hollow was vast and difficult to negotiate, and apparently no one, not even the trained rescue squad, was ready to take it on in the dark.

But Dylan glanced away and offered instead to search Harmony's numerous small coves in his boat.

"We should have a signaling system," a neighbor said, "in case one of us finds Justin."

Cuffy nodded. "We've used whistles in the past, and I have enough for everybody out in my van."

Ben Grant had momentarily disappeared down the hall— to the bathroom, Cathryn had believed. But upon returning he said, "I just got off the phone with my wife. She's already sent out an APB to everyone tuned into her program. I think we can safely assume that if Justin's on private property, he'll soon be found."

Overwhelmed, Cathryn covered her trembling mouth with trembling fingers. "Thank you, Ben."

A short time later the group moved outside, where at least thirty more volunteers awaited them. Cuffy organized the various parties, shouted instructions, and soon cars were speeding away.

Cathryn wasn't in any of them. She was still standing on the driveway, arguing with Tucker, although she sensed the battle had already been won.

"You are *not* coming with me," he said, dousing himself with bug repellent, being careful not to spray the whistle hanging around his neck.

"I *am*," she insisted, fastening elastic bands around the cuffs of her sweatshirt and jeans.

"You'll slow me down."

"I will not. I know Morgan's, too. Maybe better than you do. I've walked it dozens of times."

"I really, really wish you wouldn't do this," Tucker muttered, testing the flashlight he'd dug out of his car's trunk.

"Tough."

Ready to leave, he sighed heavily. "All right, all right. I won't say another word."

"Promise?"

He sighed again. "Yes."

Cathryn insisted on a handshake, because she knew it wouldn't be long before she'd have to trade on that promise.

WALKING INTO Morgan's Hollow at night took courage. Walking into it *alone* took something greater. That took a mother's love, and Cathryn had plenty of that as she descended the walking trail where Tucker had reluctantly dropped her off.

"It only makes sense," she'd argued. "We'll cover twice the ground if we split up." He'd known she was right.

She stopped to readjust her small backpack and imagined Tucker driving around to a trail head on the opposite rim. "Be safe," she whispered.

During the day Morgan's Hollow was a hiker's paradise. Home to deer and marsh hawks, the four-hundred-acre glacial ravine had been the first area of Harmony to be designated a wildlife refuge. Its vegetation and ancient terrain added to its appeal. On an afternoon's trek, one might pass an amateur botanist or geologist as readily as a birdwatcher, jogger or simple lover of natural beauty.

When the sun went down, however, Morgan's became a hiker's nightmare. Darkness descended quickly and densely inside the bowl, even while day's light still shimmered on beaches and hilltops nearby. Moreover, from the floor of that bowl, nothing of the outside world was visible—no lights from ships or houses, or any other markers by which a person might keep his bearings. One of the eeriest phenomena, though, was that sound carried strangely because of the many rock outcroppings, hillocks and folds in the land. Voices that were close sometimes sounded far, and far ones sounded near.

Cathryn was ready to cope with all of these unpleasantries. What she wasn't so sure about were the ghosts. According to local legend, which Cameron had recorded quite entertainingly in his most recent book, Morgan's was haunted by the spirits of native Indians felled by smallpox during early colonial days. They'd been buried here. In all her walks, Cathryn had never experienced anything remotely like a spirit, Indian or otherwise, but then, legend also claimed they only manifested themselves at night.

"There's no such thing as ghosts," she whispered, following the long bright oval cast from her flashlight onto the gradually descending path before her. "There's no such thing as ghosts." Aiming her voice high, she called loudly, "Jus-tin!" She paused, ears attuned to the slightest wind whisper, and swept the flashlight over the scrub growth to right and left. The night air shimmered with the songs of crickets and other summer insects. Nothing more. She marched on a few steps, and again called, "Jus-tin!"

While still above the tunnel-like vegetation of the lower ravine, she scanned the distance, trying to guess where Tucker might be, hoping to see a light. But across the darkness all she saw was more darkness.

"There are no ghosts. Are no ghosts…" she muttered, marching along. What she really ought to do, she thought, was pray. *The Lord is my shepherd, I shall not want…* Yes, that was better. She loved the twenty-third psalm. It was so comforting. *Yea, though I walk through the shadow of the valley of…* Uh… No, maybe not. "Jus-tin!"

Cathryn kept her equanimity by telling herself her son wouldn't be dumb enough to come into the hollow alone at night. And if he'd come during the day, he would've been long gone by now.

Unless he was hurt or lost.

No, she refused to think that. She'd just keep walking and calling and scanning the underbrush. She'd cover her territory because someone had to cover it and make sure he wasn't here.

Oh, but what if he was?

She walked on, sometimes slowly because the ground was gnarled with tree roots, sometimes faster, and sometimes stopping to pull herself free of a grasping briar, but always fighting her worst fears.

Please, God, let him be all right. If he's hurt, let him not be in pain. If he's lost, let him be unafraid. If he's been abducted...

On that image, Cathryn's defenses collapsed and she inhaled a painful cry.

"There are no ghosts. There are no ghosts," she repeated until the phrase was merely a mantra, calming her and keeping a beat for her feet to follow. At times, without intending to, Cathryn drifted into *The Lord is my shepherd* again. And once, quite mysteriously, she found herself muttering, *Half a league, half a league, half a league onward...*

"Justin!" she called, her voice hoarse, her shirt stuck to her skin with perspiration. *Half a league, half a league, into the valley, the valley of...* "Justin, are you there?"

A half hour passed in this manner, at which point Cathryn stopped and realized she'd been walking on instinct and her memory of the trails, and now was unsure where she stood. She pulled out her trail map and aimed the light on it. Was she even on a trail anymore? It was so dark. Walls of foliage rose all around her, the sky only a small patch of bright stars directly above. Great. Now *she* was lost.

The situation suddenly struck her as eminently laughable, especially considering what day this was. Her divorce day. But she didn't laugh. Tears filled her eyes instead.

Exhorting herself not to fall apart, she studied the map again, then turned a slow circle, shining her light in every direction. Just ahead gleamed a marker. She was on a trail, after all! "Justin!"

She resumed walking, but all at once her heart took a leap. "Justin?" And from some muffled distance came the gloriously familiar cry, "Mom!"

"Justin?" she called with frantic eagerness, turning a circle with the light.

"Mom!"

"Justin?"

"Mom!"

"Keep calling, honey. I'm coming. Keep calling."

Cathryn followed a trail of sound, through scratchy bayberry, over rocks and a fallen tree trunk, until at last she found her son.

"Justin!" She scrambled forward, bending low to keep from snagging her hair on the overhanging branches that concealed the shallow grotto where Justin had taken shelter. He struggled to his feet and threw himself at her, arms tightly encircling her as he burst into tears.

"It's okay, honey, I'm here. It's okay." Crying too, she kissed his head, his cheeks, his ears, anything her lips could find. "Shh. Shh," she said, cradling him close. "It's all right now."

"Oh, Mo-om, I'm so g-gla-ad you fou-ound me. I was s-so scared," he said, sobbing so brokenly she could barely understand him. "I shouldn'ta been, but I wa-as, and I s-started running…"

"Shh. Shh," she soothed, like when he was younger and had awakened from a nightmare. "It's all over."

"I didn't know where I was." He continued crying. "I finally realized I shouldn't keep walking, I might get even more lost. If I just waited for morning…so I found this place."

"You did right, honey. That was smart."

"But it's so awful here. You can't see anything, and I'm full of bug bites, and the animals..." he went on, hiccuping words. "I didn't want to fall asleep in case a skunk found me. But I didn't want to stay awake either, because of...because of..."

"What, honey?"

He went still, eyes wide, peering into the shadows beyond. "Did you walk through the icy cold spot, too?"

"What icy cold spot?"

In the circle of yellow light carved out of the darkness by her flashlight, Cathryn saw his expression slowly change, rationality filtering into it. Again, he seemed her baby, waking from a bad dream.

He lowered his head and exhaled a self-deprecating chuckle. "It was probably nothing. Just my imagination. It was dark, and, well, you know the stories about the hollow."

"And you thought that cold spot you walked through was...unnatural?"

He swallowed and nodded several times. "And because I did, I ran like a spooked horse."

Cathryn combed back his disheveled hair. "Well, that's okay. I probably would've fainted." She was overjoyed to see a brief smile.

With his sobs at last under control, she said. "Shall we get out of here?"

Justin wiped his shirt sleeve across his eyes. "I'd love to but..." His lips trembled slightly. "I fell and twisted my ankle."

"What? Are you hurt?"

He nodded. "I think I sprained my ankle again, the weak one."

Oh, great. Now what? "If you lean on me, do you think you can walk? The trail isn't far. Only a few yards."

"I'll try."

Once they reached the trail, Cathryn clamped the whistle between her lips and gave several shrill blasts. "There. Help will be here before you know it."

"Help?"

"Mmm. Did you think I was the only one looking for you?" She laughed. "Boy, are you in for a surprise."

Justin shrank into the hood of his sweatshirt like a turtle. "Sorry."

"Yeah, me, too. Me, too. While we're waiting for the troops, let's take a load off and talk about it."

Getting her son to discuss his anger wasn't nearly as difficult as it had been before tonight. Having experienced the consequences of that anger, he was more than ready to open up. Cathryn's heart nearly broke when he explained how scared the divorce made him because now he was "the man of the house," a phrase she'd used once or twice during the past couple of months to get him to do his chores.

"I don't want to be the man of the house," he confessed, his voice clogged with tears again. "I...I don't know how."

Cathryn held him to her, trying to ward off her own tears. "I don't either, Justin. I have no idea what I'm doing, and I've been scared, too."

"You?" He pulled back.

"Yes, me. I've been terrified. That's probably why I've been so tough on you and your sister and brother lately." After a moment's thought she added, "And on myself."

"I'm not sure I understand."

"Me, either. But it's sort of like you giving me lip and throwing rocks at seagulls. Pretty stupid, huh?"

"Sure is."

"Tell you what, kid. How about we both forget about being the man of the house and we just be ourselves from now on?"

Justin giggled in childlike relief. "Okay." But insecurity momentarily flickered over his young handsome face. "Are we gonna make it, Mom?"

"Yes, we are," she said with newborn conviction. "Oh, things are bound to change, but, hey, that's life." Had she really said that? She, Cathryn Hill McGrath, who'd always wanted things to remain the same? She, who'd secretly feared stepping outside her cocoon of domestic busyness?

She, who'd been so afraid of uncertainty she would have borne another baby just to continue living the familiar?

"When you think about it, Justin, change can be good. It can be a time of growth, a time of fun and adventure. It all depends on how you look at it." She stroked her son's long lean arms and smiled. "We'll be fine, honey, and you know why? Because we're blessed. We're surrounded by people who love us and care about us and want to help."

From a distance there suddenly came a familiar deep voice calling, "Shortcake!" Justin and Cathryn looked at each other, breath suspended, and then collapsed with laughter.

Standing, she hollered back, "Tucker!"

"On my way!" he replied.

"Keep calling!"

"Okay!"

Cathryn and Tucker continued to shout out to each other in this manner, their voices a gossamer thread linking them through the darkness. It seemed an eternity, but the inky distance between them did lessen. His calls grew louder and closer, and finally Cathryn heard more than his voice. She heard the snapping of twigs, the thrashing through brush, then footfalls on hard-packed trail, footfalls that increased in speed as he ran to her and she to him.

"Tucker," Cathryn cried one last time before being lifted off her feet into his arms. She wound her arms around his neck and hugged him extra tightly, forgetting every reason why she shouldn't, and he hugged her.

Eventually, he loosened his hold, set her on her feet and stepped back. "How's Justin?" he asked.

"He's okay. He's sprained an ankle, that's the worst of it."

"And you?"

"I'm great."

Tucker smoothed her hair, cupping her head in his hands. "Yes, you are." He pulled her forward again and held her close in his arms. Under her hand his heart beat wildly, a twin to her own.

What was happening to her? she wondered. She'd accepted her sexual attraction to him long ago, but this was more than hormonal chemistry. Was it possible she'd also developed feelings for Tucker? She refused to call it love. That would be indecent. She'd only become divorced that day. But *feelings* was a word she could live with. And yes, she did have them for Tucker. She'd probably had them for a while, in fact, but refused to acknowledge them.

After being reassured that Justin was indeed all right, Tucker blew a few loud blasts on his whistle. Almost immediately Cathryn heard the far-off reply of another whistle, and a brief while after that, another farther away, and another farther still, until the night was full of whistles, a chain of sound linking her and the people who'd turned out to help.

Tucker carried Justin out of Morgan's on his back, while Cathryn guided and lighted the way. The trek out didn't take nearly as long as the trek in, or maybe it just seemed shorter because Tucker and Justin exchanged war stories about the hollow all the way.

Cathryn couldn't decide whether Tucker was lying or telling the truth when he admitted to recognizing Justin's "icy cold spot."

"Takes your breath away, doesn't it?" he laughed, striding along as if he and her son were discussing nothing more alarming than a cold-water shower or an extrastrong breath mint.

By the time they reached the road, Justin had adopted Tucker's arrogantly breezy view of the experience, and whether the danger had been real or imagined, truth or lie, Cathryn was grateful to Tucker. He'd made it real, and Justin would be stronger—and probably incredibly more popular among his peers—for having survived it.

THE CROWD at Cathryn's house didn't linger. Everyone was tired, and Justin still needed to see a doctor. Cathryn thanked each of the dozens of volunteers individually, sent her father home with a hug, and told her friends she'd be in touch. After waving goodbye to the last straggler, Cathryn turned from the door and nearly bumped into her ex.

"Do you want me to take Justin to the clinic?" Dylan asked her, sipping a cup of the decaf Lauren had brewed when the search party returned.

"The offer's tempting, but I need to go, myself. I want to get the new inoculation against Lyme disease. Thanks anyway."

"You're sure?"

She nodded. "We won't be alone. Tucker's going and getting a shot, too."

"Well…" Dylan sighed. "Call if you need anything."

She said she would, and when he was at last out the door, she and Tucker and Justin headed for the island's small but efficient clinic.

It was well after midnight when they returned. Justin's

ankle had been x-rayed and taped, and each of them had been examined and inoculated.

WITH JUSTIN comfortably in bed and Cathryn yawning, Tucker put on his jacket and headed for the front door. He didn't want to leave, but it was time. Past time. Even Dylan had left, and he was Justin's father.

If he didn't go, he might very well turn careless, and Cathryn didn't need that. She was exhausted. She was also only newly divorced. She needed time to get her social bearings.

"I hope you'll be able to sleep," Cathryn said, pausing in the cool air wafting through the screen door. "It's been quite a day."

"Sure has."

She flicked a cautious glance up into his eyes, smiled and glanced away. He wished he could interpret her tense shyness as banked romantic interest, but he remembered too well her self-loathing after their last encounter.

"I'm glad you called me," he said, studying each feature of her tired face, each tangle in her silky hair. He yearned to touch it, to run his fingers through and draw her near, feel her close all down the length of him.

"I'm glad you answered," she said. She seemed reluctant to end the conversation, too. Maybe she was a bit more interested than he thought?

"Was there any doubt I would?"

"Sure. The way I've been acting?"

"And how's that?"

"Bullheaded. Too proud to see beyond my own nose."

"Oh. I thought you knew. I like proud, bullheaded women." He grinned, giving in to his longing to flirt. "In fact, I have a real thing for them."

She averted her gaze, but blushed anyway. "Thanks," she said softly.

He shrugged. "For what?"

"Being a friend."

Before he could respond she circled his neck with one arm, raised on tiptoe and kissed his stubbled cheek. Such an innocent gesture, yet it threw him off-balance. Whatever control mechanism he'd been using to behave himself went haywire, and when she settled back onto her heels, he leaned forward and planted a kiss on her cheek, too.

Tense, biting her lip, she gave him a hug, and he returned it. But when he should've pulled away, he didn't. He was an addict and she was a drug withheld too long. Still holding her close, he kissed her cheek again in one last pretense that this was just a friendly goodbye. She kissed his jaw. Planting ever more frantic kisses, he inched quickly to her mouth, and she to his.

They met greedily, groaning, as he captured her head in two hands and settled into a long, unabashedly sensual kiss. This was no one-way illusion, he realized. Cathryn was responding like a woman who'd had him—and this—on her mind for a while.

When they at last drew apart, they were both breathing raggedly.

"Oh, Lordy," she gasped, staring at him with astonishment. Her parted lips glistened. Her rounded cheeks glowed. "I'm sorry, Tucker."

With his hands still splayed across her back, he jerked back his head, surprised. "Why are *you* sorry?"

"For doing it again. Making you forget your commitment to Jenny."

"Don't be." He skimmed his hands down to her waist and drew her closer, flush against him. "I've done what I could to meet my obligations. I've proposed to her, I've

changed for her, I've promised her the sky. Now it's time
to face facts. The woman simply doesn't want to marry me.
I give up. And to be honest, I'm relieved. It wouldn't have
been much of a marriage.''

"And the baby?"

His hands slid from her waist over her hips and up again,
high, almost to her breasts in a need to feel her and prove
to himself she was real, and really here with him. "The
baby, the baby," he sighed, concern still shadowing him,
although not nearly as darkly as it once had. "Jen's parents
are good people, and it appears she wants to stay with them.
I have every confidence the baby will be raised well there.
And, who knows, maybe someday Jen'll meet a nice young
farmer, and everyone'll live happily ever after." He leaned
forward and placed a lingering kiss on Cathryn's forehead.
"Whatever happens, I'll send money and start a college
fund and see to the child's needs from a distance."

"You're at peace with that?" Her hazel cat-eyes watched
him intently.

"Yes," he said with conviction.

She bit her lip, lowered her eyes to her hands on his chest.
She'd finally removed her rings today. "Well then, since
you've given up on Jenny, and I'm not married anymore..."

Tucker felt a low chuckle rumbling deep in his chest. It
came from his heart, which at the moment was very, very
happy. "Yes?"

She lifted her eyes to his, bold need replacing trepidation.
"Kiss me again, Tucker?"

"Anything you want, darlin'. Anything at all."

CHAPTER THIRTEEN

JUNE UNFOLDED like a flower, so unlike the cold, bitter spring that had preceded it. Days were at their longest, the ocean was warming and, everywhere, roses bloomed—on arbors and trellises, over stone walls and fences, in meadows and beach dunes and even Morgan's Hollow.

Mimicking the expansiveness of the season, Cathryn quit her job with the housecleaning service and went to work as a waitress at one of Harmony's popular waterfront restaurants. She liked waiting tables only a little better than housecleaning, but the money she earned in tips compensated more than adequately for the job's shortcomings. Besides, she knew it wouldn't last forever.

Lauren had been visiting regularly to discuss career opportunities, bringing with her her many years of business savvy, and finally Cathryn was eager to listen. She would've been a fool not to. Lauren had been making money since the age of ten, and currently managed real estate valued in the millions. What especially mattered to Cathryn, though, was that Lauren loved her work and understood the value of following one's bliss. She'd be a trustworthy mentor on this unfamiliar road to independence.

Cathryn also spent more time with Julia, but for a very different reason. Without any family to help her, Julia confessed to feeling anxious over her impending motherhood and asked if Cathryn would help.

Would she *help?* Out came the books again, along with

the diapers and bath basins and dolls to be dropped on their heads. Cathryn also offered to visit Julia after the baby was born, all day, every day, for at least a week. Julia was over-whelmed.

"No big deal." Cathryn shrugged. "It's just what we do in our family when someone has a baby. And your timing's right. In September work at the restaurant should slow down." She also promised to be with Julia through labor and delivery if necessary, although both women agreed Ben wasn't likely to wimp out.

Julia's dependence on Cathryn did wonders for her ego. Julia had always been beautiful, strong, talented and on tar-get with her destined work. She'd crisscrossed the country following a glamorous radio career, seeing places Cathryn had only read about. Yet here she was now, terrified by this next step in her life and asking for help. It occurred to Cath-ryn that maybe her life hadn't been so stagnant after all.

But if Cathryn had to choose one reason for her June-busting-out-all-over mood, it was Tucker. She still wouldn't call what she felt *love.* That was a special term reserved for a special relationship, one she wasn't ready for yet, didn't know when she would be ready, or even *if* she'd ever be ready. But she did have a crush on Tucker—a full-blown infatuation, actually—and her friends noticed. How could they not? She was walking on air.

She and Tucker agreed to keep to a casual approach—no commitments, no pressure, and no sex—although in her mind the *no sex* part came with a *yet.* They were free to see other people and actually encouraged each other to get out and date. But somehow they never did. All their free time ended up being lavished on each other.

They shared long, lazy picnics on the beach, quick, ex-hilarating swims in the still-chilly ocean, shopping strolls, visits with friends, and twilit evenings with the kids, playing baseball or hide-and-seek, often with Cathryn's parents joining in. With the end of school, life only got better. All three of her children passed into the next grade. "Way to go, Peanut!" Tucker cheered, slapping high-five with Bethany when he arrived for a celebratory barbecue.

The house Tucker had inherited from his uncle was as renovated as it was ever going to get under his ownership. Its walls wore fresh coats of paint. The bathroom and kitchen were updated. Furniture was polished and slip-covered. New valances hung at the clean windows, and everywhere blue accents tied the interior to the everpresent sea beyond. It was adorable, Cathryn thought. And it was done, leaving Tucker time to concentrate on the garage, where he continued his uncle's trade.

Sitting on a stack of tires one afternoon in late June, watching Tucker perform his magic under the hood of an old Saab, Cathryn wondered if he was happy. The more she got to know him, the more she understood her father's long-ago assessment that Tucker was a complex and highly intelligent person. Yet, there he was, grease on his forearms, pitting his intelligence against nothing more challenging than mute steel.

When she voiced her question, he said, "What do you mean, am I happy?" He cast her a sidelong glance, which, as it lingered on her, grew to a heart-melting smile.

"Do you ever dream of doing anything else?"

"I've done lots of other things. You name it, I've done it."

"Is there anything you miss?"

Tucker wiped his hands on a rag. "Sometimes. I sometimes miss racing." His hand-wiping slowed. "But not enough to go back to it. It isn't worth dying for."

"Dying! Since when have you ever factored dying into anything you did?"

He hung the rag over the raised hood and stared at the engine. "Since...you."

The garage was still, absolutely quiet, sunlight pouring in great heavenly shafts from high windows, and at that moment Cathryn felt she really was in a sort of heaven. Tucker went back to work, but he was distracted, picking up tools and laying them down without ever having done anything with them.

Finally he paused, braced his hands wide on the car's fenders, his back hunched. After a while he turned his head, his expression one she'd never seen on his face before. Raw longing lay there, mixed with vulnerability and fear. "Well, aren't you going to say anything?"

Cathryn climbed off the stack of tires and walked toward him on legs that trembled. "There's nothing to say, only to do."

He straightened stiffly, unsure of what was coming at him.

"I think you'd better lock up here," she murmured, winding her arms around his shoulders.

He raised his arms out to the sides. "Cath, I'm covered in grease. Look at me."

She grinned. "Oh, I am. And I like what I see." She moved closer, fitting herself to him wherever and however she could. "I like it very, very much."

The outer corners of his eyes crinkled as he chuckled. "You asked for it." No sooner said than he'd swung her off her feet into his arms and started for the house.

On the periphery of her swirling thoughts, Cathryn wondered if she was crazy. Barely divorced a month, and she was getting involved with another man. But everything about it felt right. This had nothing to do with revenge, or with egos that needed bolstering, or any of the other reasons they'd made love the first time. This had only to do with her and Tucker and their mutual desire, their mutual joy in each other.

He carried her up the stairs and into his bedroom, kissing her all the way, and let her slowly slide down his body till her feet touched the floor. "Don't go anywhere," he said, leaving her with one more kiss. After a quick wash-up in the adjacent bathroom, he returned.

With none of the artifice of their lovemaking three months ago, they each dispatched with their clothing. Neither felt the need to speak, but they did smile at each other often. Tucker turned back the blue-and-white quilt and sat on the bed, drawing her down with him.

They kissed and caressed, remembering the myriad kisses and caresses they'd exchanged since "the night of the hollow," as they'd come to call the night of Justin's adventure. Those other kisses and caresses had been wonderful but usually ended in frustration. Not these. These they could shower without reservations.

Cathryn lay back in a splash of warm sunlight on the crisp white sheets, already aching for Tucker. His dark, long-lashed eyes traveled over her outstretched body, pale here, suntanned there, and she stretched even more comfortably, luxuriating in his admiration. Yes, she was finally slim and toned, her body fit to be admired, but the best of it was, Tucker had always looked at her this way.

"Come here," she whispered, lifting one arm to him, and he did. He joined her in the sunlight in a mating that was sweet as the roses overgrowing Harmony, expansive as the summer just unfolding, and potent as the ever-present sea.

When it was over, Tucker had only enough strength to move his weight off Cathryn. With faint aftershocks of pleasure rippling out from where their bodies still joined, Cathryn lifted her fingertips to Tucker's cheek. They smiled in contentment, still unspeaking. The summer was just unfolding, and so was life. They had all the time in the world.

FERRY SERVICE picked up in earnest by the Fourth of July. Eight runs a day to and from the mainland, all of them crowded with vacationers and daytrippers bound for the island. The only trip that could accommodate Tucker's vehicles back to Harmony was the first at seven in the morning. So, after a big race weekend in New Hampshire, he and Cathryn and her children rented rooms in a Cape Cod motel and crossed the sound with the rising sun. In the belly of the ferry sat his truck and two stock cars. In his wallet burned a hefty check—he'd done well—and in the eyes of the kids gleamed something close to idolatry.

As for Cathryn, what could he say? She was the reason he'd raced. She'd convinced him to enter the competition. Be yourself, she'd advised. Follow your heart.

He did. He was.

The ferry docked at the pier, and before long he had taken Cathryn and the kids home, promising to call them after they'd all caught up on their sleep.

He drove the two miles to his house, parked the truck in the garage, and headed indoors for a long restful nap. Before he'd even reached the top of the staircase, however, he sensed something was wrong. The house felt different. With his skin prickling, he paused, turned and looked behind him into the living room. The sight of two large suitcases by the front door nearly knocked him sideways. What the hell?

Suddenly the door to his bedroom opened. He tensed, his mind flashing *Burglar!* until he remembered burglars didn't come bearing luggage.

But pregnant ex-girlfriends did. And there stood one now.

''Surprise,'' Jenny sang.

Tucker could feel his blood draining, his head getting light.

"Oh," Jenny laughed. "I guess this *is* a surprise." She was wearing a pink nightgown that should've reached her knees, but because of her protruding belly, most of her thighs were exposed. Tucker's gaze skimmed from her short auburn curls to her brightly painted toenails, studying the changes in her anatomy.

"My God, you're big!" The exclamation was out before he could censor it.

She laughed again. "Isn't this something?" She smoothed her hands over her stomach and linked them underneath. "I'm sorry for barging in and making myself at home, but your neighbors, those nice people in the white house, had a key and said you probably wouldn't mind."

Tucker dropped a hand on top of his head, sure it was ready to spin off. "Why don't we go downstairs and have some coffee and...talk."

"Sure, just let me get my robe. And make mine decaf, will ya?"

Tucker stood in his kitchen, staring at the coffeemaker as if he'd never seen such a machine. His thoughts were swirling, and his body temperature kept swinging from hot to cold. *Concentrate, Tucker. Concentrate.*

The coffee was brewed by the time Jenny came downstairs. She'd combed her hair and put on some makeup. "I love your little house," she said, accepting a steaming cup from Tucker.

He didn't want to talk about his little house. "When did you get here?"

"Yesterday. Late afternoon."

Why? Why are you here? That was the question. It blazed across Tucker's mind, burned the tip of his tongue.

"So..." She smiled. "Are you happy to see me?"

Tucker sipped his coffee. "You're looking well."

"I'm feeling well. My morning sickness passed months ago."

"Great. Great."

"The people next door said you were away in New Hampshire, racing?"

"Yes."

"Oh." She continued to smile, but disappointment clouded her green eyes. "I thought on your tape you said you were quitting."

"I did, for a while, but I missed it. What I'm aiming for now is balance."

"Balance?"

"Mmm. Between working the garage and racing, livelihood and avocation. I think I'm on the right track." *And why am I explaining this to you?* he wondered. *This has nothing to do with you anymore.*

Jenny didn't argue his decision. If anything, she seemed intent on acquiescence. "Do you mind if I make some toast or something?" she asked him. "I'm starved."

"Oh, I'm sorry." He jumped to his feet. "Sit down. I'll get it."

"So, I guess you're wondering why I'm here," she said, while Tucker prepared a breakfast of bacon, eggs and toast for her. He himself had lost his appetite.

"The question's crossed my mind."

"Well, I watched your video and finally decided it was time to put you out of your misery. Actually, it was my folks who made me see the light. They watched the video, too, and really took a liking to you. So, here I am, in person, to say yes, I'll marry you." It apparently didn't occur to her that he might have changed his mind. "As to when and where and how, we don't have to decide the exact details right now. My only request is that we be married before the baby's born.''

"And when's that?"

"Mid-August, I figure." Jenny braced her hands on the table, hoisted herself off the chair, and excused herself to visit the little girls' room.

"It's such a pain. This month I hafta pee at least once an hour."

Alone, Tucker stared unseeingly at the bacon sizzling in the frying pan—a man drowning and not knowing which way was up. This couldn't be happening. It couldn't. Just when life was getting so good. He should've known. The gods were just, if not merciful, and were only rewarding him for his dissolute past. But did they have to be sadistic, too? Why had they given him Cathryn?

He searched for anger, for cynicism or indifference—any of the defenses that had buoyed him through bad times in the past, but they eluded him. As he stood over the stove, the only thing he could find was sadness.

He heard Jenny returning and quickly swiped his arm across his face. He tried to keep his back to her, but she came up beside him and noticed his ravaged expression anyway.

"Aw, Tucker." She touched his arm and rubbed it comfortingly. "Raising this baby really means the world to you, doesn't it? I didn't believe it at first, but now I can see it's true."

He drew in a deep fortifying breath and tried to smile. "How do you like your eggs?"

TUCKER SPENT THE MORNING driving Jenny around the island. Mostly they stayed in the car, and he pointed out landmarks. When they drove through town, she was eager to stop and visit the shops, but Tucker said there would be plenty of time for that. Actually he wasn't crazy about being seen on Water Street with her. Granted, the number of tourists was crushing, but locals were sure to be among them.

"Where does your friend Cathryn live?" Jenny asked some time later, as Tucker pulled away from a roadside ice cream stand.

He nearly dropped his half-full Coke in his lap. "C-Cathryn?" His ears turned hot.

"Yes. I'm dying to meet her." Done with her cone, Jenny wiped her hands on a paper napkin, twisted it and crammed it into the car's ashtray. "From what I saw of her on the tape, she seems like a real sweetheart. I want to thank her, too, for all the help she gave you. You're looking great, Tuck." Jenny suddenly pressed two hands to the sides of her stomach. "Oh. Oh, wow."

Tucker tensed, eyes wide with alarm. "What? What's the matter?"

She laughed. "The baby just kicked. That's all. He's a soccer player for sure. Here, feel." She took Tucker's right hand so that he had to steer and hold his soda with the other, and placed it on her rock-hard belly.

On a rational level the rippling movements under his palm registered as amazing, but on an emotional level he only fell deeper into depression and fear. He'd been driving around for a couple of hours, pointing out beaches and lighthouses and historic homes—and desperately trying to find the escape hatch in this dilemma. But so far it eluded him, and he was quickly sinking into the feeling it didn't exist.

"It's something else, isn't it?" she said.

Tucker nodded. "Sure is." He retracted his hand.

"So, where does she live?"

Tucker had hoped Jenny would forget. "Oh, about a mile back down the road."

"That close? Oh, Tuck, I've got a great idea. Let's go by and surprise her."

"No!" The response snapped out of him. Jenny jumped. "Sorry. I just don't think...I think she may be working today."

"Oh." Jenny settled into the bucket seat, frowning. "What does she do?"

When he told her that Cathryn currently worked as a waitress, her eyes sparkled. "I don't believe it! Is that a coincidence, or what? I *knew* we were going to be friends. I just knew it."

Running out of places to drive, Tucker returned to the house and suggested Jenny relax on a chaise lounge in the yard. He supplied her with magazines, lemonade, a plate of nachos and a pillow to prop up her legs. Then he concocted an errand he needed to see to and went to visit Cathryn.

CATHRYN WAS on the phone with Lauren's mother, Audrey DeStefano, when Tucker showed up. Audrey had bought a house on Harmony during the winter and was currently renovating it into a B&B. However, the topic of their conversation wasn't Audrey's B&B but a baby shower for Lauren.

"We'll host it together," Cathryn told Tucker after saying goodbye to Audrey. "But I'm not sure what to do about Julia. She's due only a month after Lauren. We could easily turn the event into a doubleheader, but maybe separate showers would be better. You know, to give each mother-to-be her hour in the limelight. What do you think?"

Cathryn suddenly noticed how quiet Tucker was, how serious, how troubled. "What's wrong?"

"After the news I have to tell you, I'm afraid you may be thinking in terms of a *triple*-header."

"What?"

"Do you have room for one more pregnant lady on your social calendar?"

"Who? What are you talking about, Tucker?"

"Jenny. She's here."

The statement slammed her broadside. "Wh-what?"

"Let's go outside."

They sat on the deck in a double-seat glider while Tucker told her about his morning. Cathryn heard the words but registered few details. Her mind kept screaming *No, no! This can't be happening.*

"I don't know what to do, Cath," Tucker finished. "Jen assumes nothing has changed since I mailed her the video. God, if I'd known the effect it was going to have, I never would've mailed it."

And I never would've filmed it, Cathryn thought, pained by the irony.

"What should I do?" Tucker took her two hands in his and squeezed them. "Say the word, just say it, and I'll send her packing."

Cathryn met his gaze, his pleading, agonized gaze. She ached to say, *Yes, send her away,* but her conscience wouldn't allow it. "I can't. You know I can't." If a breaking heart had a face, it was Tucker's at that moment. "You'd never be happy knowing you'd gone back on your word to her. I couldn't live with that."

"Cath," he pleaded. "Think about this carefully."

"I am. It's the right thing to do, Tuck. She's carrying your baby. You've told her repeatedly you want to raise it. You've proposed. You've promised to be a responsible father and faithful husband. You've even changed for her. Is there really any question?"

Tucker drew her into his arms and held her tightly. "This is so hard!"

Yes, it was. Hard, unfair and cruel. And Cathryn hurt so

much she almost changed her mind. Almost. Putting a little distance between them, she framed Tucker's rugged, ravaged face in her hands, wiped a tear with her thumb and for his sake, tried to smile. "We'll always have Paris?"

He laughed weakly. "And that's more than I ever expected."

They held each other again. "It's going to be all right." Cathryn's heart broke a little more. "Better than all right. Just think, in less than two months you're going to be a father. You're going to have your own wife, your own family."

Tucker's hold tightened. "It's what I've always wanted. All my life."

"Yes, I know." She drew back, brushed aside the hair over his brow. "And now you have your chance. Take it."

"But…"

She gathered all her strength. "No. Don't look back."

CATHRYN MET JENNY two days later. She was working the afternoon shift, busily clearing a table on the restaurant's sidewalk-facing porch, when she spotted Tucker helping a short, very pregnant young woman into a seat three tables away. He glanced her way, apology in his eyes.

Cathryn pocketed her tip and walked over, smiling as cheerily as she could. "Hi! Jenny?"

Jenny gazed up at her and beamed. "Oh, Cathryn! I'd know you anywhere." She tried to rise, but Cathryn placed a hand on her shoulder.

"Don't get up. I remember what it's like to be in the last trimester."

Jenny had intriguing looks, Cathryn thought. Her lightly freckled face was full of warm, down-home wholesomeness, yet she exuded sensuality in subtle ways. Even while Cathryn tried to accept her with a loving heart, she envied her.

Jenny said, "I've wanted to meet you for days, but Tucker's kept me so busy doing other things. I began to think he didn't want us to meet."

"No chance of that happening." Cathryn slipped her pad out of her pocket. "What can I get you?"

Jenny ordered a fried clam roll. Tucker only wanted a Coke.

"Before you run off," Jenny said, grasping Cathryn's arm, "I want to invite you and your kids over for a cook-out."

Oh, no. "When?" Maybe she'd have to work?

"The next day you're free." Jenny stared at her until Cathryn realized she was waiting for a response.

"Oh, uh, let's see..." She scratched her head with the eraser end of her pencil. "That'd be in three days."

"Great. It's a date then."

Great.

CHAPTER FOURTEEN

BECAUSE OF HER JOB, Cathryn got to overhear the full range of reaction to Jenny's appearance on Harmony. Most locals were stunned. They'd seen Tucker with Cathryn so often they'd come to accept that their friendship was more than platonic. Also, having embraced the new and improved Tucker, they were dismayed to have this remnant of his wayward past show up on his doorstep. Poor Tucker, was their attitude. Just when he was getting his act together. But there was another element on Harmony who seemed to derive cruel satisfaction from his situation. Wasn't that just like Tucker Lang? they said. Once a rotten egg, always a rotten egg.

Cathryn steamed whenever she heard Tucker being discussed, no matter how kindly. No one got the story right, yet everyone believed they had the inside scoop. When Cathryn overheard herself being whispered about, she utterly boiled over. That, more than anything, convinced her to accept Jenny's invitation to the cookout. Cathryn went one step further; she also accepted Jenny's overture of friendship.

The morning after first meeting her, with a few hours free before work, Cathryn accompanied Jenny to the food market to help her shop for her small weekend party, and the morning after that, she guided the young woman through the stores and businesses on Water Street, introducing her to any and every neighbor they met. Cathryn even took her into the Water Street Diner, a bastion of Harmony gossip.

She wanted to confound wagging tongues with her ready acceptance of Tucker's pregnant girlfriend. She wanted to silence them by flaunting inconsistencies in the tales they spread. What she didn't count on, however, was the effect her companionship would have on Jenny. When Cathryn arrived with her children at Tucker's on Saturday, Jenny greeted her like a new best friend. Lauren, already there with Cameron, pantomimed a round-eyed ''uh-oh!''

Julia and Ben had been invited, too—''to make the day less intense,'' Tucker explained to Cathryn as she followed him indoors to help prepare a tray of drinks.

''Thanks. It *is* easier with more people to carry the ball of conversation.'' She'd barely met Tucker's eye since arriving. The only times she had allowed herself to gaze at him, she'd done so from a distance when he wasn't looking back, and even then the pain of her longing had nearly killed her.

What was the matter with her? She'd had nearly a week to become used to the idea of losing Tucker. Why wasn't it getting any easier?

She turned from the refrigerator, a lemon in each hand, and whirled right into Tucker's chest. Upon contact, electricity sizzled between them. They jumped apart, reddening.

''Gonna be a long day,'' Tucker muttered.

At the counter, slicing lemons as if her life depended on it, Cathryn replied with intentional obtuseness, ''Especially with the conversation so focused on pregnancy and babies.'' Through the open windows she could hear the three quite pear-shaped women discussing methods of easing lower back discomfort. Ben and Cameron had escaped to a game of badminton with the kids.

''Does it bother you?'' Tucker asked.

"Nope. Ow!" Cathryn's left hand flew away from the cutting board. Instantly a thin line of blood oozed from a cut to her index finger.

"See what you get for lying?" Tucker turned on the faucet, adjusted the water to cold and, gripping her wrist, plunged her hand under the spray.

For at least a minute he held her wrist—and stood much too close. "You can let go now," Cathryn said unsteadily.

"I'll just go get a bandage," he replied, equally unsteady.

Tucker returned. She dried her hands and said she was perfectly capable of applying the bandage herself. But he insisted on doing it, and she complied, secretly savoring his closeness and touch.

"How are you and the kids doing?" he asked her, holding her finger with one hand and smoothing the plastic strip with the other. Low and softly spoken, his words seemed a lover's question.

"We're fine. The kids were a bit confused when I told them about Jenny, but now they're happy for you. What about you? How are you doing?"

Tucker continued to administer to her finger long past necessity. He whispered, "I miss you."

"Shh. Don't." She was about to place her bandaged finger over his lips, but then thought better of it. "We'd better rejoin the others."

Julia was discussing the helicopter service provided by the Harmony Rescue Squad when Cathryn and Tucker stepped outside. "They'll have you at a hospital on the mainland like that." She snapped her fingers.

"That's reassuring to know," Jenny said. Tucker handed her a glass of iced tea. She smiled up at him and said, "Thanks, sweetie."

As innocuous as Cathryn's stolen moment with Tucker had been, she felt like pond scum. Maybe it was time to admit that this mixing with him and Jenny was a mistake and the best thing she could do for everyone concerned was to keep her distance.

"Or you could give birth to your baby here," Lauren said. "That's what I intend to do. Harmony has an excellent midwife. She's a certified nurse-practitioner who'll deliver in your home if that's what you want, although she much prefers the clinic."

"A midwife. Now that's a thought."

Tucker remained standing, his eyes on the group playing badminton. "I thought you wanted to return home to have the baby."

"I do. I prefer to be near my mother. The girls and I are just talking...you know, in case our little soccer player decides to make an early appearance. Lauren thinks I've already dropped, and she should know. She's the oldest of five and remembers her mother's pregnancies."

To Cathryn's eye, Tucker appeared to pale. "Do you mind if I go play badminton, too?" he asked no one in particular.

"Of course not." Jenny smiled up at him again. When he was out of earshot, she said, "He's been so sweet about this whole thing."

"He certainly has," Lauren said, flicking a stealthy glance at Cathryn.

Jenny lowered her eyes, her brow pinched. "I know what you all are thinking. I'm a rotten person for putting Tuck off so long and I don't deserve him." She wisely didn't wait for corroboration. "But marriage is such an important step, and, well, it's no secret that Tuck and I aren't exactly head-over-heels with each other. There's been a lot to consider."

Jenny's eyes remained lowered, but the lines of her face

and the slope of her posture betrayed her sadness anyway. A curious sadness, Cathryn thought.

But then Jenny lifted her chin and smiled valiantly. "However, Tucker's a good man. I know that now. I also know how lucky I am to have him. And if I give our marriage even half the effort he's making, I know we'll be okay."

For all the time Cathryn had spent with Jenny, she'd never probed for personal details of her and Tucker's relationship. She hadn't really wanted to know them. Now, while part of her wished she could dislike Jenny for not being in love with Tucker—was the girl out of her mind?— Cathryn's better part applauded her honesty and willingness to work at the marriage. As she'd once said to Tucker, with that attitude, success was just a matter of time.

"Speaking of marriage," said the much-too-outspoken Lauren, "when do you and Tuck plan to tie the knot?"

Jenny swirled her iced tea. "That depends on how soon we can make arrangements." She lifted her trusting green eyes and fixed them on Cathryn. "I hate putting you on the spot like this, but I was wondering if you could help?"

Cathryn glanced behind her, but no one else was standing near.

Jenny laughed. "Yes, you."

"Me? You want me to help?"

Jenny wiggled forward to the edge of her seat. "If you don't mind. It'd mean the world to me, Cath."

Oh no, oh no, oh no!

Julia came to Cathryn's rescue. "I wasn't aware you planned to have the ceremony here. I thought you'd prefer your hometown, your family's church."

"I did consider it, but that was before I came to Harmony. It's a beautiful place to have a wedding, and it *is* Tuck's hometown, sort of, and we'll be back in Missouri soon enough.''

Anxiety and dread jostled within Cathryn's heart. ''What do you mean, Jenny?''

''My parents are giving us three acres of their land and the deposit to start building a house.''

''Oh.'' *Please, let this be a smile on my face.*

Lauren filled the awkward silence. ''What sort of wedding do you have in mind?''

''Obviously, not large. Thirty guests at most. But I'd still like to do it up right. My parents will be flying out. Some relatives and high school friends, too.''

Cathryn finally marshalled her thoughts. ''Oh, Jen, I really don't have the time to cook for that many people—if that's what you have in mind.''

''Oh, no. No!'' the girl laughed. ''All I need is your advice and organizational skills. My father will foot the bill for everything—the caterer, the flowers, the music...''

''Oh.'' Cathryn's gaze shifted to Julia, who could provide top-notch deejay services; to Lauren, who someday planned to rent out the grounds at Rockland House for weddings. Neither said a word.

''Where would you like to have it?'' Cathryn inquired.

''At this late date, anywhere. Beggars can't be choosers.''

''Thirty people?''

''Yes, at the very most.''

Cathryn sighed. Jenny was looking at her so hopefully. ''I'll call around, see what I can find.''

The young woman pressed her hands together and held them to her chin. ''Thank you!''

''YOU'RE REALLY GOING to help her?'' Lauren asked two days later.

''What else can I do?'' Cathryn fit the mattress into the

bassinet she was letting her friend borrow, then reached for a soft jersey sheet.

"It just doesn't seem fair." Lauren pouted, tying one of the white ribbons that garnished the frilly hood. "You and Tuck were on the road to something really...significant."

"Life isn't always fair, Laur. After everything you've been through, you should know that."

Lauren widened her eyes in concession, then let the thought slide to exclaim, "Oh, this is adorable!" She circled the bassinet, admiring Cathryn's handiwork.

"Enjoy," Cathryn said, rolling the small crib alongside Lauren and Cam's canopy bed. The windows were open, and sunshine and soft ocean breezes filled the "Lady Gray suite."

"I still think it's unfair," Lauren said as they stepped out to the hall. "I usually cringe when I hear the term soul mates but you and Tucker are."

Cathryn cast her an exasperated glance. "Will you stop! I have something important to discuss with you."

"Oh? What's up?"

"I'd like to rent your west lawn the Saturday after next for the wedding. I've found a tent and a caterer, but I can't find a satisfactory location."

"How about the school cafeteria?" Lauren said without mercy. "Or better yet, one of the parlors at D'Autell's."

Cathryn stopped at the top of the stairs. "This is a wedding, Lauren, not a funeral, and the groom happens to be Tucker. Therefore, I intend to do the very best job I can."

Lauren studied her determined expression. "You love him that much, huh?"

"No." Cathryn was adamant. "It isn't love. Nothing like that. I just don't want anyone saying anything negative about him, or about his wedding, or his wife. That's all."

They descended three steps and stopped again. "I understand,'' Lauren said, her hand on Cathryn's arm. "But I have to ask myself, if that isn't love, what is?''

Cathryn stared at her wise lifelong friend in stunned silence. Love? Could it be?

Lauren wrapped her arm across Cathryn's shoulder, gave her a squeeze, and they continued down the stairs. "You're right, Cath. The west lawn would be perfect.''

A WEEK INTO organizing Tucker and Jen's wedding, and with less than a week to go, Cathryn quite unexpectedly ran into her ex-husband. She literally bumped into him on the sidewalk outside the Five-and-Dime and nearly dropped the bag of wedding favors she'd just bought.

"Hey, Cath!'' He steadied her, holding her by the arms.

"Dylan?''

"Hi. Where are you off to in such a hurry?''

"Oh,'' she shrugged. "Work. I'm just trying to sneak in some errands before my shift begins. And you?'' He was dressed in a gray and blue striped polo shirt, jeans and soil-encrusted workboots. His hair was golden from the summer sun, his skin deeply tanned.

"Just coming from the diner, heading back to a job on Barney's Cove.'' He glanced at his watch. "I've already eaten, but can I treat you to lunch?''

"Thanks, but I've eaten, too.'' On impulse she added, "How about a gelato instead?''

"Great.''

They crossed Water Street and made their selections at a cart in Shipyard Park. Dylan led her to a bench near the bandstand. "Are the kids with your mother today?'' he asked, sitting with his arm draped comfortably along the backrest.

"Yes. She's been wonderful about baby-sitting while I work. I don't know what I'd do without her.''

"Well, you know my mother will watch them, too."

"Yes. And I intend to take her up on her offer."

Dylan nodded, murmuring, "Good, good."

Cathryn was struck by the novelty of the moment. They hadn't conversed amiably in months. When he came for the children, he usually stood at the door and she made herself busy elsewhere in the house.

"How's the landscaping business these days?"

"Booming." He laughed, shaking his head. "I must be crazy, selling out now."

"Is the deal already done?" she asked, surprised.

"No, not yet, but everything's in place. Jack Mendoza takes over in September."

"Then what?"

Dylan swallowed and his handsome features sobered. "I move to New York with Zoe."

Cathryn stared at her quickly melting confection, imagining the adjustments he'd have to make in the near future. "Don't be scared."

Dylan took her gelato from her and tossed it, along with his own, into a trash container. "How do you know I'm scared?"

"The same way you know I had no interest in that gelato. We were married to each other for twelve years."

He sighed, reached over and covered her hands with one of his. "Yes, we were."

They said nothing for several minutes, just sat watching boats pass in the harbor.

"I don't know, Cath," Dylan resumed as if they'd been talking all that time. "Maybe we got married too young. Maybe we should've waited like Julia and Ben and Lauren and Cam. Our personalities would've been better developed...our interests. We would've been able to make more mature choices."

"Maybe. Maybe not. I can't decide. In any case, I've come to the conclusion there's nothing to be gained in trying to find reasons or assign blame. I've lost interest in it. I just want to move on," she said, surprising herself. "We had some wonderful years together, Dylan, some wonderful times."

His hand tightened over hers.

"Those memories, I'll hang on to," she continued. "They're a much more secure base than the others to step off from. The others...I can't say I've let them go yet, but I'm getting there, and I want you to know I wish you well."

Dylan's brow furrowed as he scowled at the horizon. "I don't understand how you can be so generous."

She pulled her hands from his and to lighten the mood said, "Me either."

Out of the blue she announced, "I'm thinking of selling the house."

Dylan's head jerked in surprise. "Huh?"

"The house. I may sell it someday. Would you mind?"

"No, of course not. It's yours to do with as you please, but..."

"It holds too many memories, Dylan. Plus, I'm sure I can live more economically in something smaller."

He shrugged. "As I said, it's yours. No need to ask my permission."

"I wasn't. I guess I was just telling you." Cathryn heard the clock chiming in the Congregational Church tower. "Yikes. Gotta run." She shot to her feet. "This week my boss is out and I'm in charge of the main dining room."

Dylan rose, too. They smiled kindly at each other. "Take care of yourself, Cath."

"I will. You too, Dylan." Then Cathryn turned and dashed across the street, dodging cars just off the ferry. Fleet and light, she skimmed the ground, a woman who'd found her footing at last.

JENNY'S FOOTSTEPS crunched on the gravel outside the garage. Tucker's spirits dipped, as they always did when she entered his consciousness, reminding him of their marriage, a mere four days away.

Her shadow preceded her. So did her voice. "I love your suggestion, but let's see what Tucker thinks."

"See what I think about what?" On his back on a dolly, Tucker skated halfway out from under the Ford he was working on, just as Jenny stepped into the garage with Cathryn. He winked at his soon-to-be-bride, but the joy suddenly shooting through him came not from her but from seeing Cathryn. He hadn't expected her to come by today.

Jenny responded, "Having a string quartet instead of recorded music during the ceremony."

Tucker gazed innocuously at Cathryn, his thoughts far from innocuous. "Isn't it kind of late to find a string quartet?"

Gazing at him over Jenny's shoulder, Cathryn probably thought she was hiding the yearning in her eyes. "Yes, ordinarily. But a group that was supposed to play at another wedding just became available. The wedding was cancelled."

Tucker scratched his head and glanced at Jenny. "Hell, I don't care. Do whatever you think is best."

Jenny beamed. "Thanks, sweetie," she said, missing the point that he *really* didn't care. In fact, there wasn't one bone in his body that was interested in this wedding.

Cathryn started for the door. "Let's go book the group, then." She paused, frowning. "Jenny? Are you okay?"

Eyes wide, Jenny stood slightly hunched over, hands on her stomach, a grimace on her face. Tucker rolled all the way out from under the car, glancing back and forth from Cathryn to Jenny.

After what seemed an eternity, Jenny relaxed her shoulders and expelled her breath. "Whew!" She shook her head and laughed unconvincingly. "Junior's sure acting up today."

"Acting up?" Cathryn asked, her concern infectious. Tucker sat up stiffly.

"Yeah. Rolling around. Turning over," Jenny answered with a vague shrug. "Who knows what he's doing in there."

"How about we just stay here a moment and talk? Whose car are you working on, Tucker?"

Although he didn't understand why Cathryn had asked such a question, he trusted her implicitly and answered, and somehow they stretched it into a conversation. Just when the topic had been stretched to its absolute thinnest, Jenny stiffened again.

"Oh, no. Here he goes again."

"How does it feel, Jen?

"Painful. Like he's trying to…get…" She gritted her teeth over the rest of her sentence and leaned against Cathryn for support. Cathryn placed a hand on Jenny's stomach and glanced at Tucker.

"She's having a contraction, Tuck."

"I'm wh-what?" Jenny panted, round-eyed. "I—I—I c-can't be-e." She expelled a relaxed breath. "I have another month."

"Tell that to the baby."

Tucker was on his feet and by Jenny's side without knowing how he got there. "Sit down. Here. Sit." He swung a chair to the back of her knees and pushed her into it. "What should we do?" he asked Cathryn.

"What have you decided to do? What's your plan?"

"I don't know." He squatted by the chair. "Do we have a plan, Jen?"

"Yes, but I doubt we'll make it to St. Louis in time."

He straightened to his full height. "Now she decides to be a comedian." He squatted again. "Contingency plan?"

"The clinic. The midwife," Jenny answered him, then looked up at Cathryn. "Do you think that's possible? She's never seen me as a patient."

"She isn't going to have much choice, is she? Tucker, take Jen inside and get a small bag ready—simple toiletries, a nightgown, tapes she might want to listen to during labor. Then call the clinic and tell them you'll be coming in and you need the midwife. If she's not available, the clinic retains two doctors who I'm sure can figure out from their twenty-odd years of combined training how to deliver a baby."

"Hey, where are you going?"

"Home." Cathryn fitted the strap of her purse over her shoulder.

"But… Can't you…?"

She shook her head. "No, I can't. I…have to go to work." It was probably the truth, yet Tucker thought he saw something else in her eyes. A plea.

"You'd better run then," Jenny said graciously. "And don't worry about us. Babies take a while to be born, especially first babies. We'll be fine."

Cathryn glanced at Tucker one more time, one last plea. "Yes, we'll be fine," he told her, the words convincing because they sprang from love. "Go to work."

Cathryn wished Jenny luck and a speedy delivery, gave her a warm hug, then waved goodbye with a promise to visit the clinic later. The next moment Tucker was on his own.

TUCKER FILLED OUT about forty-seven forms at the front desk, with a behemoth of a nurse named Mrs. Beasly breathing down his neck. She'd been on duty the night he'd brought Justin and Cathryn in, too. He also remembered her from his misspent youth, from her tending to a broken wrist he'd incurred in a fall while learning to ride his first Harley.

Accepting the forms from him, she said, "You are planning to marry that girl, Mr. Tucker. Aren't you?"

"Yes, ma'am," he replied. She believed him now about as much as she'd believed him when he'd agreed to get rid of his bike.

Meanwhile, Jenny had been whisked off to the birthing room to be prepped. When he joined her, she was dressed in a hospital johnny and funny socks.

"Shouldn't you be in bed or something?" he asked, gripping her elbows from behind.

"Uh-uh. Walking's good. It speeds labor." She looked down at one of his hands, then the other, and chuckled. "I can stand on my own, Tuck. I'm not crippled."

"Oh. How about I walk beside you then?"

"Thanks. I'd love that."

A woman in her late thirties, with long brown hair plaited in a single thick braid, entered the room wheeling a monitor. A stethoscope swung over her blue smock.

"This is Louise, the midwife," Jenny said to Tucker, smiling as if the woman was already a trusted friend.

"And you must be Tucker." The woman extended her hand. "Jenny's been telling me all about you."

"And you're still smiling?" he said.

Louise's smile only broadened and in an aside to Jenny, she said, "He's every bit the charmer you painted him to be."

"How's Jen doing?"

"Great."

"You don't foresee any problems with the baby being a little early?"

"Not really." The midwife was about to add something, when Jenny braced against the wall and endured another contraction.

Tucker hovered over her, feeling helpless. "Are we close?" he asked the midwife.

"To what?" Unconcerned, she popped up from behind the bed where she'd plugged in the monitor.

"The birth."

"Sorry to disappoint you, but I believe we have a few hours yet."

A few hours! And already he felt weak in the knees? He wasn't going to make it, especially if the delivery turned out to be anything like the tape he'd watched at Cathryn's, *The Miracle of Birth*.

"Let's get you hooked up, Jen, and see how the baby's doing," the midwife said cheerfully. She fitted a belt around Jenny's waist and positioned a heavy disc over her belly.

A few minutes later Tucker held a paper coming out of the monitor in ticker-tape fashion. "This is the baby's heart-beat?"

"Yes, Steady and strong, just the way we like it."

He gaped at the line—at the visible manifestation of the life he'd created. "Oh, God. Look, Jen."

But Jenny was having another contraction and missed the wonder in his eyes. For a brief moment, he wished Cathryn were present to share his astonishment. She was so much a part of this occasion, the very reason he and Jenny were together, she should be here, he thought.

"That's a reflection of Jen's contraction," Louise explained, indicating a variation in the pattern on the paper. "It's almost over. See? It's almost back to where it was."

Tucker stared, awestruck, at the pattern on the ever-

lengthening paper—heartbeat and contraction, baby and
mother inextricably entwined. *It's time,* the pattern whispered. Time to pledge total commitment. Somewhere deep
inside, Cathryn would always be a part of him, but his life's
path didn't lie with her. It lay here, in his hands. Cathryn
had taught him he could love. Now it was time to move on
and love some more.

"What can I do?" he asked Louise.

The midwife smiled, recognizing a man who was indeed
ready to help. "Run the water in that tub, please. Not too
hot. Soaking will ease Jen's contractions somewhat."

Jenny went into deep labor early that evening, about eight
hours after her first contraction in the garage. Until then
there had been room for conversation. Jenny had even insisted Tucker have something to eat. Now, however, the
birthing room crackled with wall-to-wall tension. Tucker felt
guilty and helpless, watching the contractions come on,
wringing perspiration and grunts of pain from her. He
dreaded each onslaught, sweated through the duration,
waited, waited, barely breathing, for the comforting tones
of the midwife as she said, "Good one. You're doing great,
Jen."

He fetched ice chips and placed them in Jen's mouth. He
rubbed her back, applied cool washcloths to her face and
let her squeeze his fingers until they turned blue. And finally
the tension peaked.

"The baby is crowning," Louise said. "It won't be long
now." And a short time later, "That's it, Jen, keep pushing,
almost there, almost... Yes!"

Suddenly the baby came sliding into the world. It was
wet, bloody, wrinkled—and absolutely the most beautiful
creature Tucker had ever beheld. "It's a girl, Jen," he
choked out through tears. "A little girl."

Jenny sagged against the upraised bed, exhausted but

smiling like a Renaissance Madonna. The baby began a lusty crying and her mother's smile expanded into a joyous laugh.

Louise placed the newborn on Jenny's stomach and covered her with a soft receiving blanket. Comforted by the warmth and the closeness to her mother, the baby stopped crying and opened her eyes.

Tucker leaned down, forearms braced on the bed, and stroked the baby's sticky head with his index finger. This was exactly what he'd dreamed about back in February. He'd gotten his wish, and if his joy was bittersweet, he refused to admit it. "Hey, little lady," he whispered. "This is your old man looking at you. I love you."

Louise, busy with cleaning and stitching, smiled as the familiar process of bonding unfolded. After a while she asked, "Would you like to cut the umbilical cord, Tucker?"

"Me? Uh, no. I'll let you do the honors. Thanks anyway."

A staff nurse joined them, placed the swaddled infant in a clear plastic bassinet and wheeled her off to an examination room.

"Dr. Lawrence is going to run some routine tests," Louise said. "You can go too, Tucker. It shouldn't take more than a half hour."

"No, I'll stay with Jen."

Tucker got Mrs. Beasly to bring Jenny a sandwich and milk. She was famished, not having eaten all day. After Jenny ate, the nurse returned, helped her into a clean nightgown and wheeled her into a regular-care room.

Watching his soon-to-be wife settle into her pillow, Tucker thought, *I should tell her I love her. For what she's just endured, it's the least I can do.* But Jenny closed her eyes and within seconds was asleep. *I will,* he promised her silently. *I will.*

A short, stout man of about forty, with a balding pate and smooth red cheeks, returned the baby. Positioning the bassinet alongside the bed, he introduced himself as Dr. Lawrence. Although he was quiet about it, Jenny woke instantly, already developing a mother's radar. He placed the baby in her eager arms, said she weighed in at seven pounds, eight ounces, and if she was early, he couldn't see any evidence of it.

While he continued with his report on the baby's health, Tucker became uncomfortably aware of the doctor's scrutiny. As he spoke, he gazed continually from Jenny to Tucker, Tucker to Jenny, his eyes searching. For what? Tucker possessed a certain radar of his own. "What's the matter?" he finally asked. "Is something wrong with the baby? What are you not telling us?"

"Oh, good heavens, no." The doctor chuckled. "I'm so sorry." He waved his hands like windshield wipers, whisking away the unfortunate misinterpretation. "I'm just stymied, trying to figure out which one of you is of Asian descent."

Tucker felt like a cartoon character, head spinning, neck coiling higher and higher. "What are you talking about?"

"The baby. She's definitely…I mean, her features are…" The doctor paused, swallowed and pulled on his collar as if it was choking him. "Oh, dear," he muttered softly.

Tucker glanced at the baby in Jenny's arms and for the first time noticed the wisps of straight black hair, the round face, the distinctive slant to the eyes.

Simultaneously, Jenny gasped. With her mouth hanging open, she turned white, then red, and her expression crumpled. She lifted the baby, buried her face in the pink receiving blanket and broke into heart-wrenching sobs.

Tucker and the doctor rushed to her side in alarm, partly for her sake, mostly for the baby's. But there really was no cause for worry. Jenny lowered the baby unharmed, and though she continued to cry, Tucker realized her tears sprang from joy.

Now he was really confused.

CHAPTER FIFTEEN

THE RESTAURANT WAS short on help but hardly on customers, and Cathryn's shift stretched from seven hours to ten. By the time she got home, the children were in bed and her mother was dozing in front of the TV.

Cathryn sagged onto the sofa beside her, tired and unsettled. She was making good money at waitressing, but the hours weren't worth it. If she wasn't careful, by the time she had supper with her children again, Justin would be married.

She'd been thinking of quitting the restaurant, but the help-wanted ads in the *Island Record* only listed more of what she'd already done. Two days ago, however, while visiting a flower shop to order bouquets for Tucker and Jenny's wedding, the owner, who also served as a wedding consultant, had mentioned she was looking for a part-time assistant, and asked if Cathryn was interested. Cathryn didn't have any formal training in floral design, so she'd immediately said no. Right about now, though, she was willing to wing it. If the job didn't work out, well, c'est la vie. First chance she got, she decided, she was going to pay the florist another visit.

"Oh!" Her mother woke with a start.

"Hi, Mom. Only me."

"What time is it?"

"After ten." Cathryn asked the usual questions: How were the kids? Were there any phone calls? Where was the day's mail? Finally she felt she could approach the subject that had been on her mind all day.

"By any chance, do you know if Jenny's had her baby yet?"

Her mother sat forward, energized by the reminder. "Yes, I called the clinic around eight o'clock. It's a girl."

"Oh, great." Cathryn smiled in relief.

Her mother added, "Seven pounds...something."

"Really?"

"Hmm. That surprised me, too. It's probably best Jenny had her early. Imagine if she'd gone full term?"

"Mmm. So, how is everyone?"

"Apparently, fine. That's all the desk person said. I think it was Martha Beasly, and you know how she is. The delivery went well, and mother and daughter are fine. End of report."

Cathryn longed to ask about Tucker, too, but that would aim a spotlight on feelings she preferred stayed hidden. "Do you know how long she'll be at the clinic?"

"Oh, heck. I forgot to ask."

"It doesn't matter. She's sure to be there tomorrow."

Her mother's tone changed ever so slightly, revealing she knew all about Cathryn's torment. "Are you going to visit?"

"I should." Cathryn swallowed.

Meg reached over and rubbed her daughter's back, her silence eloquent.

"I'm all right, Mom. Really."

Nodding, Meg got to her feet. "Well, give Jenny my best and tell her I'll see her at home."

"Will do." Cathryn kissed her mother's cheek, told her to drive carefully and went upstairs to bed.

CATHRYN STOOD in the doorway of Jenny's room, obscured by a large bouquet of garden flowers which the children had helped her pick. Her first impulse, to see if Tucker was in the room, infuriated her. He wasn't. Jenny was alone, sitting up in bed, nursing her baby. "Jenny?" Cathryn said.

The young mother lifted her eyes slowly. "Cathryn, hi!" She beamed.

"Congratulations, Mom." Despite her lingering feelings for Tucker, Cathryn stepped into the room smiling, remembering well the joy of being in the younger woman's place. "I'm so happy for you," she said, pressing her cheek to the crown of Jenny's head.

"Me too. Isn't she beautiful?"

"Oh, she is!" Cathryn exclaimed softly, although she couldn't see much of the capped and wrapped infant. "So tiny. I always forget. Have you named her yet?"

"No, I'm waiting for…" Jenny lowered her eyes and grinned. "…input from her daddy."

"Oh, I brought you these."

"Thank you. How pretty."

"How was your delivery?" Cathryn asked as she arranged the flowers in a vase.

"Awesome!" Jenny prattled on and Cathryn tried to follow, but after a while she realized the only details she absorbed were the ones that involved Tucker. He'd been a champ, apparently. The images Jenny painted of him made Cathryn proud…as well as brokenhearted. After sharing such a momentous experience, Tucker was indisputably Jenny's now.

Dipping her nose into the bouquet, she asked as casually as possible, "Where is Tucker, anyway?" Cathryn expected Jenny to say he'd gone home to nap or to shower. When she answered that he'd gone to the airport, Cathryn swiveled. "The airport?"

"Yes." Jenny chewed on her lower lip, looking as if she was making a decision. "Have a seat, Cath."

"I…" Cathryn couldn't think of an excuse.

"Please. I owe you an explanation."

Cathryn sat, watched Jenny stroking her baby's cheek with the tip of a finger, gathering her thoughts.

"When I met Tucker last fall I was just coming off a bad experience involving another man. His name was Lee Quan." Seeing Cathryn's puzzlement deepen, she added, "Yes, he's Chinese. We met at my dentist's. Lee had just graduated from dental school and was working as an associate." Jenny grinned. "I know. It's a crazy place to meet a guy, right?"

Cathryn shrugged. "Whatever works."

"Anyway, we dated about five months and fell very much in love, despite his family's opposition to the relationship. They're old world and had already arranged for him to marry someone else. My parents weren't exactly crazy about us, either. They don't see many mixed-race couples where they live, and still think of them as, I don't know, abnormal or something."

Cathryn's breathing had become shallow, her spine rigid. "What happened to you and Lee?"

"His parents had their way. They forced him to break up with me."

"And he did, even though he loved you?"

"Oh, yes, and I've never blamed him. It was a complicated issue…you know…family honor?"

"Your parents must've been relieved."

"Oh, they were. The things they said really angered me. To get back at them, I'm afraid I went a little wild. They wanted me to date white guys? Sure, I said. I could do that. So I went searching for the most unacceptable white guys I could find, guys who'd make my parents think twice about race and a man's true worth.''

''And you found Tucker?''

Jenny nodded. ''Although, to be honest, it only took a couple of dates for me to realize he was a pretty decent person.''

''But not enough of one for you to want to marry him when you got pregnant.''

Jenny gazed at her slumbering baby. ''That had more to do with how I still loved Lee. But as the pregnancy progressed and Tucker kept calling…well, you know the rest.''

Cathryn blinked, stupidly she imagined. ''Yeah?''

''The upshot of this is a real kicker, Cathryn. I hope you're prepared.''

Cathryn heard her heart beating in her ears. ''Go on.''

''It wasn't until last night, after the baby was born, that I realized Tucker wasn't the man who'd made me pregnant. It was Lee. He and I slept together the night we broke up. We were kind of careless about birth control, but it wasn't a likely time of month for me to get pregnant, so I never thought any more of it. Then, just a couple of weeks later, I was with Tucker.'' She lowered her eyes and tears coursed down her cheeks. ''It was a terrible thing to do. I'm not proud of it.'' She sniffed, reached for a tissue and pressed it to her nose.

''So T-Tucker i-isn't…'' Cathryn clung to the arms of the chair. She hadn't experienced this weightless, breathless feeling since she'd gone through Space Mountain.

''No, he isn't the baby's father.''

Cathryn laughed, sort of. Actually it sounded to her like a strangled yip. ''Are you sure?''

''Yes. We did blood tests last night. Besides,'' Jenny said, smiling down at her baby, ''I'd know Lee's mouth anywhere.''

Cathryn laughed again. "What are you going to do now? Is the wedding still on for Saturday?"

Jenny's eyes gleamed. "Yes."

If hope had found a ray of sunlight in which to blossom, it died with Jenny's answer. Apparently, Tucker was willing to marry her anyway. Such was the power, the miracle, of birth.

"The only difference, of course," Jenny said, chuckling, "will be in the groom."

"Huh?"

"The groom. Tucker insisted I call Lee last night. I was ashamed to, but Tucker said a man has a right to know when he's become a father."

"Then—" Cathryn's spirits zoomed again "—you're not marrying Tucker?"

"Oh, no. I could never do that now. Poor guy. He took the news surprisingly well, though."

"And the airport?"

Jenny smiled. "Lee's arriving on the eleven o'clock shuttle. Tucker's gone to pick him up."

Cathryn laughed incredulously again. "But what about Lee's family?"

"I come first, he says, and if they can't accept me, that's too bad. He's marrying me anyway."

Just then, Cathryn heard Tucker's voice in the corridor. Every cell in her being came vibrantly awake. He paused in the doorway to let an excited young man precede him into the room.

"Lee!" Jenny cried.

The young man hurried to her side, and whether they hugged or kissed, Cathryn was unaware. Her eyes had met Tucker's and never strayed, as she stood and walked toward him.

"You understand the situation?" he asked her, gesturing toward the reunited couple.

"Yes. Jen explained."

Tucker's jaw was shadowed with more than a day's growth of beard, his hair was disheveled and in need of a trim, and he was wearing tight jeans and an old black T-shirt that contoured his muscular chest. On it was the logo: Live fast. Die young. Leave a good-looking corpse. He looked delectable.

Tucker saw her staring at the shirt. "I haven't done any laundry since Jen arrived. It's the only clean shirt I could find." Then, pointing his stubbled chin toward the bed, he said, "Let's give them some privacy."

Cathryn walked out to the corridor and he closed the door. For a while they simply stood there, staring at each other. It was over. The door was literally and figuratively closed on Jenny. They smiled, sighed deeply, and their breathing took on a more relaxed rhythm.

"Have you had lunch?" Tucker asked.

She shook her head. "Let's go see what's available."

On their way by the front desk, Mrs. Beasly glanced up from a chart she was reading and scowled at Tucker over her glasses.

"Morning, Nurse *Beastly*." He grinned and winked. The woman snorted. Leaning toward Cathryn he whispered loudly, "She's very confused."

They bought soda and candy bars from a vending machine and went outside to a wooden bench in the shade by the side door. Tucker's Mustang, parked alongside her van, shimmered with heat in the paved lot before them.

Tucker unwrapped his Snickers and took a bite. "Quite a development, huh?" he mumbled.

"Sure is." Cathryn sipped from her can of Orange Crush

and shot him a sidelong glance. "You look tired. Have you gotten any sleep?"

"Some."

He also looked a little sad, Cathryn was dismayed to see. "After all these months, it must be a tremendous letdown, finding out the baby isn't yours."

He agreed with an expressive lift of his eyebrows. "Especially after going through labor and delivery. I really reached a point last night where…" His words faded. He shrugged. "But it has a happy ending, and that's all that matters." He brightened. "And you know what? They want me to be the baby's godfather."

"No! Well, that's something." She peeled back the wrapper of her Butterfinger and took a bite. The chocolate was beginning to melt in the July heat.

"Damn right. It's a responsibility I don't take lightly."

"When's the christening?"

"I'm not sure. Soon. Jen's just waiting for a friend to fly in to be godmother."

"Gonna be busy around here. They want to get married Saturday."

Tucker popped open his Coke.

"Mmm, I know."

After guzzling half the can, he rested it on the seat beside him. "The wedding'll probably be smaller than planned. She's going to call her folks today, and after they hear her news, she doubts they'll come."

"Sad."

"Yes. And so unnecessary." Tucker spoke around another bite of candy.

"Does Lee have a place to stay tonight?"

Tucker stretched out his long legs and crossed them at the ankles. "Yeah. He'll sleep at my house, but he's hoping to find a rental cottage for a week or two, someplace where Jen can rest before they fly home.''

''At this time of year? Good luck.''

''I know.'' Tucker's drone expressed his dread. ''They can stay with me, of course.''

''But a week or two of houseguests, Tucker?''

He sighed and finished off his Snickers.

''I have an idea,'' she said brightly.

He squinted at her, one eyebrow cautiously arched, reminding her of someone peeking out of a bunker. ''It was an idea of yours that got me in all this trouble to begin with.''

''Was not. You did that all on your own. Anyway, here's the idea. How about you let Lee and Jen use your house and you come stay at mine? I have tons of room, including a pull-out couch in the basement.''

Tucker gazed up at the summer-fluffy clouds in the summer-blue sky, a suppressed smile tugging at his lips. ''Not a good idea, Cathryn.''

''Why not?''

''I might be tempted to…well, you know…pick up where we left off.''

Yes! sang her heart. *Yes, oh, yes!* She'd never gone hanggliding, but she imagined her exhilaration was similar to what a person must feel while riding a wind current.

''Is there something wrong with that—with our picking up where we left off?'' she asked him.

Focused on the tips of his shoes now, he said, ''There could be. Before long everyone's going to know the baby isn't mine, but since I was ready to marry Jen, I must've believed it was. From that they'll deduce the obvious, that I was sleeping with her, a woman so indiscriminate she didn't even know who'd gotten her pregnant. It'd be incorrect and unfair, but they wouldn't know that, or care.'' He glanced at Cathryn quickly before he returned to studying his shoes. "I don't want any of my garbage spilling over on you."

"And how, may I ask, would that happen?"

"Just by association. People might say you're no better than me, or just like Jenny, or on your way to a life of dissolution."

Cathryn groaned. "I've created a monster. You really care about what people might say? And I repeat *might*."

"Only if it bothers you." He turned his head and gazed at her, his eyes lingering this time.

"It doesn't. In the first place, what I do and who I associate with is nobody's business. And, second, I can handle any misconceptions that arise—if they arise."

He nodded as if mentally eliminating one objection from an invisible list. "How about the fact that I chose Jenny over you? When it came down to you and her, I let you go. You must be angry as hell over that. Hurt, too, I bet."

Cathryn expelled a sigh of exasperation. "You had no choice in the matter. You would've been a jerk not to choose her. And if I remember correctly, I was the one who made the decision, not you."

"But I went along with it. I didn't have to."

"Tucker, read my lips. I am not mad. I am not hurt."

He nodded again, his compressed lips turning up at one corner. "Okay, what about the kids? How can I possibly explain this baby mix-up to them?"

"Don't underestimate what my kids can and can't understand. They'll surprise you every time."

"Yes, but wouldn't it bother you that I'd be a bad example to them? Or that people might think you're crazy for letting me hang around them?"

Cathryn had heard enough. She hauled back and whacked his head. "Snap *out* of it!"

"Ow!" He glowered at her. With his lips still forming an *O* she kissed him, hard and fast.

"I don't care about any of that," she said.

"I didn't think you did. I was only asking to make sure."

Cathryn cradled the head she'd just whomped and rubbed it. "Sorry." But she grinned because he was grinning, and everything was right with the world.

"Ah, Cath…" He sighed, running his fingers up her neck and over the sides of her face into her hair. "We came so close to losing each other forever. I've never felt so miserable or scared in my life." He laughed softly, incredulously, drawing her toward him and resting his lips on her forehead. "Even last night, when I decided it was time to forget you and commit myself to Jenny, I knew it wasn't possible. I knew I'd always love you."

Cathryn stopped breathing. Slowly, she backed away.

His eyes roamed her face, unashamedly devouring her. "Yes, you heard right. I used the L word. What are you gonna do about it?"

"There's nothing I can do except…tell you I love you, too."

Tucker pulled her against him and held her so close she could barely breathe, but she didn't mind. There was no place on earth she preferred to be.

"However…" she said, muffled against his neck. He released the pressure of his hold and let her speak. "However, as soon as we get up off this bench, we're going to pretend we never said it—that word. Okay? We're going to take things nice and easy for a while."

"Fair enough." Tucker sat back.

"Hey, where are you going?" She gripped his shirt. "Kissing is allowable, and I wasn't done."

"Cathryn, we're sitting outside the cl—"

His words got swallowed up in her kiss. At first Tucker

responded with self-conscious stiffness, but she persisted and soon heard the familiar wanting sound deep in his throat that signaled his growing need.

They were still kissing when the side door opened and the desk nurse came marching out, car keys in hand. She noticed them and finally her outrage spilled over. "Mr. Lang!"

Reluctantly Cathryn lifted her mouth from Tucker's and, still embracing, they peeked up at the formidable woman standing over them, hands on her wide hips.

"A man with lower morals I have never met!" she said. "You deserve to be hung by your heels and flayed!"

"Pardon me?" Tucker said politely. "Did you say *flayed* or *filleted?*"

The woman's enormous bosom heaved. Her eyes and nostrils flared. "I never!" she sputtered, stalking off toward her car.

"It makes a difference," Tucker called after her. "What do you think she said, Cath, flayed or filleted?"

The nurse left rubber, peeling out of the lot. Tucker chuckled. "See what I mean? See what you'll be getting into? My reputation in this town is dirt. Always has been. Always will be. And this time it wasn't even my fault! *You* were the one doing all the kissing and groping."

"I have to confess, you're right. But we can change that, you know. I don't mind if you do all the kissing and groping for a while."

Tucker threw back his head and laughed, drawing her against his rumbling chest. "You're incorrigible."

"No, no. We don't have to do it right here. We can go to my van. Come on. I've always wondered what it'd be like to make out in a van." She stood and tugged Tucker's hand.

Laughing and shaking his head, he got to his feet and followed her.

CHAPTER SIXTEEN

Two Years Later

CATHRYN AND Tucker were married on a sunny day in July in a traditional church ceremony amid two hundred of their closest friends.

They had tried to approach their romance slow and easy. Tucker had wanted Cathryn to take time to discover herself and enjoy her independence. He'd even encouraged her to date other men, and she had. He'd also figured the kids needed a transitional period to get used to not having Dylan around before they had him.

But the kids were fine with Tucker's being around and actually played matchmaker when they could, and after a while he and Cathryn gave up on slow and easy—what was the point, when it only made them miserable?—and set a wedding date. Today's date.

Cathryn had put her house on the market and it sold over the winter, just in time for her and Tucker to buy the property adjacent to the one he'd inherited from his uncle. They'd moved in during late spring.

It wasn't a fancy house nor a particularly large one, but it was sturdy and had other advantages, and its location was ideal. Tucker remained just a path's walk away from Lang's Auto Repair, which he continued to operate. And his uncle's house, which he now rented to a young couple, was never far from view. He also gained another garage with the new house. That came in handy for storing his stock cars, which he still occasionally raced, but only as a hobby now, and only because Cathryn and the kids got such a kick out of traveling off-island with him and watching the races.

The children liked the new house, too, because they had the entire upstairs to themselves. They also enjoyed living less than a mile from town. They could walk to school if they wished and visit many more friends. To have doting grandparents just up the road was kind of neat, too.

Cathryn thought she'd gained most from the move, however. She'd gained an entire barn to house the office, workroom and storage area of her fledgling business as a bridal consultant and organizer of weddings and special events.

A year of employment with Flowers by Scott had convinced her of two things. First, that she had a natural talent for creating and pulling together beautiful, and often unique, weddings—a talent that had been fostered over the years by just about everything she'd done, from crafts to gardening, choral singing to chairing fund-raisers for the PTO. The second thing she'd learned was that enough wedding business was coming to the island to justify her branching out on her own.

Actually, if the number of weddings she had booked for the fall was any indication, she'd struck a mother lode. Apart from the living she could make, she realized there was a very real need for her services, a need that was growing rapidly with the popularity of island weddings among off-island brides.

When they arrived for a consultation, Cathryn presented them with photographs and computer files chock-full of information on churches, reception sites, caterers, menus, bands, florists, accommodations, cake bakers, tent renters—everything a bride needed to assemble a wedding. She usually let the young women wander into her workroom, too,

where, amid sewing machines, glue guns, flower arches and
bolts of material, their imaginations could run wild.

Cathryn loved her work, and although her days were hec-
tic during the wedding season, that season was short—May
and June, September and October. During the heart of summer the island was simply too busy handling vacationers to
accommodate weddings.

The rest of the year Cathryn could slow down, work on
the occasional island event, and take time to shop, create
new props, sew up table linens or chair covers, read about
the industry and update her files. But the aspect she loved
most about her work was the opportunity it gave her to be
with her children. With Tucker, too. There certainly were
advantages to both of them being their own bosses and
working so close to home.

Surprisingly, Tucker had become an asset to Cathryn's
business, as invaluable as her creativity and organizational
skills. A consultation with her also included a tour around
the island with him in one of his growing fleet of vintage
vehicles, which he hired out and sometimes drove himself,
dressed in full heart-stopping livery.

As a tour guide, pointing out locations where weddings
had been or could be held, Tucker was informative, humorous and utterly charming. Quite often, in fact, he
charmed a bride and her mother or whoever came with her,
right into ideas they hadn't thought of before. Weddings at
a lighthouse, for instance, or in a meadow, or on a beach
or yacht or the porch of an inn. Weddings with fireworks,
trolley rides, hot-air balloons. Weddings featuring mariachi
bands, calypso themes and activities to entertain guests during their two-or-three-day stay.

All of which meant extra business for Cathryn, whose job
it was to make all the arrangements and stay on top of all

the tiny details, so that when the bridal party and guests arrived, it was done. *Voila!* The wedding of their dreams!

Today Cathryn didn't need anything elaborate or unique to fulfill her dreams. The traditional ceremony she and Tucker had agreed upon would suffice quite nicely, thank you. Waiting in the vestibule of the church while her parents were ushered to their pew, she realized she was happier, stronger and more at peace with herself than she'd ever been in her life. How far she'd come since that fateful Valentine's Day two years ago!

Although she resisted thinking about her former husband on the very threshold of marrying Tucker, her thoughts turned to Dylan anyway. As planned, he had sold his business on Harmony and moved to the state of New York with Zoe, and it appeared everything had worked out well for him. His new business, geared to a far wealthier clientele, was thriving. He was married to an absolutely stunning woman. They traveled, attended the theatre and ballet, lived in a house the kids described as palatial, and summered in their two-million-dollar cottage here.

Cathryn didn't envy him a bit. In her opinion he'd lost something far more precious than what he'd gained. He'd lost seeing his children regularly and being an ongoing part of their everyday lives. What was especially pitiable was that she suspected he realized it, too.

He tried to be a good father. He called the kids at least once a week, sometimes more. He cleared his work schedule during school breaks to vacation with them, and he saw them on summer weekends when he joined Zoe at the cottage. Still, it wasn't the same. It wasn't enough to fill the emptiness the divorce had created, and since Zoe had no interest in having a child of her own, Cathryn could only see that emptiness going on and on.

No, she didn't envy her ex one bit.

With her parents seated, Cathryn gave her wedding attendants one last inspection—perfect!—and nodded to the first usher to proceed. Ben saluted her and started down the aisle. He was followed by Cameron, who was followed by ten-year-old Cory, all of them extraordinarily handsome in their black tuxedos.

Julia stepped forward next, with Lauren a few feet behind her, both women dressed in palest-of-pale-green organza gowns, offset by leaf-green sashes of shiny satin. Next came eight-year-old Bethany, similarly attired, tossing rose petals into the air with all the bearing of someone announcing a queen.

Finally, only Cathryn remained in the vestibule. For her second time around she had chosen an ankle-length gown of swishy organza, too, except that hers was more detailed and tinted pale-blush and had a raspberry sash for accent. In her hair, worn up for the occasion, were tiny rosebuds and baby's breath.

From where she stood, everything looked as it should— the flowers, the candles, the bows on the pews. The videographer was present. The photographer, too. And above her in the loft, the choir was doing a commendable enough job without her.

But the most precious feature of the setting was Tucker— Tucker waiting for her at the altar with Justin, his best man, at his side. When Cathryn caught sight of Tucker, love picked her up and zoomed her to the moon.

Meeting her gaze, Tucker broke into a smile so goofy with love that several people in the congregation laughed out loud. Cathryn smiled back and continued smiling all the way down the aisle. When they met she stepped into his arms automatically. Neither of them waited for the ceremony to be over. They simply kissed, which made their audience laugh all the more.

"I love you," Tucker whispered, framing her face in his hands.

"And I love you," she replied, pouring her soul into the words. They turned, smiling happily, and let the ceremony commence.

From the church the celebration moved to Rockland House for cocktails on the lawn and dinner later, served inside an enormous tent which Cathryn had transformed with hundreds of flowers, miles of tulle and raspberry ribbon, and thousands of tiny white lights.

Soft recorded music, courtesy of Julia, accompanied dinner, along with toast after toast to the newlyweds. One of those toasts came from Justin. It wasn't the most eloquent or humorous toast heard that day—he simply wished his mother and Tucker a long, happy life together—but it was definitely the most touching because it came from him.

After dinner Cathryn and Tucker obliged their guests with the customary cutting of the cake, followed by a romantic first dance. Taking a bow when it was done, they invited everyone to join in and then retired to the head table to enjoy their cake.

Among those out on the crowded dance floor were three adorable toddlers: Leah Quan, Adam Hathaway and Michael Grant. To get them out from under people's feet, their parents held them in their arms as they danced. Cathryn made sure the photographer took lots of pictures.

She was thrilled that the Quans had made it to the wedding. They seemed a happy couple, and it was a treat for Tucker to see his little goddaughter. Her birth had not only brought her parents together, it had also reunited them with their parents. Jenny's folks had toppled like a house of cards the moment they'd laid eyes on their grandchild, and Lee's parents had tumbled soon after.

The births of Adam and Michael had likewise brought

blessings to their families. Adam's had put an end, finally, to the hard feelings between the Hathaways and DeStefanos. Having produced such a delightful little person, they no longer saw the advantage of holding grudges. Cameron's parents seemed especially relieved to see this twelfth-generation Hathaway born. In Adam their heritage would live on.

Michael's birth reaped a boon of a different kind. Julia had no living relatives, but now she had a family. Not just her small nuclear family, but Ben's large extended family as well. They'd always been loving and accepting, but now they were also *there,* visiting from Boston as often as possible. Yes, they loved Ben and Julia, and they loved being on the island, but it wasn't the beach they ran for when they arrived, nor was it Ben or his wife. It was Mikey.

Seated at the head table, watching the three couples dance with their children, Cathryn and Tucker smiled, happy for their friends, and happy in their own decision to have a second family—but not quite yet. They wanted to lavish a little more time on the three children they already had.

The dancing continued well into the evening, a testimony to Cathryn's ability to organize a hard-to-leave party. But with the bride's bouquet tossed and the groom's yawns becoming increasingly exaggerated, the reception finally broke up. After saying good-night to the last of their guests, Cathryn gave good-night hugs to Justin, Cory and Beth and sent them home with their grandparents. Then, although the mess inside the tent was immense, they too left Rockland House. A professional cleaning crew would handle the chaos in the morning. Right now, they needed to get a few hours' sleep. They were booked on an early-afternoon flight out of Boston tomorrow. Their destination—Paris.

While Cathryn removed the dainty flowers from her hair, Tucker hung his tuxedo jacket and removed his tie.

"I think I'll go check on the outbuildings before I'm too tired," he said. "I want to make sure they're locked up and nothing's lying around the yard that shouldn't be. Do you mind?"

"No, of course not." Cathryn turned from the mirror, looped her arms around Tucker's neck and kissed him lingeringly. "As long as you come back."

He grinned. "Count on it."

She watched him leave their first-floor master bedroom through the sliding patio doors, continued watching as he headed for the barn, and only when he disappeared from view did she resume what she'd been doing.

She turned on the clock radio, tuned it to WHAR, and after brushing out her upswept hairdo, removed her wedding gown and slipped into a comfortable nightshirt. Then she opened the first of three suitcases that needed to be packed.

The popular Latin number playing on the radio came to an end, and instead of hearing the voice of the college intern who was filling in for Julia tonight, Cathryn heard Julia herself.

"Good evening, Harmony. Julia here, just back from the nuptials of Tucker and Cathryn Lang and feeling a bit mellow about the whole thing…and about them…and love and marriage in general. So I think I'll shift into a lower gear here…" From the radio drifted the first faint strains of Rod Stewart's "Have I Told You Lately That I Love You?"

"I suspect the Langs have better things to do tonight than tune in to WHAR, but I'm sending this out to them anyway. In fact, all my music will be for them. Happy marriage, guys. This is WHAR, Harmony radio, 91.2 on your FM dial. And I'm Julia Grant. Stay with me awhile…"

Cathryn's jaw had dropped sometime during the last minute and remained that way through the entire song. "I don't believe you!" she murmured, shaking her head at the radio as Julia introduced the next number, the romantic old standard "The Twelfth of Never" by Johnny Mathis.

Cathryn was sorely tempted to open her journal and record her friend's gesture, along with all the other wonderful details of this most wonderful day, but there was no time tonight. However, she'd already slipped a new notebook into the outside pocket of her carry-on and fully intended to log everything during the long flight tomorrow.

Some time later Tucker tapped on the sliding glass door and walked in from their private patio.

"Everything okay out on the north forty?" she asked.

"Yep." During his travels he'd managed to unbutton his pleated shirt and pull the tails out of his pants. "Hey, is that Julia?" he asked, kicking off his shoes.

Julia's rich, sultry voice drifted from the radio, reading from *Sonnets from the Portuguese.* "How do I love thee? Let me count the ways..."

"Yes. Do you believe it? Nothing keeps that girl from her work. And guess what. She's dedicating all her music to us."

"Cool!" Tucker opened a bureau drawer, scooped out a fistful of underwear—during the past year he'd reverted to briefs—and dropped them into a suitcase.

Julia finished reading the sonnet and swung directly into more music. "That was the talented Sarah McLachlan doing 'Sweet Surrender,'" she said when the tune ended. "And the weather for the rest of tonight..." She did a brief weather spot, finishing it with, "Looks like tomorrow's going to be a great day to fly. Of course, any day's a great day to fly if your destination is Paris. Have a ball, Mr. and Mrs. L." Strains of "April in Paris" filled the room.

Cathryn lowered the lid of a suitcase and zipped it shut. "That *is* pretty cool, being on the receiving end of all those dedications."

Closing a different suitcase, Tucker said, "We'll have to send her a special thank-you."

"Yes, definitely."

They'd just finished lining up their bags in the hallway when Julia came to the end of her show.

"This last recording is a departure from the others we've heard tonight, but as I was looking over the shelves here, it simply jumped out and cried, Play me. In a way it isn't really a departure. Love is love, no matter what form it takes. Good night, Cathryn and Tucker. Good night, Harmony. Until tomorrow…"

Cathryn took off her watch and laid it on the nightstand, pausing in her curiosity. What on earth was Julia talking about? And then it began—the song that the Ecumenical Choir sang at each Harmony graduation in June, the old spiritual, "May the Circle Be Unbroken."

She lowered herself to the bed, her back to Tucker, her eyes on the darkness beyond the sliding glass doors…seeing all the way back to childhood, to four little girls on their first day of school. To days of innocence and sharing games of fantasy with tea sets and dolls. To sleepovers and giggles and notes passed in class. Swimming lessons, secrets, snow forts, and sex manuals sneaked from mothers' bureaus. To boyfriends and love, boyfriends and pain, a baby miscarried, a mother gone. To SATs and beauty pageants, Valentine dances and Christmas concerts…and one last beach party to say goodbye…

Cathryn's friends had left Harmony and she'd remained, holding in her heart the words of the song now playing, "May the Circle Be Unbroken." Even then she'd realized it was unrealistic and overly sentimental of her to think the others would someday return and they'd all live as friends again. At best the circle would be one of spirit, of memory and fond feeling. Still, she'd hoped—and look what happened!

Of course, Amber wasn't with them anymore, and that would always be a source of sadness. But she was never far from thought and so remained, in a way, a part of the group.

Cathryn felt blessed. Friends might not be the center of life, but they were close. They shared your problems in a way that was different from the way parents or children or even husbands shared them. Laughter with friends was different, too. And if you were lucky enough to have *old* friends in your life, what a wealth of history you shared. Even when you didn't remember it all, it was there, resonating off everything you did.

There was an old Simon and Garfunkel song called "Old Friends" that an English teacher had once asked Cathryn's class to analyze, and a line in the lyrics had always stayed with her. It painted a picture of two elderly friends sitting on a park bench "like bookends." In Cathryn's estimation, nobody had ever said it better.

The spiritual ended and WHAR went to static. Tucker came around the bed and turned off the radio. "Are you all right?"

"I think so. Just a little…sentimental tonight."

He drew the drapes and sat beside her, hip to hip. "Good sentimental or bad sentimental?"

"Good. Yes, definitely good."

He draped an arm across her shoulders. "Shall we move on then?"

"Oh? To what?" She looked at him askance, suppressing a grin.

"Showering—so we won't have to waste any time in the morning."

"Augh!" With a flick of her shoulders she cast off his

arm. "Married less than a day, and already you can only think of practicalities?"

Cocking one eyebrow at her as if he'd been dared, Tucker shot to his feet and hauled her off to the adjoining bath. Before she realized what hit her, she was in the shower stall, minus a nightshirt, and Tucker, still in his tuxedo pants, was soaping her down.

One very long shower later, they flopped into bed, almost too tired to speak.

"What a day!" Cathryn sighed.

"What a night!" Tucker sighed, too.

"Is the alarm set?"

"Yep. For 5:30. Five hours from now."

Cathryn moaned and curled against his side. "By the way, what did you say to Lee just before the Quans left the reception? He looked a little strange."

"Nothing. Just…that he'd better take good care of my little goddaughter, or I'd hunt him down and break his knee-caps."

Cathryn braced up on one hand. "Oh, you are *bad*."

"And you love it."

She chuckled. "That and everything else about you."

Tucker traced her hairline over her brow and down the side of her face, his eyes growing serious and adoring. "I love you, Cathryn."

"I love you, too."

"No, I mean I really love you. With all my heart. With all my soul. I *love* you."

Cathryn wasn't crying. It was her wedding night and she refused to cry. But a tear managed to drop onto Tucker's shoulder from *somewhere*.

Tucker's tender touch traveled down her neck and over her collarbone, back and forth. "I didn't think I'd ever know such happiness, and to find it with you, and to have all this…'' His glance lifted briefly. He swallowed. ''People I've known have called me the luckiest guy on earth. Right about now, I believe it.''

Cathryn cuddled into the curve of his arm, her cheek resting above his strongly beating heart. ''We're both lucky.'' Her heavy eyelids closed. ''I don't want to make comparisons with…anybody, but with you I feel more in touch with myself than I ever have before. I'm finally on the right track.''

''You always were, Cath.'' He pressed a sleepy kiss to the top of her head. ''All the rest of us—me, Lauren, Julia, so many others—we had to knock ourselves out before arriving at what you knew all along.''

Cathryn yawned, snuggling deeper into his side. ''What's that?''

Tucker yawned, too. ''The secret,'' he mumbled against her hair.

''Secret?''

''Hmm. Meaning of life.''

''Oh.'' Cathryn listened to the sea murmuring in the distance awhile. ''You're sure the alarm is set?''

''It's set. Good night, darlin'.''

'''Night, Tucker.''

Cathryn and Tucker Lang fell asleep, wrapped in each other's arms. Over their heads stretched a sturdy roof. In their pantry lay a store of good food. Their children were healthy and safe. Their work was fulfilling, and they had friends—friends who'd be there the inevitable day when the roof sprang a leak. In each other's arms, wrapped in a circle of love, they slept, no longer dreaming of Paris, because Paris was theirs.

Daddy's little girl... **THAT'S MY BABY!** by

Vicki Lewis Thompson

Nat Grady is finally home—older and wiser. When the woman he'd loved had hinted at commitment, Nat had run far and fast. But now he knows he can't live without her. But Jessica's nowhere to be found.

Jessica Franklin is living a nightmare. She'd thought things were rough when the man she loved ran out on her, leaving her to give birth to their child alone. But when she realizes she has a stalker on her trail, she has to run—and the only man who can help her is Nat Grady.

THAT'S MY BABY!

On sale September 2000 at your favorite retail outlet.

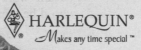

HARLEQUIN®
Makes any time special ™

Coming this September from

AMERICAN ◆ ROMANCE®

You met the citizens of Cactus, Texas, in
4 Tots for 4 Texans when some matchmaking
friends decided they needed to get
the local boys hitched!
And the fun continues in

Don't miss...
THE $10,000,000 TEXAS WEDDING
September 2000
HAR #842

In order to claim his $10,000,000 inheritance,
Gabe Dawson had to find a groom for Katherine Peters
or else walk her down the aisle himself. But when he
tried to find the perfect man for the job, the list of
candidates narrowed down to one man—*him!*

Available at your favorite retail outlet.

Makes any time special ™

HARLEQUIN® SUPERROMANCE®

You are now entering

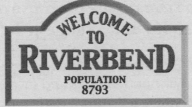

WELCOME TO **RIVERBEND**
POPULATION 8793

Riverbend...the kind of place where everyone knows
your name—and your business. Riverbend...home of
the River Rats—a group of small-town sons and
daughters who've been friends since high school.

The Rats are all grown up now. Living their lives and
learning that some days are good and some days
aren't—and that you can get through anything
as long as you have your friends.

Starting in July 2000, Harlequin Superromance brings
you Riverbend—six books about the River Rats and
the Midwest town they live in.

BIRTHRIGHT by **Judith Arnold** (July 2000)
THAT SUMMER THING by **Pamela Bauer** (August 2000)
HOMECOMING by **Laura Abbot** (September 2000)
LAST-MINUTE MARRIAGE by **Marisa Carroll** (October 2000)
A CHRISTMAS LEGACY by **Kathryn Shay** (November 2000)

Available wherever Harlequin books are sold.

HARLEQUIN®
Makes any time special ™

Visit us at www.eHarlequin.com

HSRIVER

**Don't miss
an exciting opportunity
to save on the purchase of
Harlequin and Silhouette books!**

Buy any two Harlequin or
Silhouette books and save
$10.00 off future Harlequin
and Silhouette purchases

OR

buy any three
Harlequin or Silhouette books
and save **$20.00 off** future
Harlequin and Silhouette purchases.

**Watch for details
coming in October 2000!**

PHQ400

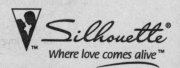

Romance is just one click away!

online book **serials**

➤ *Exclusive* to our web site, get caught up in both the daily and weekly online installments of new romance stories.

➤ Try the Writing Round Robin. Contribute a chapter to a story created by our members. Plus, winners will get prizes.

romantic **travel**

➤ Want to know where the best place to kiss in New York City is, or which restaurant in Los Angeles is the most romantic? Check out our Romantic Hot Spots for the scoop.

➤ Share your travel tips and stories with us on the romantic travel message boards.

romantic reading **library**

➤ Relax as you read our collection of Romantic Poetry.

➤ Take a peek at the Top 10 Most Romantic Lines!

Visit us online at

www.eHarlequin.com
on Women.com Networks

HARLEQUIN®

SUPERROMANCE

COMING NEXT MONTH